ROSA'S GOLD

ALSO BY RAY KINGFISHER

HOLOCAUST ECHOES
The Sugar Men

Tales of Loss and Guilt
Matchbox Memories
Slow Burning Lies
Easy Money
Bad and Badder
E.T. the Extra Tortilla

ROSA'S GOLD

Holocaust Echoes

RAY KINGFISHER

LAKE UNION
PUBLISHING

Text copyright © 2016 Ray Kingfisher

Published by Lake Union Publishing, Seattle

www.apub.com

Amazon, the Amazon logo, and Lake Union Publishing are trademarks of Amazon.com, Inc., or its affiliates.

ISBN-13: 9781503936584
ISBN-10: 1503936589

Cover design by Debbie Clement

Printed in the United States of America

FOREWORD

Although this is a work of fiction, many of the places and events depicted are real. As befitting the subject matter I have tried as far as possible to create a story that could, realistically, have happened, and included many events that actually did. I hope my writing does justice to such an important subject, but if the story contains historical inaccuracies or I have taken liberties with some events, then I apologize beforehand.

PROLOGUE

The old leather briefcase had lain undisturbed for six years, and its secrets for over sixty.

The buckle was now pockmarked ginger with rust, and the leather, a hundred shades of brown, was alive with creases and cracks. But it was still as tough as the day it was made.

It was just sitting there, guarding its contents much like a faithful old collie dog might stick by its owner. And those contents were Mac's life's works. Mac hadn't even looked at them for the last five years, ever since his eyes had clouded over a little and his hip complained at the mere thought of clambering down those narrow stairs to the cellar. That amount of effort now seemed pointless; Mac had lost hope of anyone ever being interested in his story, let alone finding those friends he'd spent so long looking for.

His first stroke left him barely able to look after himself, let alone the house.

His second, although he couldn't have known it at the time, was ultimately to see him reunited with those old friends.

CHAPTER ONE

A s if things weren't bad enough, it was pouring down with rain when Nicole Sutton and her mother moved into their new house.

Okay, so people (mainly her mum) had told her that Henley was a charming market town nestled on the banks of the glorious Thames, overlooked by the unspoiled splendour of the Chiltern Hills. But as their car meandered through streets of dull-brick houses it just looked tired and dreary to Nicole.

And those thoughts didn't change when they drew up outside number 77 Victoria Road, a distinctly creepy-looking two-bedroomed terraced house with its own waterfall pouring from a gutter joint.

Perhaps the inside would be a little more exciting, more like the big house in Wimbledon they'd said goodbye to only an hour or so before.

Well, no. Actually it sucked.

The second they opened the front door the reek of 'single old guy' hit them as sure as garlic smelling salts would. Mum didn't acknowledge it, of course; forcing a smile was more her style.

Nothing – *absolutely nothing* – looked remotely new (or even clean). None of the fittings had been replaced for decades. Dirty floor mats lay inside the front door and at the threshold of both downstairs rooms, all pretty much worn through in the centre. Mum threw those out even before the removal truck arrived. Indiscriminate streaks hung suspiciously mid-dribble on the wallpaper. Indescribable stains colonized the carpets – especially in the bathroom (Mum said that would be the second thing to go and that only a single man would put carpet in a bathroom).

Between the two of them they would make the place habitable, Mum said, but that looked a long way off. They had a weekend before Mum started work, but judging by first impressions they'd need a month.

To get out of the way of the removal men Nicole went up to check out her new bedroom. It was certainly a step down from her previous one, both in size and décor. She looked around the room, ignoring the ancient wallpaper, trying to decide where everything should go, trying to care.

Trying to care.

God, that was hard. What the hell did it matter?

No, that would be no good – too *self-indulgent*, as Mum kept saying. Think how life would be in her new bedroom, in her new house, in her new town, a few months down the line.

Think how 2011 could be the start of a new life for both of them. Think practical.

Really? Well. The practicality was that the carpets – even if steam cleaned and disinfected – were just *so* uncool, seventies swirly-patterned affairs that turned up near the edges like week-old bacon sandwiches. The smell wasn't too far off that either. Still, once the removal men brought in her bed and Mum bought her some furniture . . . and they'd hired one of those industrial carpet cleaners . . . added a few posters and a ton of air freshener . . . yes, it had possibilities.

The shouts from downstairs took her away from imagining those possibilities. They'd obviously smashed the fridge-freezer or the cabinet into a wall, or dropped something heavy on a stray foot.

No, don't think like that, Nicole. These days her first thought always seemed to be that someone had been hurt. She had to stop thinking the worst.

The accident could have happened to anyone.

She dismissed the thought and stood next to her new bedroom window, peering out towards the river. Yes, she could just see a little triangle of murky Thames water between the houses opposite, even without standing on tiptoe.

Being tall helped with that. It also made her the best 400-metre runner in her year. The plan had been to fit training and summer athletics tournaments around her final exams. The accident put paid to both of those aspirations.

At least Mum had let her have the back room. She didn't want her bedroom to look out onto a road. Especially one dark and shiny with rain.

Mum kept telling her to be positive, that the flashbacks to the accident would go away eventually, that it had only happened three months ago after all.

It had happened a few weeks before her final exams, and by the time she'd recovered, her school friends were tied up in school-leaving euphoria and had forgotten all about her – or so it seemed. And as for seeing them on a more social basis, well, Mum and Dad told her there was no way she was drinking or partying so soon after a fractured skull, and the headaches repeated those warnings most days.

Mum and Dad kept telling her the headaches would eventually subside, and they were right, although they were also right to say 'subside' as opposed to 'stop'. Any form of studying would have to be put on hold because lengthy periods of reading brought on headaches too.

At least she was alive. Mum and Dad said that too. But they hardly ever mentioned Darren. And Nicole tried not to dwell on what might have happened had she let Darren sit in the passenger seat that day.

'Nicole!'

Her mother's call from downstairs brought her back to the present.

'Nicole! Are you up there?'

You saw me come upstairs, Mum. Where else would I be? On the roof?

Nicole stood up and stomped over to the doorway. 'What?' she shouted, unable to match the antagonism in her mother's voice.

There was no reply. But she could hear Mum's erratic voice.

'No, put that in there . . . We really need that in the kitchen but leave it in the hallway for now . . . Who labelled this box? Doesn't say what it is . . . Put it in the lounge and we'll sort it out later.'

There were concurring grunts from the removal men, then there was some short disagreement about moving things 'down there', wherever that was.

Best to go downstairs, Nicole thought.

'Where have you been?' her mother said while she was still on the stairs. 'Come on, no slacking. Show this man where the two bedrooms are.'

Nicole turned to the man in question and pointed a finger upwards. 'Mum at the front, me at the back, bathroom in the middle.' She flicked her finger vaguely in the relevant directions as she spoke.

'Nicole!'

'What? You asked me to—'

'Don't be stroppy. Show him where we want things put.'

Nicole sighed, rammed her hands into her pockets, and started walking back upstairs. The wiry man with wiry hair and a bedside cabinet under each arm turned to his side and crabbed up the stairs behind her.

He left one cabinet in the front bedroom, then took the other into Nicole's, and placed it where she was pointing. He drew the back of his hand across his brow, peered through the net curtains and pulled one aside. They both stepped back at the puff of dust that floated towards them like ghostly fog. Nicole caught her heel on a rippled section of carpet and stumbled.

'I'm sure your dad can fix that,' the man said.

Nicole gave him an acid look.

'Oh, or . . . is it just you and your mum living here?'

She started to give a glum apologetic nod, then firmed the nod up. *What did she have to apologize for?*

'Sorry. I thought . . .' The man pointed to nowhere in particular. 'I thought the guy at the house you moved out of . . .' He waited for clarification. None came. 'Right,' he said, strolling to the door. 'No rest for the wicked.'

As his footsteps thumped on the stairs, Nicole looked down and gave each corner of the carpet a cursory examination. She picked the least stained option and sat down, pulling her knees up to her chest.

It was the same conversation – give or take a word – that she'd had with her Aunty Sandra, then with a random hospital porter she'd met when going for a check-up, and finally with the creepy neighbour who was, of course, now an ex-neighbour.

'Henley, eh? Nice place. Fresh start and all that. Quiet compared to round here. You must be looking forward to it. Oh, only you and your mother going? Oh, I see. Oh, well, yes. Anyway, nice place, Henley.'

It was certainly quiet – they'd traded size for tranquillity. Okay, Mum had asked her how she felt about moving, but at *not-quite-seventeen* she was old enough to have an opinion yet also old enough to know her opinion counted for little. The move was likely to happen whatever Nicole said about missing her friends. It turned out that Mum had arranged a job transfer to the Henley branch of the bank, and what were the chances she'd sewn the whole thing up before she'd even asked Nicole about the move? Would Mum pull a trick like that? *Mmm.*

Mum had changed. God, everything had changed – since that day.

It had been an ordinary day – although a very wet, ordinary day. Dad turned up at school to collect them. He told them Mum had a heavy cold so he'd had to make his excuses at work and leave early.

Nicole dodged the rain and hopped into the passenger seat first (that was just one of the perks of being the older kid), so Darren jumped in the back. Then Dad sped off. Although, being Dad, he first checked they had their seatbelts on. Yep, ordinary day.

On that average afternoon of that ordinary day, Dad was driving around a bend he'd gone round hundreds of times before – albeit more slowly than today.

The next thing Nicole knew, her world was turning upside down and inside out, her body pulling on the seatbelt so much it felt like she was being torn apart.

And the next thing she remembered was her head being clamped between two blocks of polystyrene. She felt herself being lifted onto a trolley and into an ambulance.

Also she remembered complaining about the mother of all headaches, and hearing someone say something about bleeding from one of her ears.

It was what they called a 'simple' fracture of the skull. No worries. No surgery. Just a short stay in hospital and a long time staying at home doing pretty much nothing.

Dad said he just skidded due to the torrential rain, then lost control. He had concussion and went to hospital for observation. There was more to his story, but Nicole only became aware of that a few weeks later, when the nasty argument happened.

Darren was killed. The autopsy supported the scene-of-accident officer's preliminary report that the violent twisting motion in free space had broken his neck, killing him instantly, and leaving Nicole an only child. And also messing up Mum and Dad more than she could ever have imagined.

Immediately after the accident Nicole's focus had been on making a physical recovery – that and getting over the black hole in her life that was Darren. Although her fracture didn't need treatment she was told to avoid stress.

Avoid stress. Yeah, *that* was a laugh, considering what happened a few weeks afterwards.

There was strictly no going out, so she relied on texting, emails and Facebook (when the headaches weren't too bad) for keeping in touch with friends. But it was never going to be the same. She was simply out of the loop; keeping track of who was going where and who was seeing who caused too much fuzz around her mind. What little information she managed to glean suggested all her friends were going their separate ways – to either college or jobs – and Mum pointed out that they all probably would have found new friends by now.

Thanks, Mum.

CHAPTER TWO

I suppose you might call this an author's foreword.

It seems strange to think of myself as an author, and even stranger to pretend I'm starting this story with any notion of where it might end.

All I know is that today is Saturday, 24 February 1990, that yesterday I retired, and that Doctor Green suggested I do this. He said it would keep me active in my retirement, give me a purpose in life. But he was being kind. We both know the real reason he suggested I do this.

It was Dylan Thomas who said, 'He who seeks work finds rest.' I wonder whether they took that idea and twisted it into *'Arbeit Macht Frei'* – the words erected across those dark, threatening gates like a mantra to the suffering masses. Was it a mantra? Was it a prayer? Or was it there merely to taunt those people that little bit more? Either way, 'twisted' is the correct word; everything in that horrid place in those horrid times was twisted in one way or another.

Now I've officially entered old age everyone appears to think I'll turn into a bumbling old fool overnight. Of course, I'm sure I will eventually.

But don't we all end up that way?

Well, the lucky ones, at least. And, believe me, I do count myself lucky. I was never successful in marriage. Or, to be accurate, I was unsuccessful twice. That wasn't anybody's fault, and I'm glad no woman has been burdened with me for life. Actually, that's not true; there was one woman I would have traded my soul and all my worldly goods to have spent my life with, to still have by my side. But I'll come to her in good time.

But I've had a happier existence than those around me would believe. I have no family and, on the face of it, little to live for. But I can truthfully say that to me every day is still a sunny day.

What follows is a true account as much as I can remember it. And I have a pretty good recollection of the events, oh, yes, I do. That's partly because I kept lots of photographs, letters and scribbled notes – but also because the events kept racing (and still *keep* racing) around in my mind like a circus ringmaster reminding the audience of the acts to come.

I should mention before I continue that I've been here before. Twice. I first had the idea to write my story when I was in my mid-thirties. They were dark days when I was coming to terms with my own failings as a husband and as a human being, still searching for the reasons that were hidden in the shady corners of my mind.

I returned to the task when I reached my half-century. I thought the time was right, that I had a story to tell. But although by then I had come to terms with my personal shortcomings, there was still some confusion in my mind. Every time my pen hovered over a pad of paper – when I had to stop merely thinking about my feelings and compose sentences to describe them – my mouth became dry, my chest tightened, and I ended up telling myself there was no point, that it was backward-looking when I should be forward-looking.

The reason I say this is that I could well falter again. I feel a curious mix of uncertainty and determination, although, at the moment, the words do seem to be flowing.

But enough foreword. Tomorrow I will write more, and start at the beginning.

∽

It's now the middle of March. Yes, I had a break of almost three weeks. I doubted my reasons for continuing my story. But I've come back to it, and I think I always will, even if it takes years.

It's a crisp and chilly morning, which makes the sun seem all the more sharp and piercing. But even if the skies were leaden and it was teeming with rain it would still be a sunny day in my world. That's partly because I'm retired, but mostly because of the way I am – the way I choose to be.

But I do wonder why I'm writing this memoir. Was Doctor Green's oblique suggestion more of a joke, or does he really think it might be good for me? Who knows?

Blimey, I just called this a 'memoir'. That sounds grandiose. It isn't really; I'm just an ordinary man, one of many who were lucky to survive.

Anyway, perhaps the real reason why I'm writing this will gradually unfold. Or perhaps it won't.

There's one more thing I need to get off my chest before I start, and that's the insomnia. Some nights the sleep simply won't come. I've always tried to be an optimistic fellow, but the truth is that for most of my life I've hated whatever it is that gets between me and my sleep.

Do those thoughts stop me sleeping? The hiss of deathly steam trains, the clank of gates, the devil's dance of flames, that stench of evil itself.

The soulless faces.

The screams.

Or do those thoughts simply take advantage of my insomnia to play their old tricks on me?

Either way, it doesn't bother me too much these days, especially since I retired and am able to have a nap at any time I please during the day. And I get to witness the glory of sunrise more often than most.

Also, I've learned by now that the mind is in turns a curious and powerful force.

I've been having those night-time thoughts for so long they're almost comforting, like old relatives you don't like but secretly worry about when you don't hear from them for a while.

So I have no idea where this piece of writing will lead. I do, however, have a good idea of how to start it.

CHAPTER THREE

F or Nicole, the front door of 77 Victoria Road shut with a sense of finality.

The removal men had left. Mum hadn't called it off at the eleventh hour. Life was never going to go back to the way it was.

For a few minutes she wandered aimlessly around the kitchen and the living room. Each was littered with bags and boxes, and the only clear spaces were walkways to get from one cluttered area you couldn't even swing a kitten in to the next.

She went to the hallway to find Mum standing with hands on hips, gazing at the bags and cardboard boxes piled up there.

She looked like she was about to cry.

Well, Mum, it was your choice to come here, to do this without Dad.

But they'd had that particular argument. More than once.

Immediately after the accident Mum and Dad had found solace in each other, sharing grief at their shared loss. But very soon afterwards something changed. Or rather, Mum changed. Nicole didn't ask because she didn't know what to ask; it didn't seem right for her to say, 'I know something's wrong, what is it?'

Not while they were making arrangements for Darren's funeral.

*

'Right,' Nicole's mother said, her arms now suddenly springing to life. 'Let's get this lot down the cellar.'

'We've got a cellar?' Nicole said.

Her mother nodded. 'Yes, and the sods wouldn't take anything down there, said we hadn't paid for that.' She picked up two plastic bags. 'Don't daydream. Grab what you can and we'll have this cleared in no time. No clothes because they'll rot down there.'

Nicole did as she was told and they both struggled to the door next to the kitchen. It was a bilious green colour, with gobs of sap that had seeped through the layers of paint as if they were refusing to be imprisoned in the cellar and wanted their freedom.

Nicole's mother dropped her bags and opened the door. They both recoiled as a musty smell flew out of the darkness. Opening the door wider threw some light on a section of craggy wall, in the middle of which lay a grubby, old-fashioned light switch.

'Is it safe?' Nicole said as her mother reached out to it.

Her mother retracted her hand slightly, hesitated, then said, 'The electrics have all been checked, don't worry.' She reached out again, as though holding a match to the blue touchpaper of a suspect firework, and quickly flicked the switch.

The light below came on, and what Nicole saw scared her more than the darkness. On one side, cobwebs were trying their best to disguise more rough brickwork; on the other, a rickety-looking handrail beckoned the foolish.

Nicole's mother picked up both of her bags in one hand and pressed the palm of the other against the handrail. She gave a distinctly uncertain nod, then started descending the wooden steps. Halfway down she flicked her head back and said, 'You too, it's not like it's haunted.'

'How do you know?' Nicole mumbled.

'The survey said so. Now come on.'

Nicole followed her mother, slitting her eyes just in case stray cobwebs (or anything worse) lay in wait. As her foot stepped onto the concrete base she opened her eyes fully and looked around.

Everything was neat and tidy. At one end brooms and shovels hung on hooks, with smaller tools resting on a shelf at chest height. On the other side there seemed to be some sort of desk with a wooden chair in front of it, and shelves above holding rows of jars and tins. Nicole stepped across to take a closer look. Everything was covered in dust, so much so that it looked like a bucket of grey icing sugar had been sieved over every surface.

'This is disgusting,' she said, dropping her bags where she stood. 'It's filthy, it's horrible.'

'It's a cellar. Cellars are supposed to be filthy and horrible.'

Nicole felt a lump in her throat. 'I . . . I don't . . .'

Her mother peered at her through the dimness. 'What?'

'I . . . don't want to live here, Mum.'

Her mother groaned. It was her special *here we go again* groan. 'Don't start, Nicole. Not now.'

Nicole started sniffing back a few tears.

'Oh, come here,' her mother said, placing her bags on the floor. She opened her arms and Nicole, four inches the taller, stooped to place her head onto her mother's shoulder.

They stayed together for a few moments, Nicole's mother enveloping her, rocking them both side to side.

'I'm sorry, love.' She gave her daughter's hair a few long, lingering strokes. 'But I can't say it's what I want either.'

'Well . . .'

Nicole paused for breath and her mother interrupted with 'Ah, ah, ah!' She held her daughter's shoulders and pushed her away to arm's length. 'Nicole. You're seventeen now. Pull yourself together. I don't want to live here—'

'But—'

'No. Listen to me. I don't want to live here any more than you do. But we both know whose fault it all is, don't we?'

Nicole wiped the wetness from her eyes and saw that sternness on her mother's face again. It was almost cruel. *She never used to be like this.*

'Now stop crying, pull yourself together, and let's get some work done.'

Nicole sniffed, then nodded.

Her mother pointed to the desk. 'You can clear this area and start piling the bags on top; they won't get so damp on there.' She turned away and started clumping up the stairs.

Nicole blew her nose, then looked at the desk. 'Desk' was probably too grand a word for it. It had a large hole at the front in the middle and . . . were they metal hinges screwed into it at the back?

She snorted out a short laugh.

It was a door.

She stepped back to look underneath. Yes, someone had actually nailed an old door onto wooden blocks and put a chair next to it. At least they'd bothered to take the handle off.

She touched it with one finger, immediately snatching it back and wiping it on her jeans. She winced in disgust at the smooth, almost oily residue that still clung to her finger, then wiped it again.

She glanced at the top of the stairs. Perhaps she could tell Mum everything was too horrible to touch. *Would that work? Mmm.*

'It's only dust,' she muttered. 'Only dust.'

Old papers and magazines were stacked up on one side of the desk. She ran a forefinger across the top one to reveal the date. 8 August 2005. Six years ago. She checked a couple more. Much the same. She gathered them up very slowly, keeping her head back to avoid the plumes of dust.

Then she spotted the old briefcase at the far end of the makeshift desk.

Yeah, she could dump them in that.

She leaned across and dragged it over.

God, what a crappy old thing. Who would keep that?

It was like some cruddy antique. Probably leather, brown or black – it was hard to tell through the carpet of dust. The buckle, speckled with ginger rust, somehow still possessed a sparkle that broke through the dust.

And was it really that heavy, or was there something inside it?

She carefully pressed the buckle. Nothing happened. Probably locked or jammed.

She shoved it to the right and then to the left, and almost jumped as the thing clacked sharply, the flap over the top springing out towards her. She lifted the flap and slowly opened the briefcase, its leather creaking ominous.

Damn. It was full to the brim. She pulled out a sheaf of papers.

What the . . . ?

There were lots of letters, correspondence to and from the Jewish this and that, and to and from the American this and that. Government stuff. All sent to a John MacDonald at 77 Victoria Road, Henley.

And all obviously crap.

Oh well, she would just have to bin the crap and bin the crappy old briefcase too.

She put her hand back in and pulled out a large hardback note-book. She opened it at the first page and started reading. There was a date, and then something about this being an author's foreword. A bit of random stuff about Dylan Thomas. And something in . . . German?

It was about an old man. Obviously the old guy – John MacWhatever – who owned the house before them. Written in 1990.

God, before she was even born.

It was a bit rambling, not exactly *The Hunger Games.*

He was now retired. *Blah blah blah*. Mental problems. *Blah blah blah*. A few marital issues here and there. *Well, who hasn't?* Trouble sleeping. *Mmm . . . Nothing to see here.*

She closed the notebook, then tilted the briefcase to see what else was inside.

Did something just glint?

Yes, something at the bottom of the briefcase definitely glinted, which was going some considering the puny light bulb behind her. Taking great care so as not to throw up even more dust, she opened it wider and peered inside.

Yes, definitely something shiny there, something a magpie would grab.

She reached in and plucked it out.

It was a ring.

And miraculously it wasn't dirty or dusty, but bright and like new. It was roughly made, not perfectly round, and had a criss-cross pattern cut into its face. It was hardly precision-made, but had a certain rustic charm. She popped it onto her finger, then drew her hand back to admire it.

A shout from upstairs spoiled her daydream.

'Nicole? Have you finished making room down there yet?'

She groaned, took a breath and shouted back, 'Nearly.'

'Well, get a move on. We haven't got all day.'

Actually, they did have all day. And all weekend. And all week, and all week after that. It might take that long to sort the house out.

But Nicole kept those thoughts to herself and said, 'I'll just be a few minutes.'

That's right, put Mum off for a while longer. Don't let her think she's the boss.

She admired the ring again, then glanced at the notebook. Perhaps it would explain where the ring came from. She opened it and started reading again.

19

This time it might be an idea to read properly, from the start.

He was retired. Mental problems. Sunny day. Marital issues. Trouble sleeping. Aah, now it started to make more sense, starting at the beginning, where he was born.

She read on.

CHAPTER FOUR

I was born in February 1925 as John Charles MacDonald in Henley, or Henley-on-Thames as some people like to insist. I can't be fussy about names; I was only ever known as John before I went into the forces. There my name was changed to Mac, and I've been Mac ever since.

For anyone who grew up along this stretch of the river Thames, rowing was in your blood. Or, as the locals would have it, you have Thames water flowing through your veins. For me it's still true. These days I might struggle to get into a boat, but once I'm in I enjoy gracefully pulling myself along as much as I ever did. My hip does complain the next day, however. Increasingly I do a lot more coaching than rowing; it's easier on my hip that way.

Luckily I grew up to be an inch over six feet tall, with long arms and legs and a fairly wide chest – a big lad for those days and well suited to rowing.

As a kid I never really had many troubles, but those I had just fell away as soon as I settled into my scull and started pulling it along, gliding across those glassy waters. I've never found anything quite so relaxing in my entire life as rowing. Even when I really went for it, perhaps racing my pals – when my lungs were bursting and telling me to stop, when my legs and arms were burning and my head was as dizzy as a spinning jenny – even then I still felt a sort of homely calmness in concentrating on maintaining my stroke rate.

I wasn't much good at school because I was more into sport than books. Although as I've got older and less inclined towards physical pastimes I've become more well read, appreciating the poetry and literature that soothes my soul the way rowing used to. And my soul needs that.

As a teenager I had ambitions of starting up my own business, but knew I had time for that later. Fighting for king and country came first, so although I became a porter on the railways after leaving school, I was always biding my time until I could join the forces. I'd followed the build-up to the war, including Churchill's speeches, and just wanted to get stuck in and help out as much as I could.

I got my chance when I turned eighteen in February 1943. Up until then lads under twenty weren't sent overseas, but they'd just changed the rules. The change was touted as good news at the time, but in hindsight it might have been because things were getting desperate in Europe and the Far East. Inspired by the Battle of Britain, I applied to join the RAF, but they didn't want me. My mother and father were quite pleased about that because of the high mortality rate, but I was genuinely upset. At the time I tried to kid myself it was because I was too big to fit into some of those cockpits; the truth is I wasn't clever enough. So the army it had to be.

I joined the light infantry division as a cadet and went off for six weeks of basic training – the first time I'd been away from home. On the first day the lance corporal lined us up in the barracks and asked us our names. We all gave our second names, then he told us to be at ease and asked us our first names. Someone before me was called John, so when it came to me and I said 'John', the lance corporal gave me a queer sideways look and asked again.

'John,' I said again. 'John MacDonald.'

'Already got a *John*,' he said. 'Can't have *two* Johns. Very confusing.'

I didn't have a clue what to say to him, I just watched him give his chin a thoughtful rub with his fingertips.

Then he looked up and down the rows of men. 'Do we have a Mac?' he said.

Silence.

Without another thought he turned to me and said, 'Right, your name's *Mac* from now on. Understand?'

I nodded slowly.

'Not *John*.'

I didn't know whether to nod or shake my head, so I did neither.

'So let's try that again. You. What's your name?'

'Mac,' I said.

He smiled a proud smile. 'Good lad.'

And that was it. I was known as Mac throughout my time in the army. Even when I left the forces and got a job as a clerk for the council it seemed natural for me to carry on being called Mac, so I've been called that for the rest of my life by almost everyone.

Perhaps it's just as well I never had children; more than one Mac in a house might have been confusing.

Anyhow, I really enjoyed the six weeks of army training. They taught us how to use weapons, some unarmed combat, and how to march in formation. Being a sporty type I was in my element and sailed through it. At the end I got my first posting – my only posting, as it turned out. I remember my father being really proud of me, and I remember my mother crying. I knew she wasn't crying with joy.

I was posted to Tunisia to join the Eighth Army. That was a surprise as everyone knew our lads had all but won the battle for Africa at that stage. I was later told the send-off from Southampton was a fancy affair, but it completely passed me by at the time, I was too upset by my mother crying again. Between the tears she gave me some envelopes and notepaper and told me to write whenever I could, but especially at Christmas. My father told her not to fret so much, that I'd be back before then on leave.

He was wrong.

CHAPTER FIVE

*N*icole!'

Nicole almost dropped the notebook at the shout from above.

Yes, it was definitely one of Mum's special shouts with a rasp on the last syllable.

She put the notebook and all the papers back in the briefcase and scurried upstairs.

'Sorry,' she said. 'Got carried away down there.'

Her mother pointed to some boxes. 'Take those—'

Nicole's phone started ringing. She shrugged apologetically to her mother and answered it.

'Dad?'

Even as the word left Nicole's lips she saw her mother's nostrils twitch and her face give that sour look it had seemingly rented long term. Nicole took her phone into the living room.

'It's . . . good,' she said. 'It needs a bit of work but it seems a nice area, just a stone's throw from the Thames.'

'I'm glad,' he answered. 'Maybe I can pop up and see you when you're settled in properly.'

'Cool.'

'Yeah?'

'Yeah. I'd like that.'

'And your mum, she good?'

'Oh, same as me, getting used to it, cleaning up, unpacking, seeing what needs mending. You know.'

There was a pause before he started speaking again, a tremble in his voice: 'Tell her I'll be happy to mend anything, or pay for anything that needs doing.'

'I will, Dad. Thanks.'

'And remember, I'm not too far away.'

'No.'

Nicole screwed up her face to throttle the tears that were forcing their way through her system. She swallowed, took a breath, and said, 'I've got to go, Dad. Mum's calling me for something.'

'Of course. Give her my best. Tell her to let me know if there's anything I can do, anything at all.'

Nicole nodded to no one and forced out, 'Sure, bye.'

'Miss you, poppet.'

'Miss you too, Dad,' she mumbled, then closed the call and clasped the phone to her chest.

She took some strong, deep breaths, wiped her face, and went out to the kitchen.

'What did he want?' her mother said.

'Just making sure we've got ourselves moved in okay.'

'As long as he isn't planning to see us anytime soon.'

Nicole felt herself blush. 'Why not?'

'And if he's offering to help, tell him he can stuff it.'

'Oh, *Mum!*'

'Don't *Mum* me, Nicole. You're old enough to understand now. I don't want to hear from him. And I definitely don't want to see him.'

'But—'

'And you know why.'

Nicole felt her sap rising, and the fact that there were some things she *didn't* understand wasn't helping. 'I know Dad denies it,' she said, snapping the words out.

Her mother's face turned to stone. 'And you believe him? You really believe him over me?'

'Well, no . . . I . . .' Nicole gulped. Then she turned and headed for the hallway.

'Nicole? Where are you going? There's work to do.'

But Nicole was gone, leaving the front door to strain its hinges and bounce back.

Turn right or left?

Who cares? Just run!

She ran, but after a few long strides – a few thumps to her system – a mild fuzz started in her head, and she slowed to a walk. It didn't matter. Within minutes she was at the banks of the Thames. She sat down on a bench, huffed to herself, and held her head in her hands.

No, this life here wasn't going to work.

There had to be another way.

She looked up and down the river, at how serene the whole area seemed.

Yes. Calm. Calm.

Beyond the barges and Sunday cruisers moored in front of her, a rowing boat drifted by with four men pulling in unison, gently, yet strongly. Working hard, yet relaxed.

If only everything could be as simple, as calm. As constructive.

She huffed again.

Why was Mum being so horrible?

No, why was *her life* so horrible? She'd hardly finished pining for the brother she'd lost forever and now it looked like she'd have to start pining for Dad too. Mum seemed to have turned into a twisted, selfish cow, her school friends had forgotten her, and she was now in a town where she didn't know anyone.

She looked up the river again, towards the single bridge.

How had she ended up in a one-bridge town like Henley?

The bridge blurred in tears as the memories echoed around in her head – the memories of those arguments. They'd started soon after the accident, culminating in that big, snarly one only two months ago.

Mum comes home from work. Saying nothing. Face trembling.

Something wrong. Seriously wrong.

Nicole doesn't dare speak for half an hour, then says, 'What's wrong, Mum?'

'I think you should go to your room.'

'But what's wrong?'

'Nothing. Just go to your room. I need to talk to your dad.'

'What about?'

'Oh, please yourself, you're almost seventeen.'

The door opens. Dad walks in. Ignores Nicole. Says to Mum, 'Karen. I'm sorry. I can explain.'

'You can explain?' she replies with mock laughter. 'This'll be good.'

'Nothing happened. We just went out for a drink.'

'And then went back to her place?'

'No.'

'And with *her* too, Barry. That bitch you'd been drinking with when you had the accident.'

'That's not fair. I wasn't over the limit and you *know* that.'

Mum starts crying now. '*Oh, Barry!* Why did you do this to me?'

'Oh, Christ. It's nothing. I'm . . . I'm just in a bad place at the moment.'

'A bad place? *What?*'

'Mum, Dad,' Nicole says. 'What's happened?'

'Go to your room, poppet,' Dad says.

'Do you call *her* "poppet" too?' Mum says.

Dad shakes his head angrily. 'Oh, you're being ridiculous. And before you chop my head off—'

'It won't be your head, you *shit*.'

'If you'll let me explain.'

'No, Barry. You don't need to.' She bangs a fist on her chest. 'Because every horrible feeling you have, I have too.'

'What are you talking about?' says Dad.

Now she snarls and spits the words out. 'Everything you feel, I feel too. *Guaranteed.* In a bad place? *Me too.* Head in a mess after losing Darren? Not as much as *mine.* I carried him for nine months.' Now she shouts, her face almost melting with rage: 'Feel unloved, do you? *Me too.* Desperate for affection? Guess what, *me too!*'

Dad turns to Nicole. 'Go to your room, Nicole, *please.*'

But she just stares back.

'The only difference,' Mum continues, 'between me and you is that I didn't drop my knickers for the first man to—'

'Now just hold—'

'Shut up! I didn't drop my knickers for the first man to show me a bit of attention. You know why? Because I *cared*, because I loved you, because I loved Nicole, because I loved Darren's memory.'

'That's out of order!' Dad shouts.

'No, Barry. What you did with your damn girlfriend, *that's out of order!*'

'I just work with her, *for Christ's sake!* Now stop this. Please. You're upsetting Nicole.'

'Wrong, Barry. *You're* upsetting *everyone.*'

Dad holds his hands up. 'All right, all right. Let's just calm down.'

Mum shoves him out of the way. '*Too late!* It's over.'

Dad groans. 'No, Karen. Please.'

'And Nicole's sixteen. She can decide who she wants to live with.'

But neither of them looks at Nicole. It's like a dream. She freezes, mouth open, feels faint. Her head is throbbing, her heart hurting – really, actually hurting like someone's pressing on her chest. And the room, the house, everything except Mum and Dad is normal, as it should be. It's only Mum and Dad who aren't right.

Dad says, 'There's no need for this. I know it's been hard since . . . Look, we can work this out. *I want to work this out.*'

'Well, I *don't*. I can't stand the sight of you and I don't want to hear you, okay?'

Dad starts to cry. 'No, look. We can—'

'No! I don't want to see you. I don't want to talk to you. We're finished.'

Dad clasps a hand onto his head. 'You want me to leave? Is that it?'

Nicole can't control herself any longer. Her body jerks the tears out.

'You're not using me to soothe your guilty conscience,' Mum says. 'If you want to go, go. If not you can sleep in the spare room until we sell the house.'

Nicole stopped gazing aimlessly up the Thames and leaned forward on her knees, gazing down between her feet instead.

Whatever she did or didn't understand about Mum and Dad, the fact was she had ended up in a one-bridge town like Henley, and it was up to her to find a way out of it.

CHAPTER SIX

To illustrate my first experience of real army life, I've copied out the letter I wrote and sent soon afterwards to my parents. My mother kept it safe and treasured it until she died many years later.

The words of my eighteen-year-old self tell the story far better than I could now. They show how simple my thoughts were at the time.

2 July

Today is my third day on the ship the army has commandeered from the merchant navy. It's an enormous thing, it takes me half an hour to walk all round the deck. Mind you, I gave that up when we rounded Spain because it was as hot as a baker's oven out there. I could almost feel the sun's rays singeing my arm. Billy and Slim from training are with me, and at first we tended to keep ourselves to ourselves, but now we've got to know plenty of the other lads. None of us know what we'll be doing in Tunisia; it's common knowledge we've won the whole country bar the odd skirmish here and there. We all think they've made a cock-up and we'll get sent back home when they realize there's nothing to do there.

3 July

We docked in Tunis this morning, I think that's the capital of Tunisia. When I got off I thought it was hotter than anything I'd ever known. But that was just the *morning*, it's even worse now. You can't do anything physical like sports because it saps your energy in seconds, I don't know how anyone sleeps, let alone survives it. Perhaps the lads are right and we'll all be sent home. I'm starting to hope so because a few of the lads have got bad sunburn and April showers are now a pleasant memory. What we wouldn't give for some clouds!

5 July

We've started to wander around the barracks in the morning and evening when it's cooler. It's a right League of Nations here: Americans, Canadians, Australians, Indians, South Africans; also a few Europeans – mostly Poles, I think. Anyhow, we're all in it together, and we all get along well, even those who don't speak English.

6 July

While I was shaving the other day I got to know an Australian chap who insisted on being called Joey. I don't know what his real name is, he said he didn't really have one. He's a real character, saying how the heat here is nothing compared to Wagga Wagga. I had to ask what he was talking about, apparently that's a place in Australia. He seems like a veteran at twenty-two, all swagger and confidence – but then again he *is* twenty-two.

9 July

This evening, just as we've been here a week and starting to get used to it, we found out what's happening. I know it's what I joined up to do, and I wouldn't tell any of the lads this, but I'm getting a bit scared now. To be honest I think all the younger ones of us are, you can tell by that little bit of shock on our faces. But we all support each other, and we all accept we're here for the best of reasons. Anyhow, I must try to get some sleep; in the early hours we invade Sicily. That's an island at the end of Italy, apparently.

10 July

It was all a bit of an anti-climax.

I was all geed up to fight, to use some of my training. The crossing was a bit choppy, and as we left the patrol boat I actually felt fear in the pit of my stomach for the first time in my life. I didn't feel sick (I think those hours rowing on the Thames must have stood me in good stead) but it was still horrible. I felt a bit weak and shaky, but I just kept my chin up and did some deep breathing. That helped a lot. Most of the lads suffered, though, because we just kept yawing from side to side. Joey, in particular, was very sick; he's obviously used to heat but not water.

But the thing is, the boat crossing is the worst thing that's happened. There we were, all patting each other on the back as the doors opened, all lost for words but all wondering whether the others were as frightened, and as we ran out onto the Sicilian beaches, all bluster and false courage, there was absolutely nothing. There was nobody. No people at all, never mind Italian or German soldiers. We just walked up the beach and clambered up some of the cliffs and beyond into the scrub, and there was nothing but a few wild goats to resist our advance into enemy territory. This is war? It feels more like a stroll along Brighton seafront at dawn.

12 July

I spoke too soon. After a couple of days of marching inland – all at an easy pace and in good spirits – we were opened fire on. Nobody I know of got hurt, but it halted our advance. We're laying low for the day.

13 July

I feel physically sick. Joey was shot today and I can't get the image out of my mind. He just dropped to the ground and, at first, nobody knew why. Even when four of us surrounded him to take a closer look, he seemed to have nothing more than a hole in the middle of his tunic, which was oozing blood. One little hole not even the size of a penny, that was all it took. We just watched him die, none of us knowing what to do, like it was a show at the theatre or something. Poor Joey was just coughing and spluttering and holding out his hands, grasping for someone to help him. Nobody could.

I know I expected to see people die out here, but when it's someone who's been a pal – even for a few days – the feeling isn't anything like you expected; it makes you go a bit numb and you don't feel like talking, or doing anything, or even looking anyone in the face.

One of the four soldiers who watched him die was a bit older than the rest of us, and although he didn't do anything it didn't seem to bother him as much, he just said we had to leave Joey and find some cover behind one of the rocks around us.

14 July

We've advanced about fifteen miles now, and I saw another pal of mine – some chap from up north I knew from training – take a bullet in the arm. He's in terrible pain, but carrying on regardless. I'm starting to feel very lucky.

That was, in effect, the end of my letter to Mother and Father. I handed it in to be posted back home, not knowing whether it would get there.

It did get home, but it was to be the last letter I would write to my parents for many months. I can only imagine what they went through in the intervening period, not knowing whether I was alive or not.

On the next day I wouldn't have known what to write anyway. I was in perpetual panic.

We were trying to capture a farm. The theory, I was led to believe, was that if you controlled the farm buildings you controlled the surrounding land to an extent. One of our lads who spoke a bit of Italian asked the owners whether any Italian soldiers had been here and they said no, never. We weren't so sure, so we searched the house and outbuildings. Just as we were preparing to move on, somebody opened fire on us from somewhere. Two of our lads were killed instantly and the rest of us ran for cover. I ended up in a hayloft and didn't know what to do; I was shivering with fear. There was a break in the gunfire and I heard footsteps above me, then more gunfire. I heard the bullets ricochet everywhere but I had no idea where they were coming from. I crawled across to an opening in the front of the hayloft and slowly poked my face into the streaming sun. I felt quite weak with fear at what I saw: across the farmyard our lads were shooting up towards the roof of the hayloft I was in. Well, there was nothing I could do; there was no point me running out there, it would just have confused things and probably got me shot one way or another. I crawled back to the far side of the hayloft and curled up into a ball.

I have no idea how long it lasted for, but I could hear our lads retreating away from the farmyard and behind the main house. I crept down from the hayloft and stood just inside the doorway, in the relative cool of the shade, watching the main house. For a few seconds I thought about making a run for it. I decided not to, kidding myself that it would have been madness. The truth was my legs were like jelly so I'm not sure whether I could have run without falling over. I admit I didn't have a clue what to do. All that training and yet there seemed to be no other option than to do nothing, to stand still. Although I was shivering I also felt the sweat gliding down past my eye.

Then I heard a click, and my senses were heightened for a second. I stopped breathing to listen. I felt something hard and cold on the side of my neck, digging itself in.

I started breathing heavily. I felt a trickle of cold saliva dribbling from the corner of my mouth. I heard a single word. I didn't understand it but I turned around very slowly. It was then I noticed I'd wet myself. I didn't care. The Italian soldier said nothing else but pointed to my weapons and to the floor, keeping the muzzle of his gun rammed deep in the tense flesh of my gullet.

I did as I was told, even though my hands were trembling. I even put down the knife I was carrying, later realizing I might have got away with keeping it. But I wasn't thinking straight. In fact, my only thought was that I was going to die, that I was never going to see my mother and father again. I felt the urge to pray, but couldn't remember the words to any prayers. I was so full of fear I could almost hear it buzzing in my head like an electric charge.

Another soldier appeared. He searched me, looking for weapons I assume, but didn't take anything else.

Once they started talking to one another I calmed down, even having a little presence of mind to be embarrassed about wetting myself. Now I merely felt alone, as if my pals had deserted me.

The soldiers forced me onto the floor, face down, hands behind my back, and talked for an hour or more. It was uncomfortable, nothing more.

I heard a truck pull up outside. I was kicked and shouted at. I got up. The barrel of a rifle helped my hands find their way to the top of my head. I was shoved outside and towards the truck.

Inside the back of the truck were two other prisoners, lots of straw and animal excrement of some sort. The two other chaps were an American called Burt and an Indian called Devendra. Both of them could see the state I was in; my eyes must have been as wild as the barren countryside around us. They seemed to understand what had happened to me and started talking, asking me questions and telling me their own stories.

I didn't take much notice for the first few hours; I was shivering with fear. And after that first experience of an enemy rifle pressing into my body I was all the more scared about what was going to happen.

I don't know whether it was because of Burt or Devendra talking to me or just sheer exhaustion after the adrenaline rush had worn off, but I eventually calmed down enough to think properly.

For the next day or two the possibility that we were all being taken to our deaths never left my mind – it was there in the background as sure as breathing was – but we had little choice other than to get to know one another. We were confined together in that goat barn on wheels, eating and sleeping and performing nature's chores in front of one another.

I didn't have a clue where we were going, but through the uncertainty there was a glimmer of relief at still being in one piece.

CHAPTER SEVEN

Sitting on a bench by the Thames in the one-bridge town of Henley, Nicole dried her face and gave a few puffs of recovery.

She checked her watch.

Too early. She couldn't face going back home just yet. *Give Mum a little more time to worry.*

That's right. Don't go back yet.

Or even . . . at all? Mmm. Right. How well would that work?

She absent-mindedly brought her hand up to her face to give her finger a frustrated bite. There was a metallic click on her tooth.

The ring.

She showed the back of her hand to her face.

The ring might be valuable.

Thoughts started whirling in her mind – thoughts of the life she wanted. And all whirlwinds start with a small eddy. With a seed, a decision or a lucky break.

She got up – almost jumped up – from the bench and headed for that single bridge.

There was bound to be a pawnbroker in town.

The High Street?

Mmm . . . unlikely.

She crossed the road and headed for what Mum would call the 'less salubrious' part of town, looking down this road and that. *So where would a pawnbroker be?* Pawnbrokers, cheap burger bars and tattoo parlours. They all went together.

A few minutes later she'd found one, its shop window full of utterly, utterly random crap. Jewellery rubbing shoulders with guitars rubbing shoulders with laptops, then there was more jewellery, some designer handbags, a set of golf clubs, an old—

'You going in, love?'

Nicole jerked at the ragged voice and moved to the side. 'Erm . . . sorry, no.'

'Tough choices, eh? Know what you mean.'

The man, greasy skin sprouting waxy grey hair above a melee of baggy clothes, opened the door and went in.

Nicole looked again at the sign in the window.

It said, 'Gold and other jewellery bought and sold here'.

It also said, 'Proof of ID required'.

This needed a little more planning. She would go home, then perhaps come back with some ID. She just had to find which packing box it was in.

When she got back home the place looked worse than it did before.

But Mum didn't say anything. There was no *Where have you been?* No *I've been sick with worry.* In fact, not even a *Hello*.

But eventually she did speak. 'I've cleaned the kitchen floor,' she said. 'But I need to clean out the cupboards and drawers before we can put anything in them.'

Nicole matched her mother's pause, then said, 'Are they dirty?'

Her mother's hair shook as she shuddered in disgust. 'You do not – *you do not* – want to know.'

Nicole was pretty sure she didn't, so asked if her mother had seen the box of books.

'Did you label it?' her mother said.

'Not sure.'

'Well, there you go. Anyway, there are more important things for you to do, like the bedrooms. Why don't you find the vacuum cleaner and the bags with the bedding in them?'

Nicole kept her sigh to herself. 'Yeah, cool.'

But she did find time to open a few boxes and dig out her ID.

Later on, with two bedrooms habitable and a small area of the kitchen usable, Nicole's mother called time. She said it was enough work for one day and they needed to eat and get some sleep.

They opened one of the boxes in the hallway and took out just what they needed, and soon were eating together at the kitchen table. It was tinned soup and the crumpled remains of the loaf Nicole's mother had managed to cram into the box that morning.

'So, do you know who lived here before?' Nicole asked.

Her mother shrugged her shoulders as she chewed and swallowed. 'Some old guy,' she said.

'What? On his own?'

A pair of eyes scanned the room in a theatrical fashion before glaring at Nicole. 'What do you think?'

'Yeah. Sorry.'

'Single men are the worst – no, *old* single men are really the worst. I tell you, if I'd known it was this bad . . .' A quick shake of her head finished the sentence.

'Didn't you see it before you bought it?'

Nicole's mother hesitated, then said, 'Well, at the time we didn't have much choice, did we?'

'Didn't we?' Nicole said.

The question went unanswered and they finished eating in silence. Afterwards they both sat back.

'So where did he move to?' Nicole said.

'Where did *who* move to?'

'This old guy.'

'Oh, I don't think he *moved*, as such. More *got taken out*.'

Nicole stopped to think, then said, 'You mean *he died*? In *here*?'

'Well, I don't know whether he died actually in here. I think the estate agent said something about him having a stroke and not being able to look after himself. And it was the council selling it, so I assume he didn't make a will.'

A disdainful grimace took hold of Nicole's face.

'Oh, it's nothing,' her mother said. 'This house is over a hundred years old so he's probably not the first to cop it in here anyway. People die. Fact.' Her face cracked a little. She looked down, blinked a few times and let out a long breath. 'Sorry,' she muttered. 'That didn't come out well.'

Nicole did her best to smile warmly. 'He'd understand. Anyway, I wasn't thinking about Darren. It's just sad when that happens, when you don't have anyone to leave your house to.'

'Well, what's done is done. And it's our gain.' She stood up. 'Come on, I'll wash up and you can dry.'

For a few minutes they stood next to each other, passing plates but not speaking.

Then Nicole spoke.

'Mum?'

'What?'

Nicole glanced at her mother out of the corners of her eyes, trying to work out what sort of a *what* that was.

'What is it?' her mother said.

'I was just wondering . . .'

'Just say it, Nicole, *please*.'

'I was just wondering . . . everything in this house is ours, isn't it?'

'What d'you mean? Like what?'

'Well . . .' Nicole thought *ring* but shrugged as she searched for any word apart from that one. 'Like, all the stuff down in the cellar, tools and stuff.'

Her mother gave a shorter, less procrastinated shrug. 'Well, of course. Anyway, the old guy won't need any of that lot where he's gone.'

Nicole nodded agreement and carried on drying plates for a few minutes.

'Mum?'

'Oh, what now, Nicole?'

No. Leave it, Nicole. It could wait. She shook her head and said, 'Oh, nothing.'

Her mother stopped washing up for a moment. 'And don't keep saying "Mum", then "it's nothing". That is *so* annoying.'

'Well, I was just wondering . . . about Dad, that's all.'

A cloud of suds flew off the rubber glove her mother was wearing. 'Just *don't*, Nicole. We're just settling in. Let's make it our home. So just *don't*. All right?'

Nicole fell silent again and carried on drying, but only for a minute. Then she dropped the tea towel on the floor and ran to her room, burying her head in the pillow.

When Nicole woke it was dark. She sat up and for a bright split second thought she heard Darren's voice from next door.

Were they all still in London? Mum, Dad and Darren and her?

Perhaps the Henley thing had been a bad dream.

For an instant her heart felt light enough to fly right out of her chest. But the pillow was wet and her cheekbones had that damp tenderness that made reality hard to ignore. And there was that faint musty aroma. It smelled like *old guy*.

She fell back onto the pillow, wishing for a different reality. Whatever Dad had or hadn't done, she wished they were all still in

London, *together*, that the accident hadn't happened, that Darren was still alive, that Mum wasn't so bitter, that Dad was back to normal, that . . .

But there was only one reality. No seven-day cooling-off period. No twenty-eight-day returns policy.

No choice.

Ten minutes later – ten minutes of turning and sighing and giving the bedclothes a petulant tug every so often – and the result was the same. She was alone with Mum in a town where she didn't know anyone.

And she wasn't going to get any more sleep.

She was, however, still fully clothed, and had found her ID. And she still had the seventy pounds Dad had given her when they'd said their goodbyes that morning, she in a cold daze of fear, he with a firm chin, and forehead pulled tightly over his eyes.

And she still had the gold ring. To do with as she pleased.

So she could just leave the house now. Add the money the pawnbroker would give her to the seventy pounds, and yes, that would last a few days until she got a job. There were the squats she'd heard so much about; they were everywhere, or so Andrea had said last term. There were bound to be some in Henley, it was just a question of finding them.

Or she could even go back to London and live with Andrea or Chloe or one of her other school friends. They wouldn't mind.

Whatever, she could decide that later. The most important thing was to get out.

With the stealth of a fearful cat she got off the bed and opened the bedroom door.

Silence.

Mum must be asleep.

She turned, grabbed her handbag, and slowly descended the stairs.

The streetlight threw an amber glow through the glass rectangle in the door and onto the one remaining stack of boxes. Nicole's coat lay on the top. She picked it up, slid it on quietly, then looked through that murky rectangle of glass to the outside world, peering left and right along the street.

Right. She would turn right. Towards the town centre.

She stepped back to take a last look upstairs.

Good. Mum was still asleep. Neither of them would want a tearful farewell.

As she turned back towards the front door she caught sight of herself in the mirror on the wall and froze.

Mum had obviously hung the mirror up in a rush; it rested crookedly on its hook. And right now the mirror painted a self-portrait that was dark as well as crooked. There was a definite ruddiness under her eyes, and an uncertain fear within them.

She tried to send herself an encouraging smile. It was then she noticed her mouth was so dry her lips were sticking to her teeth.

Who was she kidding?

Friends? Was she thinking of Andrea and Chloe, who had visited her every week at first?

At first. Yes, *at first*. But the visits tailed off as they got on with their lives.

And as for squats, who was she trying to fool? How would she find a squat, never mind work out how she could 'join' one?

And just how upset would Mum be? She had a hard shell, for sure, but Nicole had seen her cry many times since the break-up. Although never before. Never.

She wasn't sure about God and the afterlife, but if Darren – just *if* – he was up there looking down, what would he say? Would he be telling her to leave?

The mirror had dumped her back into reality. This was now her home. That was reality. Perhaps it would be better to wait. Yes.

Leave it a few weeks, by which time she'd have more money.

Where would she get more money?

She glanced at the cellar door.

From more gold, perhaps?

She took off her coat, placed it back down on the box, and tiptoed over to the cellar door. It opened with a creak she hadn't noticed before.

She waited to hear if the creak had disturbed her mother, then stepped into the blackness and reached for the light switch. She tensed her neck as she flicked the switch and took the steps slowly and carefully.

Soon she had the briefcase in her hands, keeping the thing at arm's length, trying not to breathe in the dust. She opened it, lifted out the notebook as though it was made of ancient bone china, and pulled out all the scraps of paper. She put her hand inside the briefcase and ran her fingers around the bottom. The tips of her fingers found nothing.

Oh, well. It was worth a try.

She lifted the scraps of paper up from the desk like leaves out of a gutter, and placed them back in the briefcase. A couple of them broke away and fluttered to the ground. She bent down and picked them up, then took a moment to look. They were photos, battered and faded old things. One was of a man in army uniform, grinning as though he was in a show rather than the forces. The other, larger one showed four men rowing along a river. Perhaps that was the Thames. She held the larger photo up to the light. One of the rowers was definitely the man in the other photo. The man who everyone called Mac? The man who had never replaced so much as a mat or a pair of curtains in decades? She put the photos back in the briefcase and noticed, between the piles of letters, one or two more. It was the same man, in various situations, but always smiling.

She put all the loose sheets in the briefcase and picked up the notebook. She opened it and skimmed a few more pages of the old guy's writing. Life in the forces. Tunisia. Boats. Invasion of Italy.

There was no mention of any ring. She would have to read it properly – and there was a lot of writing in the notepad.

Nicole's thoughts were interrupted by a faint creaking of floor-boards from above.

It was still the middle of the night, and she was in the cellar of a house she didn't really know. Alone.

The hiss of a toilet cistern made her heart jump. Then there were more creaks.

She put the notebook back in the case, closed it, and rushed out of the cellar.

'Are you downstairs, Nicole?'

She closed the cellar door, holding the handle down until door found frame before gently releasing it. 'Just getting a drink, Mum.'

Then she had an idea.

She *would* get a drink, and she *would* go back to bed. But first she would go back down and get the notebook. She would hide it under her bed and read it without having to go down into that dungeon of a cellar.

She waited for Mum's door to close.

CHAPTER EIGHT

I can't remember exactly how long we stayed on the goat truck, but I know we very soon crossed over into mainland Italy and spent ages winding around the country lanes there.

It felt like a week but was probably only two or three days. Throughout that time my head was a fog of fear. I knew at any time the truck could stop. And with it so could my life. But gradually my nerves settled, and Burt, Devendra and I started to talk more. The stench of goat excrement was always there but was the very least of our concerns. Both Burt and Devendra had fought in the siege of Tobruk and told me all about it, so I had a great deal of respect for them, thinking they were better soldiers than I would ever be.

Burt told us how he loved cars. He had a Studebaker pick-up for practicality but hankered after a Lincoln Zephyr, and had plans to be a car dealer when he returned to Boston after the war. Devendra was a much more studious sort, and said how he hoped to continue his medical training and become a doctor in the Gujarat area. Devendra was a vegetarian, and I'd never met one of those before; I actually had to ask him, just to be sure what it meant. We made a good team because Burt and I weren't too keen on vegetables, so we would swap food whenever the guards saw fit to feed us. The food was palatable but we were hungry most of the time. However, the choking thirst was the worst thing. Twice a day we were allowed out to drink water that tasted more of rust than anything else. The whole thing was horrible, but in hindsight we were treated reasonably well considering a few days before we'd been trying to shoot them in their own country.

We asked them where they were taking us. They said they didn't know. That plied us with adrenaline again. We thought they must have had some idea, and we'd all heard rumours of summary executions of enemy prisoners. Now any talk of plans for after the war was forgotten; we thought plans the guards had for us were more important.

As it turned out, however, they weren't.

The suspension on the truck was non-existent, and over the rough roads we were being jolted back and forth, side to side, so closely packed that elbows and shoulders rammed into chests and arms with every bump and change of direction.

It was hot during the day – like being stuck inside a tent – but quite cold when the sun had been down for a few hours. So we were all fed up with the journey, fearful of what awaited us wherever we were going, and, yes, tiring of each other's company.

It must have happened during the early hours of the third or fourth morning.

We were starving and exhausted from lack of sleep, and aching from the jumble of bodies. I just wanted somewhere quiet and still to curl up into a ball and switch off.

But I was aware of the roads – or the driving – getting worse. The truck had been veering left and right a little more than usual for some time, as if the driver was either drunk or as tired as us. Our worries for our future became more immediate with every lurch of the truck. It was dark outside, God knows what time it was. And, of course, it was dark inside too. We had nothing to hold onto to steady ourselves, and no way of knowing which direction we were going to be thrown in. Bodies were starting to get flung about like rag dolls, except that when one hit you it didn't feel like a rag doll. I held my hands up to protect my face and curled up as best I could. I still got hit a few times; the only warnings were shouts of despair and a sense of which direction my own body was being thrown in.

It was inevitable something worse was going to happen.

Strangely, I remember no screech of tyres, just one lurch that lurched too far. I felt myself being launched into the air and landing very painfully. My right arm caught on something and my shoulder felt like someone had twisted it, much like a chicken leg would be twisted to remove it from the carcass. The pain brought tears to my eyes but also a rush of adrenaline to my head, which banished the pain as suddenly as it had appeared.

And in a second all became still and quiet, which was just what I'd been praying for.

Then the shouting started.

I looked up and could now see the sky and a half-moon masked in drifting cloud. For a fleeting split second there was beauty in that sight. Then a deathly hissing sound came from close by and I realized there were other things I could see. The truck had ended up on its side, and the wooden boards that lined its sides – the ones I'd been leaning on – had been split and torn away in places. I struggled to get up onto my knees, and that was when the hissing sound became more desperate. I looked down and saw Devendra struggling to breathe, his face trembling, his eyes large and pleading with me.

A section of wood from the other side of the truck now lay across his neck, pressing down on his windpipe. I found my hands either side of it, pulling, crawling aside to make sure I wasn't on it. The problem was that others were. As Devendra stopped making even those hissing noises and simply stared at me, I pulled harder at the wood. As I lifted, he gasped for his life. But others in the cramped space were moving too, and yet more weight fell upon the wood – too much weight for me to fight. It trapped his throat again. I tried to shove men away, but it was hopeless. I had no idea which of them were lying on the plank but they were all fighting their own battles to live. I grabbed the plank again, this time lodging my forearm underneath it for more strength. It gave him a few more precious breaths. But the movement brought back the bolt of pain in my shoulder. I fought against the demon shredding the sinews in my arm until I cried.

That was when I looked up and saw, straight ahead of me, open countryside. I saw another prisoner running away, and caught the shimmering trail of something beyond him.

It had to be a river.

Once again there was movement next to me. A man shouted in agony and by the moonlight I saw him clutch his knee as he fell onto the plank. The kneecap pointed in a hideously wrong direction. Black-dark blood streamed down the hands that tried to hold the knee together. I still wonder whether I did the right thing – whether I could have shoved him out of the way, off the plank, and saved Devendra's life.

But I had no time to think anything through. At least, that's what I've told myself ever since. I jumped forward through the smashed roof of the truck and fell onto the road, then picked myself up and started running, clutching my shoulder as every step felt like it was being hit with a lump hammer. I didn't look back. Not once. If they were going to shoot, then what the hell. I fell a couple of times over the rough, rutted terrain, but eventually reached the river. It was wide, shallow and slow flowing. I didn't stop running and fell into it; if it had been a torrent I would have done the same. The crash, the frenetic shoving and pulling to save Devendra and the run with the fear of bullets in my back at any moment – all of these had soaked my filthy clothes in sweat. My throat had been sticky with thirst for days, so I stayed there for a few minutes, soaking my clothes and slaking my thirst. The risk of a bullet and recapture was worth it.

I'd somehow lost my jacket – or it had been ripped off in the accident – but I didn't care. I took a few minutes to drink until my stomach threatened to burst, to wash the sweaty dirt from my face and hair, and only then did I turn back to face the truck.

It lay on its side like some pathetic dead animal. Light spilled from its headlights, one creating a bright, almost angelic white line along the road, the one above it diffusing into nothingness. There was no movement; I assumed anyone who could have escaped had already done so. But what about the guards? I looked more closely, and stilled myself to hear any shouts or gunshots. I heard nothing but the rush of water around my legs, and realized I had to press on.

I gave my face a final splash, then struggled through the shin-deep water to the other side. Again, I ran without looking back.

By sunrise I had slowed to a walk, and then a stagger. I hadn't had a proper meal since leaving Tunis, and I could almost feel my body eating into my muscles for energy.

More importantly, hours after leaving the river I hadn't come across any other water source, and was suffering from that raging thirst once more. I was also cold again after slowing down, and feeling the signs of sleep deprivation – dizziness and delirium.

I was ready to collapse and accept whatever that brought. I found a dip in the terrain, dropped myself down under a bush, and immediately fell asleep.

I woke to find nothing much had changed. I was eighteen years old, had been a serving soldier in the army for a little over a week, and had no idea how to do what I was trying to do – survive. I knew little of Italy other than that it was enemy territory, and I had no idea how to stay alive in the wild.

The sun was now well above the horizon and starting to warm my shivering body. But my stomach ached with hunger and the insides of my mouth felt like they were lined with glue. I crawled out from under the bush, pulled some foliage from a nearby plant, and put it in my mouth. I think there was a part of me that figured that if rabbits and deer could live on grass and leaves, then so could I. I spat it out and tried another handful, with the same results. Even hunger felt better than the bitter taste I experienced. I concluded I should carry on walking – keeping my wits about me – until I came across a farm, or even just a wild fruit bush or anything I recognized that might taste good. However, I did get some moisture from the morning dew, so licked another few plants before setting off again.

I reached a long, uphill section, and after a few miles of it my legs threatened to give way. The only thing that kept me going was the hope of coming across some sort of civilization on the other side.

And I was not disappointed.

I reached a ridge, which afforded me a good view of a small town, with a farm of some sort on its nearside, and in front of that a large tree. It was a solitary thing which looked like it was a sentry guard protecting the farm. I crouched down and crawled along the dirt, and could make out pigs on one side of the farm, chickens and ducks on the other, and between them the regular lines that spoke of crops of some sort. Beyond the farm lay the town – clumps of stone buildings so large they must have contained many dwellings, probably a few thousand.

And then, from my vantage point, I could see a much bigger conurbation in the distance, a wild sprawl, which included chimneys and factories of some sort as well as blocks of houses.

The only choice I had was whether to go down now and search

for food or wait until nightfall. At first I decided to do the sensible thing – to wait until dusk at the very least – and looked around for somewhere to shelter from the sun, which was now getting stronger by the minute. My resolve lasted about half an hour, and in all honesty I was so weak and dehydrated I'm not sure to this day whether I'd still have been alive by sundown.

I started walking down the hillside, taking slow and careful steps, always crouching, always with my head up to spot signs of movement on the farm. I stopped and hid behind that single tree for a few minutes, waiting and watching for signs of life. The tree was a huge, gnarled old thing. I later found out it was an olive tree. At the time I didn't even know what an olive was; I'm not sure many British people did in 1943. But it certainly had a presence, the lines of bark swirling up its trunk lending a ghostly feel, enhanced by sparse branches reaching out like arms ready to gather up the unwary.

After those few minutes, during which I saw no sign of human life on the farm, I sneaked out and ran towards the tallest things there: rows of trees about my height. They turned out to be grapevines. As soon as I reached the first one all thoughts of possible danger vanished; I started plucking grapes and cramming them into my mouth. I hardly tasted them, but just swallowed as quickly as I could. Before then I'd never even seen a real one, let alone tasted the sweet, tangy secret it held inside. It was food and water in one, and it was probably the best thing I've ever tasted before or since.

The rush of sweet water brought me to my senses, and I looked beyond and all around me. Still there was nobody, so I wrenched a whole bunch from the plant and fell to the dusty earth below. I finished off that second bunch, then was halfway through a third, and starting to feel full and queasy, when I heard voices. Feeling queasy turned to feeling sick and downright frightened. I had no idea what I wanted to do but knew I didn't want to go back on one of those trucks again, let alone to wherever it had been taking me.

I listened and quickly realized there were two pairs of voices — an elderly man's and a woman's from one direction, and two young men from the other. Sure, I could hide behind a spindly grape-vine, but not from all of them. I poked my head around the vine, under cover of the foliage, and saw the two younger men pushing wheelbarrows towards me. They were young and fit, just like me, probably a little smaller. Then again, they had probably been well fed and didn't have damaged shoulders. And even if I could over-power them, what then? The other pair — the man and the woman — would have had time to alert the authorities or fetch firearms of some sort. Either way, I was caught in a pincer movement worthy of any field marshal and had to do something. I got up onto my feet and stepped around to the other side of the vine, gearing myself up to make a run for it.

That was when I stepped too far, stared for too long, and the woman saw me.

I very nearly fainted with fear; these people were officially my enemy.

The woman immediately turned her face away as if she hadn't seen me, and looked over to the two men with wheelbarrows. Then she stared at me for a second. I could see the shock on her face, and felt my legs trembling, but also tensing up in readiness to race back up the hill. The elderly man with her had his back to me, but he noticed her stare and went to turn to look in my direction. I was about to break into a run when the woman tossed her long dark hair back with the help of one hand — as if to prepare herself — and clutched her stomach, crying out in agony.

The young men immediately dropped their wheelbarrows and rushed over to her; the elderly man tried to hold her, to comfort her. I didn't see what happened between them next because I was quietly edging away towards the big old olive tree, where I hid and looked back. Nobody was looking in my direction and I was out of earshot, so I ran for my life back up the hill. I just made it to the top before collapsing, exhausted, onto my belly. I turned back to see what was happening. The woman was still being consoled by the three men. Then she looked up.

Towards me?

I wasn't sure at the time, but I crawled back away from the ridge, got to my feet, and walked about half a mile to a field of long wheat grass, where it felt safe for me and my full belly to hide and rest for some time.

As I fell asleep I thought of the woman, and I couldn't stop thinking about the obvious reason for her behaviour – that she was helping me. Something else became clear to me too as I drifted off to sleep. The reason I'd stared at her for so long was because she was so beautiful. She was unlike what I'd been led to believe was a typical Italian frame; this woman was full-figured, with prominent high cheekbones and wide eyes that stirred something in me in spite of my wretched condition. For that reason alone I thought perhaps I should move on, look for somewhere else to steal food.

Still, that could wait until I'd rested.

CHAPTER NINE

The next morning Nicole was woken by her mother, mug in hand, opening the door.

Her face said 'peace offering', but it was obviously meant to be understood without being said. It was Mum's way – these days, at least.

'You all right?' Mum said, as if Nicole had stubbed a toe the night before.

Nicole sat up in bed and rubbed her eyes. There was still a little tenderness around them. Did it show? Would Mum notice if it did? And would she say anything if she did notice?

Her mother placed the mug down on the bedside table. 'Here, have that. We've got a busy weekend ahead of us. I've had a proper look around the place. Everything's filthy dirty, worse than I thought.'

Nicole stared straight ahead.

'I tell you, every last cupboard and drawer in that kitchen needs scrubbing to within an inch of its life. Bathroom's not too bad, mostly flat surfaces and . . .'

Her words trailed off. She let out a long, exhausted sigh and sat down on the bed. 'I know it's difficult for you, love. I know that.

On Monday I start work, I've got something to occupy me during the day, people to meet and all that.'

She waited; still Nicole didn't speak.

'You need to do the same, sweetheart. You've missed out on so much this year. Have you thought what you're going to do?'

Another long pause.

'Why don't you go to the college and see about a course? Might be a bit more interesting than just looking at the website. You can go on Monday when I go into work, or we can go together in the evening if you like. It's up to you.'

Nicole shrugged and said, 'I'm . . . I'm not sure.'

'Trust me, darling. You need to get out. Meet people. Sort out a course at the very least.'

'I don't know what to study.' Nicole paused, almost wriggling her body. 'Not sure I want to study at all to be honest.'

Her mother reached out, held Nicole's hand, and gave it a little squeeze.

'Have you thought about starting where you left off?'

Nicole shook her head. 'I don't know. It all seems so long ago. Not sure I can do any of it. I don't think my head's in the right place.'

'What's that supposed to mean?' her mother said. 'You need to do some study or some training, or . . . get a job of some sort. Something where you meet people and get on.' Now she gripped her daughter's hand. 'Nicole. I know you get headaches if you read too much, but that should be getting better. You need to do *something*, whatever it is.'

Nicole pulled a swathe of hair down and spent a few seconds chewing it.

'Promise me you'll think about it.'

Nicole nodded. 'Yeah. I'll think about it.'

Her mother's lips grew wide and thin. A smile from her was rare these days. It gave Nicole a warm feeling in her stomach that was unexpected, almost uncomfortable.

'You're right, Mum. I know you're right. I need to do something.'

'Good girl.'

They looked each other straight in the eye and Nicole tried to smile.

'So . . .' Her mother stood up. 'We've got today and tomorrow to sort this house out. We need to finish cleaning the kitchen and bathroom, then unpack as much as we can. You'll feel better by Monday. I know you will.'

'Yeah.'

'I've found the toaster,' her mother said, standing up. 'See you in ten, downstairs, okay?'

Nicole nodded and watched her mother leave the room. Yes, there was definitely something there that warmed her stomach, she just wasn't sure whether she wanted it to.

Ten minutes later and there was, indeed, toast on the kitchen table, and a buttery aroma was trying to overpower the stale odour that hung around the house like words spoken in anger and regretted. Also there was tea. A large pot, in fact.

Mum always thought tea could solve all the world's problems.

They sat opposite each other, listening to the local radio tell them about sunshine with a risk of light showers, which didn't matter as they both were going to be stuck indoors all day.

'Mum?'

'What, love?'

'I know you don't like me saying it . . .' She paused, waiting for the knock-back, but it didn't come. 'But . . . when can I see Dad again?'

Her mother shrugged, pushing the corners of her mouth downwards. 'Do you need to actually *see* him? You've your phone, you can talk to him any time you want.'

'But it costs a fortune.'

Her mother harrumphed a laugh. 'When did *you* start caring about money?' She prodded a finger to her breastbone. '*I* pay the bill.'

'But it does, Mum. I feel guilty if I'm on it too long.'

'You've got Skype.'

'Yes, I know. But it's . . . it's not the same.' She looked up, leaden-faced. 'I want to *see* him, Mum. I want to meet up with him and . . .' She sighed.

'You'll have to talk to him about arranging that; *you* might want to meet him but *I* certainly don't.'

'What? Like, *ever?*'

Her mother stopped chewing and put down her slice of toast. 'Look. I really, honestly have no objection to you seeing him. He's your dad, and yes, I know he was a good one – at least, until recently.'

'But you can't just say you'll never see him again.'

'I don't want to talk about it. Just remember you can see him as often as you like. Bring him here as long as you're sure I'm out, but as far as I'm concerned he doesn't exist, okay.'

The last word was clearly accented as a statement, leaving no room for dissent. She resumed eating her toast and twirled a finger at Nicole's plate for her to do the same. 'Now, come on. Let's have a decent breakfast and crack on. We've got so much work to do here, more than you think.'

An hour later it seemed like a mountain of work – and not one with an appealing snowy-topped summit. While her mother set to on the bathroom, Nicole cleaned out all of the kitchen cupboards and drawers, each one filthy with unidentifiable substances. The task took most of the day, and by the end of it everything reeked of disinfectant scrub.

Sunday was easier and a lot less disgusting, populating those chemical-smelling kitchen drawers and cupboards with pots, pans, crockery, cutlery and the myriad tools and gadgets Mum had insisted on bringing even though she hadn't used them in years.

After cleaning the carpets and walls of the living room (and throwing away the disgusting lampshade, which Nicole's mother said was probably hideous when new but was now fifty per cent dust) they set about arranging the furniture. Then they dealt with the last few packing boxes and bags.

It was seven o'clock in the evening by the time they got to the final box, which was labelled 'Nicole's stuff'.

'Looks like this one's already been opened,' Nicole's mother said.

Nicole said nothing.

'I thought you'd have taken the lot up to your bedroom – all your posters, books, cuddly toys and stuff.'

Nicole almost said she didn't give a damn about the crap in the box because she might not be living here much longer anyway. But as the words formed in her mind she realized that wasn't exactly how she felt. She had a half-hearted sift through the box before lugging it upstairs and dumping it in the corner of her bedroom.

On Monday morning Nicole got up and trudged downstairs to find her mother rushing around the house like she was on an elastic leash – into the kitchen to throw the last of her coffee into her mouth, into the living room to put her jacket on, back into the kitchen to turn the radio off, then to the hallway to check how she looked in the mirror that still hung crookedly there, then back into the living room to grab her handbag, and back to the hallway to retouch her make-up in the mirror.

'Have you had any more thoughts about college?' she said as she pulled her coat on.

'No.'

Only now did she look at Nicole. 'Oh, well. No rush.' She almost jogged over to her, gave her the briefest of hugs, and left the house.

It was quiet enough for Nicole to clearly hear the clicking of her mother's heels on the pavement as she headed for town. Then there was complete silence.

Nicole stood for a moment, not moving, wondering what to do.

She wasn't going to college, but she had to go somewhere, just to get out of this place. It might be cleaner now but it still wasn't home and never would be.

Fifteen minutes later she had her coat and shoes on and was opening the front door. She checked she had her key, her gold ring, her ID and her seventy pounds, then shut the door and started walking. It was a bright morning, but still cold.

As she turned right, she glanced into the corner shop and her eyes met those of a man. He gave her a friendly grin – almost *over*-friendly. She looked away and carried on walking. Within a few minutes the river Thames hove into view, wide and murky but full of life. People walked dogs along the path, boats as sleek as any sports car cruised majestically down the middle, keen rowers pulled themselves along nearer the water's edge. There was that peculiar boggy smell – almost sewer-like but not completely unpleasant.

Nicole's stomach gurgled, and a gust of wind seemed to whip her face. There was nothing wrong with the place; it wasn't dark or frightening or unfriendly. But she felt an urge to go back – back to that house that wasn't home and never would be.

She watched as a bright white boat with blue graphics artistically sketched along its side glided past and the man at the helm gave her a wave.

She waved back.

Then she turned and headed for home, past the corner shop, past the man who smiled at her again, and to the house that wasn't home.

After another glance at her sorry face in the mirror she took her coat and shoes off and poured herself a bowl of cornflakes. She opened the fridge, lifted out the bottle of milk, and tilted it to highlight the last few frothy dregs. A curse escaped from her lips – aimed at her mother – then she put her coat and shoes on again and headed for the corner shop.

'Legs are killing,' Nicole heard someone say.

She looked over to the till. It was the man who'd grinned at her when she'd walked past but was now ignoring her. Okay, so he wasn't exactly a man yet, but tall, broad-shouldered yet slim, and sprawled across the counter like a beached octopus. He was talking to an older man, something about doing so many miles last night, and after a run earlier in the day too.

She pulled two bottles of milk out of the fridge, walked over and placed them on the counter.

The older man loitered for a few seconds, and then said something to the younger one about seeing everyone later that evening. He said, 'Take care, Shaun,' then left.

Shaun turned his attentions to Nicole. 'Hello again,' he said, now retrieving his cheery grin. Nicole said, 'Hi,' and he came back at her with, 'All right?', another smile, then, 'Just those, is it?'

God, he sounded as chirpy as a pet budgie.

Nicole nodded, paid, and left the shop.

A few minutes later the cornflakes were drenched in fresh milk, and a few minutes after that they were no more.

Nicole put the kettle on and sat down at the kitchen table. What could she do today? Watch daytime TV? Listen to music? Unpack her box of 'crap'?

The ring on her finger clanked on the handle as she made herself a mug of tea. Yes. The ring. The book. The story. The story that might explain the ring and whether there was more. Yes, she could read it in small doses to keep the headaches at bay.

She carefully carried her mug of tea upstairs, lifted the notebook out from under the bed, and started reading it again.

This time it was different. She didn't skim. She didn't idly flick through the pages. She knew she wouldn't be disturbed. It was just her, a large mug of sweet tea, and some doddery old man's war-bore scribbles.

Except . . . that was being a bit unfair. It was actually starting to get interesting, doddery old man or not.

She read on.

CHAPTER TEN

I slept for a long time in that safe sea of wheat grass, and I needed to. By the time I woke it was dusk, and I feared the coming of another cold night. For an hour or more I hugged myself in my dirty pit to keep warm, even folding some of the grasses onto me for insulation. But I knew staying out all night wouldn't do me any good. I tried to remember whether there had been an outbuilding or shed on the farm I could use. Even a pig shelter would do.

A shiver of my shoulders told me there was no choice. I would have to find out. And with darkness falling, I decided that now was as good a time as any.

I got up and started walking, stumbling in the half-light over the rough earth, and eventually reached the ridge overlooking the farm. I crouched down there and looked below me. Apart from the animals there were no signs of movement, so I made my way down to that single giant tree again – the one as lonely as I was – and hid behind it.

And I found something there.

It had definitely been put there recently, because I'd been standing on that precise spot just a few hours before and would have remembered. It was a large bundle of material of some sort, and had clearly been placed against the trunk rather than accidentally dropped.

I wondered whether it could have been a trap – even explosives. I gingerly prodded it with the end of my foot, and started thinking why anyone would leave anything there – explosives or otherwise. I pulled it towards me and opened it. It was clothing. Civilian clothing. Trousers, shirt, jacket. And most important of all, a beret-type woollen hat. No, most important of all, inside the hat – protected by it – was a bottle of water. And then I found something else in the middle of the bundle: an apple and also a few chunks of cheese wrapped in thin paper. I sniffed the cheese and wondered whether anyone would have poisoned it. On the other hand, why would anyone leave a set of clothes there if not to help me? The time for equivocation had passed. Somebody was on my side, and I had a good idea who. If the woman meant me harm surely she would have given me away earlier.

I hurriedly re-packaged the bundle, then ran back up the hill out of sight. There I ate the cheese and the apple and drank the water. Like the grapes earlier that day it all tasted like I had landed in heaven. I licked the paper to clear up any stray morsels of cheese and was about to throw it away when I made out some writing. I tilted it up to the arc of sun on the horizon.

There were four words: 'Follow me at dawn'.

Follow me at dawn?

It was written in English, so the woman – or whoever was behind this – must have had a reasonable command of the English language. I thought that was unusual for a farmhand, so decided to sleep on it. I went back to my makeshift bed in the wheat field, put the new clothing on over my own, and slept again, this time all the more soundly for feeling much warmer.

I awoke in the early hours of the morning, well before sunrise, and started thinking about the note. Whether it was because of those thoughts or not, I couldn't get back to sleep.

Follow me at dawn?

Well, it wasn't yet dawn, so it wouldn't do any harm to see if anything interesting was happening at the farm. I roused myself and made my way back to the top of the hill. I lay on my belly and looked down on the farm. I waited and watched by the light of the sun's first rays, but nothing much was happening. Nothing moved. Even the chickens and ducks lay still, huddled and silent.

Then a solitary pig emerged from a hut. Daily life on the farm was about to start. I continued watching, and soon spotted someone walking along the rows of grapevines. I could only make out a silhouette.

Was this the woman?

The figure looked up, and I didn't know what to do. Should I wave? Would a wave be seen? Should I go down to meet whoever it was? Before I had time to do anything the figure approached the big old olive tree and looked up at the ridge – towards me. Now I was almost certain it was her. At first fear held me back and I did nothing. But she looked down on the ground, where the bundle had been. So yes, whether it was intended for me or not, it was she who had left it.

She looked up to the ridge again, then back to the farm. She tossed her hair back again in that distinctive way of hers, and I was certain. She turned and strode purposefully over the rough ground, heading to my right. When she looked up towards me again I took my chance and started walking along the ridge, still crouching, parallel to her. She carried on and we walked together for a few minutes until a road leading out of town appeared ahead of us both. I carried on walking towards it, crouching, stumbling, keeping one eye on her, and I saw a gate at the corner of the field I was in. It made some sort of sense. We walked closer and kept glancing towards each other. I reached the gate just as she stepped onto the road, so I clambered over it. The first rays of sun beamed from the horizon and now I recognized her. However, as I got to within a hundred or so paces of her, she turned and started walking along the road into the town. I hesitated for a few seconds, then followed.

There was no doubt in my mind that she was helping me. My logic was that if it was some sort of trap she would have waited to meet me face to face, but if she was genuinely trying to help an enemy soldier – a serious offence – then making me trail behind was more defensive.

I stayed about a hundred paces behind her, with my beret hanging forward to cover my eyes, with my chest thumping and my legs starting to feel weak. I was acutely aware that my life could easily have been cut short in a second.

She led me through cobbled alleys, under ornate bridges and past rustic stone buildings that all conspired to form a labyrinth of sorts.

Then I lost her. I'd followed her into a small square and taken my eye off her, my attention drawn to the cafés and shops, thankfully dark and yet to open. There were four exits – two major roads and two alleys. I heard a motorbike. I turned to see it heading towards me. I jumped over a small wall and clattered down as the drop on the other side was lower. As I staggered to my feet I heard a whistle. I looked up and saw her head poking out of one of the alleys. I walked briskly towards her, and followed her round two or three more corners.

Then, with no warning, she stopped outside two doors, which were almost next to one another. One was painted white and had a number on it; it looked like a main front door. The other was set lower in the wall and was much smaller. She didn't say a word, but looked all around her. I looked too and could see no signs of life at this early hour. She unlocked the smaller door, opened it, and pointed inside. Now there was total silence, so much so that I could almost hear my heart thumping away. I looked at her, to see any signs of emotion in her eyes, but saw nothing but my own fear reflected.

I looked around once more, then went in.

Four steep steps led me down to what initially looked like a cave. At that stage I saw nothing more than a stone floor and stone walls. It had the feel of a prison cell, and was about the same size. Just as I noticed the low ceiling a couple of inches above me I heard the door shut behind me. I turned to see the woman standing on the top step.

'Are you British?' she said. She pronounced the question with what I can only describe as that Italian 'sing'. It was an accent I would come to know and love, but other than that it was perfect English.

I didn't do or say anything. I was too confused and still scared.

'Are you British?' she repeated, now with more emphasis. 'A truck carrying prisoners had an accident about twenty kilometres away. Are you one of the British soldiers who escaped?'

I nodded, uncertain, waiting for something to happen, I didn't know what.

'You will be safe here,' she said. 'You will find milk in here.' She pointed, and as I glanced behind me she opened the door.

'Wait,' I said. 'What happened? Do you know how many prisoners escaped?'

'They said four prisoners escaped. Three have been found and shot.'

'Were they all *British* prisoners?' I asked, feeling another pulse of adrenaline hit me.

She nodded. 'They said English. They meant British. I will speak to you later – after work.'

Then she left. I heard the lock engage and her footsteps die away.

For a moment I stared at the door, half expecting it to open again, half wondering whether I was in a dream.

Then I looked all around me again. I had been wrong about this being a prison cell. Yes, it had a low ceiling and no windows, but there were wall lights, and there was thick matting on the floor together with some blankets – obviously a makeshift bed. There was also an ornate wooden chest against one wall with padded cushions on it – a seat. On the other side was a cabinet with a covered stone jug on it. I lifted the cover and found the milk I'd been told about, which the jug had kept cool. I drank the lot like a man possessed, savouring the creaminess all around the insides of my mouth. Then I looked around again. My 'cell' might have been quickly cobbled together, but it had clearly been cobbled together with some care.

I sat down on the wooden chest to think. Something still wasn't right. This woman spoke very good English. No, more than that, she *wrote* good English – better than many of my British comrades. And she was obviously strong-willed, intelligent and resourceful, as well as being beautiful.

But there was even more. I remembered her words: 'They said English. They meant British.' As now, the two were often mixed up; only someone familiar with Britain would have appreciated the distinction.

But why would anyone so well educated be labouring on a farm? It didn't make sense, she should have been a professional something or other in a big city.

I lay down on the matting and covered myself with the blanket. I rested for a time but couldn't sleep. What felt like an hour or two passed, and I realized I was likely to be stuck in here all day. I also realized I'd go mad if I just rested for all that time.

I tried doing a few press-ups, more to test my shoulder than anything. It still hurt too much for that. I went over to the door I'd come through and peeked through the cracks. It was still early morning, and now I saw the bright sunlight getting blotted out as people walked past, heard footsteps and what sounded like cordial greetings being exchanged, and even some laughter.

I turned back and had a better look around the room. Next to the cabinet I'd found the milk on there were steps leading up to a door, which I guessed led to the rest of the house. I gently lifted the handle and pulled and pushed, but it wouldn't budge. I turned my attentions to the cabinet itself. It had two doors, handles next to each other. I opened them, and had to laugh at what I found inside. Then I stopped, sad for a second, realizing how long it had been since I'd laughed. There were a few books of English poetry, and what looked like the entire works of Charles Dickens and Shakespeare, also a few other English books, and even a smattering of American books like *Moby Dick* and *The Adventures of Tom Sawyer*.

I laughed some more. Whatever I'd expected to find inside the cabinet, this wasn't it.

Then again, I'd come to expect the unexpected, and to accept I sometimes had no influence over what was happening to me. I knew I was in Italy, but had no idea whereabouts; I'd been imprisoned by a goddess of a woman whose name, let alone intentions, I didn't know; and I'd just found an English library in her cellar.

I picked up *Oliver Twist* – mainly because it was one of the few I'd heard of, and I'd seen it at the cinema a few years before so thought I could follow the story.

I took the book across to the wooden chest and sat down there. Before I opened it I took a few seconds to look at what I was sitting on. Though detailed with carvings, it was also very solid, and the metal hasp holding the lid down was padlocked. I thought nothing of it and started reading.

I'd got a fair chunk through the book when I heard a rattle. It was coming from the internal door – the one I presumed led to the rest of the house. I stood up and looked for somewhere to hide. There was nowhere. I even tried to open the wooden trunk I'd been sitting on, but the padlock held firm. Fearing the worst, I retreated as far as I could to the exterior door – the one leading to the street outside.

But the door didn't open. I heard children talking – asking or complaining – followed by the louder, rasping voice of a grown man. I couldn't understand what they were saying, and when they stopped I let out a deep breath to relax myself. I looked again out of the cracks in the exterior door to the street outside, but saw or heard nothing that told me where I was or what was happening.

I spent another few hours reading, and then heard a key in the door to the street. Again I stood and steeled myself for something unpleasant or unnerving. This time the door opened.

It opened for barely a blink, but that was all the woman needed. She locked the door from the inside and stepped down towards me.

I backed off. I must have looked like a frightened wild animal.

'You are safe here,' she said gently. 'But you have to tell me who you are and what your plans are.'

There was a tense moment. I'd come to realize in my 'solitary confinement' that if anything untoward was going to happen – such as me being shot – it would have already happened. I also thought for a few seconds that these people could have been enemy agents trying to gain my confidence and find out what I knew about the Allied forces, but that only went to demonstrate my state of mind at the time. And this woman had obviously been working on the land. The sweat-packed hair on her temples and the dirt on her hands and grey flannel work suit spoke of honesty. Looking back, I feel a little ashamed of my naivety, but I was barely an adult. The optimist in me guessed they were probably resistance fighters of some sort, so I followed that idea and decided to trust the woman and whoever else was in the house to a large degree, but be careful about telling them any specific details.

'My name's John,' I said.

'John,' she repeated.

'But everyone calls me Mac.'

She frowned and said, 'Why?'

I couldn't answer because I was so nervous, and it hardly seemed important.

'Never mind that,' she said. 'What are your plans?'

I just shrugged and said I didn't really know.

'We can talk about that later,' she said. 'I will call you Mac. My name is Rosa.'

I tentatively put my hand out and she grabbed it and gave it a shake worthy of any farm labourer.

'Could you tell me what's happening?' I said. 'Such as where I am and why you've helped me?'

She nodded and pointed to the wooden chest. We sat on it.

'You are in Valleverde, on the outskirts of Rome. I live in this house with my parents.'

'I heard some children,' I said. 'On the other side of that door.'

'Lorenzo Junior and Anna.'

'Lorenzo Junior?' I said. 'So . . . is Lorenzo Senior your husband?'

'Lorenzo Senior is my stupid brother.'

I looked towards the interior door. 'He lives here too?'

'His children live here.' She looked down to the floor.

I could see sadness jostling with frustration on her frown. Then she said, with some difficulty, 'And . . . he is not so stupid.'

'What do you mean by that?' I said.

Now a little pain flashed across her face. She shook her head and said, 'Oh, you wouldn't be interested.'

But I was. I was keen to know what the hell was going on around me and any information would have helped. Also a part of me simply wanted to see and hear her speak again. 'Please,' I said. 'Tell me about him.'

She hesitated but I told her to go on.

'It all happened last year. We were protesting against the fascists and their new laws. Myself, Mama and Papa. Also Lorenzo and his wife, Donna. We were attacked by the forces. Donna had a blow to her head. She fell and died.'

'Oh, God,' I said. 'That's terrible.'

'And now Lorenzo is away fighting with even more passion. He is like a man possessed. I think that is the right phrase.'

'I suppose it is,' I said. 'Do you mind if I ask . . . How do you speak such good English?'

'I was an English teacher.' Then she lifted a hand up between us and corrected herself. 'No. I *am* an English teacher. I *am* an English teacher.'

'So why do you work on the farm?'

She gave me the look of a fierce woman scorned, then drew breath, and I thought she was going to shout. 'No,' she said. 'It's not your fault. Perhaps you don't know what is happening in Italy.'

I shrugged. 'Well, actually, no, I don't. I joined the army to fight the Germans.'

'You are not very good at it, are you?'

I didn't know how to respond to that. It seemed a cruel thing to say. But she apologized. Then she told me she was only joking and smiled with warmth in her eyes, and I could only see the good, kind woman who was trying to save my life.

I couldn't help but laugh a little at her humour in what were clearly hard times for her. This woman had trusted me, had told me so much in so few words, and now it was clear exactly why she had helped me. It was her form of rebellion and showed great courage in its own way.

By way of balancing our conversation I told her about my life and my army career. It didn't take long.

Then she talked about the rest of her family, how they had all led relatively carefree lives until about five years before. We had become relaxed in each other's company in a remarkably short space of time, and she spoke freely and with passion.

She told me how 'Mama and Papa' were born with nothing. But when they met they both worked hard – he as a civil servant in Rome, she looking after the home where they took in lodgers. After a time they had enough money to buy a small farm, and Mama had time to start a family. Papa kept his job and took care of the farm in the evenings and at weekends.

Then she hesitated. 'I had a very happy childhood, until . . .'

She took a few deep breaths.

'Until the war?' I asked.

She shook her head. 'You really don't know anything about Italy, or about Mussolini, do you?'

'I know I'm not on his side.'

'Why are you not on his side?' she asked, and gave me a haughty look, like she was asking a school child a testing question.

'Because . . . well . . . I suppose because that's what my orders are.'

She laughed, although she was almost in tears too. 'Let's eat,' she said. 'We can talk more later.' She took another key that dangled from her waistband and opened the interior door.

CHAPTER ELEVEN

H ello again,' said the chirpy budgie at the till as Nicole stepped inside the corner shop.

'Hi,' she answered, and forced a smile.

'You live around here, then?'

'Yes.'

'I'm Shaun, by the way.'

'I know.'

'Oh, right.' The chirpiness dropped for a second. 'It's just that I get to know most people who pop in here.'

'I'm sure you do.'

Now he looked like he'd just been slapped. *Perhaps she should cut the poor thing some slack.*

'I'm Nicole,' she said. 'Just moved in about ten doors down.'

On hearing her words his face beamed so much it looked like his head was about to fall off. 'Oh, you mean *Mac's old place?*'

'Do I?' she said, knowing that was exactly what she meant.

Shaun flushed slightly. 'Sorry. You wouldn't know. The guy who lived there before you. Everyone knew him as "Mac" but it wasn't his real name. Used to coach a lot of the rowers around here. Great bloke. Bit of a legend in these parts.'

'That's very good to know. Thanks.'

Then Nicole watched with a mixture of shock and disgust as Shaun leaned over the counter and gave her figure a look – no, a proper visual examination – up and down. She looked too, just to check she hadn't put her knickers on outside her jeans.

'Excuse me?' she said.

Now he looked back at her face and said politely, 'Oh, sorry, I was just looking at your body.'

Nicole's jaw opened slightly but no noise came out.

He held a hand up and then spoke with his head jiggling about slightly. 'Hang on. No. That didn't come out right. It was just talk of Mac and rowing. Made me think.'

'That explains it perfectly,' Nicole said flatly.

He shook his head. 'No. Sorry. What I mean is, *Do you row?*'

She continued staring at him, then shook her head.

'Ever tried it?' he said.

'Never even thought about it.'

Now he had the enthusiasm of a puppy, almost panting his words out: 'You should give it a go. You'd be good at it, you would. Bein', like, tall and rangy.'

'Thanks. I'll remember that. In the meantime I need some bread.'

He pointed. She walked over to it and bought a loaf without saying another word.

Then she walked home, made herself a sandwich, and spent a little more time reading until she could feel a headache coming on.

At about five o'clock she changed into her smartest jeans and set off for town.

She strolled up Henley High Street, scanning the shop signs, trying to look like she knew where she was going.

The name 'Benton's' knocked around her head as she looked up; she even muttered the word once or twice.

That was where they were to meet. For some reason she had a mental image of a select and sophisticated coffee-bar-cum-bistro – perhaps the finest in Henley-on-Thames, where they would be waited on, drink the finest Italian mocha, and eat delicious French pastries.

But there was no coffee bar of that name – only the usual stores. She took out her phone and dialled.

'Can't find it,' she said.

'Where are you?'

'I don't know. Outside some posh clothes shop. Opposite a pub.'

'What pub?'

'Erm . . . the Red Lion.'

A groan. 'Turn back towards the town centre. Up the hill. Into Oxford Street. It's on your right.'

She closed the call and followed the directions.

It was a doorway between two charity shops, which didn't look good. It didn't smell good either. She trotted up the stairs, then looked around. She quickly spotted him and ran over.

'Hello, poppet,' her father said, squeezing her tightly. It was probably tighter than he'd ever squeezed her before.

Or perhaps it just felt like it.

She'd never been away from him for more than a day – apart from the school trip to Austria the year before. But now she wasn't going to see him at all apart from these visits. It felt strange; they'd only been apart for three days but it was like they were long lost friends getting to know each other all over again.

They parted. But Nicole sat down next to him and kept their arms touching, occasionally bouncing off one another.

'Have to stop saying that, won't I?' he said.

'What?'

'Poppet. I can't keep calling you that forever. It's going to sound a bit daft when you're thirty.'

Nicole wanted to say that she didn't mind, that he could call her 'poppet' every day for the rest of her life if he wanted to, but also that she didn't want him to at all, because it made living miles away from each other even harder.

'Guess so,' she said.

Only now did she look left and right, and breathe in the scene before her. Plastic bucket chairs were bolted to the floor. The table tops were shiny, polished Formica. Little trays at each table held red and brown plastic squeezy containers with congealed sauce around their spouts. In short, it was more truckers' greasy spoon than Italian bistro or French café.

'What do you want?' her father said.

'Just a coffee, please.'

'Sure you don't want anything to eat?'

She glanced at the congealed sauce again, then over to the serving counter. Two flies swirling around each other distracted her.

'It's okay,' she said. 'I'm not hungry. Really.'

He tutted. 'All right. I get it. Not exactly up to the standards you're used to.'

She gave an inverted smile as she tried to come up with a denial. 'Well, it *is* a bit of a dump,' she muttered eventually.

'All I can afford now. You should see the apartment I'm in.'

'I'd like that.'

She was about to ask when she could come and visit, but didn't get the chance.

'No, you wouldn't,' he said with a laugh. 'You wouldn't like it at all.'

He tried again (and failed) to persuade her to have something to eat, then trudged over to the counter and ordered two coffees and a grilled cheese and ham sandwich with fries.

'My dinner, that is,' he said when he returned to the table. 'Bloody cheese and ham toastie.'

'You could come to our house next time,' Nicole said. 'I could cook us something.' Somehow the words jarred. They felt wrong as soon as they left her lips.

Was that a flicker on Dad's face? A crack of pain or discomfort?

Then she realized. Inviting Dad to 'our house' just didn't seem right.

'Sorry, Dad. I didn't mean to . . .'

To what? To rub it in? To make him feel small? Perhaps he deserved that, perhaps not.

'Oh, that's all right,' he said. He pasted a smile onto his face but it soon fell away. 'Thanks, but I'm sure your mum wouldn't want me there.'

'Oh, it's cool with her. She said you could visit the house.'

'Really? She said that?'

'Yeah. Just as long as she isn't there at the time.'

His face dropped just that little bit more. There was silence for some time.

This wasn't how it was supposed to be. She'd looked forward to meeting him all day, her heart fluttering as she'd left the house and walked into town. Whatever he had or hadn't done, today it didn't seem to matter.

'You know I've been a bit of an idiot, don't you?' he said.

Nicole shrugged. 'I . . . Well . . . It's none of my business, I guess.'

'But you know it wasn't true, don't you? What your mum said about me and that woman?'

'You told me that before.'

'As long as you know.' He glared at her, as if that would make her believe him. 'But also I could have handled it better. And if there's any chance . . .'

He shook his head as his words ran out of steam. Then he frowned and looked down. Nicole noticed a few lines around his eyes she hadn't seen before.

He tried again. 'It's just . . . I mean . . . Does your mum mention me much?'

'Oh, all the time.'

'Mmm.' He took a long, deep breath, then stared at Nicole for a few seconds. 'Look at me, moaning and getting all self-obsessed. I forgot about you. Sorry.'

'Oh, I'm good. Really.'

'But I know it can't be nice for you, Nicole. And you know I never wanted any of this, don't you, not for me or your mum or you.'

She forced a smile. 'I know, Dad.'

Their coffees came and they each took a tentative sip.

'But I still want you to be happy in the house – both of you.'

She shrugged. 'It's cool. It's a house.'

'Yes,' he said. 'And in time it'll become a home too.'

Nicole nodded and said, 'Mmm.'

Her father made a stand with his forearm and propped his head up on his hand, gazing high above Nicole. 'I remember moving into the house in London. No character at first, until your mum got to work on it. Pictures, paintings, lamps, ornaments, good old scented candles, you name it. Did the trick though. I'm sure she'll do the same for this new house.'

He sighed, brought himself back from his reverie and took another sip of coffee. 'Have you met anyone yet?'

She hesitated. She could mention Shaun . . . but no. 'Not really,' she said. 'I've only been here a few days.'

'Decided what you're going to do yet?'

'About what?'

He shrugged. 'Studies, job, whatever.'

I'm going to run away because I hate it here.

'I thought about a course at college,' she said.

He nodded firmly. 'You should. Don't let the headaches stop you. They getting better now?'

'Mmm . . . not completely gone – not yet. But I won't let them stop me.'

As the grilled cheese and ham sandwich was placed on the table, Nicole's father picked up a knife and tapped it towards her. 'You make sure you don't. Wherever you are, you're still my daughter. I don't want you frittering your life away.'

She paused for a couple of seconds, then said, 'I won't, Dad. Honestly.'

'Good.' He cut the sandwich in half, placed the knife down and said, 'I'll do you a deal. The sooner you get some qualifications, the sooner I'll stop calling you "poppet", yeah?'

She burst out into a fit of giggles and took out a tissue.

It was good; she could pretend they were tears of laughter.

CHAPTER TWELVE

As we stood together in the cellar and Rosa turned the key I must have flinched, and she laid a calming hand on my shoulder.

'It's all right,' she said softly. 'I told you, you're safe in this house.'

Her hand lingered on my arm, I felt it tighten ever so briefly before she let go. Only now was it clear how much smaller than me she was. Her eyes looked bigger and clearer looking up to me.

She gave my chest a pat. 'You are very brave,' she said, 'escaping from that truck when you could easily have been shot.'

I said nothing, and just kept looking down, caressing her features with my eyes.

'Come on,' she said, pulling the door open slightly.

I placed my hand out to stop her opening it fully. 'But what about the others?' I said.

'Nobody is at home now,' she answered.

She pulled the door again and this time I didn't resist. We stood there, listening. There was nothing.

She stepped forward and beckoned me but I couldn't move; my throat tightened and I struggled to breathe. All I could do was peer through the doorway, and all I could see was a dimly lit wall.

She held my arm again and said, 'Come on. I've told you, you're safe here. There's only Mama and Papa. And of course Lorenzo Junior and Anna. We have to be careful the children don't meet you; they might talk. But today I've asked Mama and Papa to take them to Mama's sister.'

'Thank you,' I said.

She smiled politely. 'Oh, it's not only for your benefit. Mama's sister might have the chance to leave the country soon if the situation gets any worse. I want Lorenzo Junior and Anna to go with them.'

Thankfully I relaxed, then followed her up the stone steps and into the main part of the house. It was basic and cramped, but also clean and tidy.

Soon we were sitting at the kitchen table eating soft herby bread with cheese and tomatoes, which was like a banquet to me.

'So,' I said, 'what does Lorenzo think about his children being taken to another country?'

'He's not here to ask,' she replied quickly.

She spoke with bitterness. I said nothing and looked away.

'I'm sorry,' she said a few moments later. 'It sounds like I am holding a . . . "grudge" is the word?'

I nodded encouragement.

'But I know my brother. He would want his children to be safe even if his acts don't show that. Anyway, the problem is Mama and Papa.'

'Oh?'

'Lorenzo Junior and Anna are their grandchildren and they love them. They don't want them taken away, possibly living with strangers in a foreign country.'

That made me think about my own stable upbringing, about how I'd taken it for granted compared to this family, who were struggling to even stay together because of the political situation.

Rosa drew breath. 'But you don't want to hear about that. I need to tell you about Mussolini.'

I would have been happy to hear her talk about anything, but I nodded. 'Yes,' I said. 'I suppose I should try to understand what's happening in your country. But what about you and your family? Why don't you live at the farm?'

'That would be telling you about Mussolini.' She ripped a chunk of bread off with her teeth and spent a few seconds chewing before speaking again. 'It's all linked. Us. The farm. Mussolini. The war.'

'But I'd like to know,' I said. 'To understand.'

'All right.' She nodded, then drew breath. 'We had to leave the farm.'

'Why?'

'Because we didn't own it anymore.'

I tried to make sense of that for a moment. 'I don't understand,' I said eventually.

'It was taken from us. I think "confiscated" is the word.' It was actually pleasant to hear her struggle over a word just for once, to watch her mouth work around it.

'Why was it confiscated?' I said.

'Because we are Jews. Surely you know that much?'

'But . . . I thought that was just in Germany. And surely you can't have things taken from you just like that? Not if you own them?'

She wagged an admonishing finger at me. 'Welcome to the great world of Il Duce.'

I didn't know what to say. I felt so ignorant. 'Couldn't you appeal?'

Then she laughed – a big belly laugh that almost made her choke on her food. It was a friendly – albeit slightly pitying – laugh, and made her eyes look so warm and friendly. It also made me feel downright stupid, but I joined in just the same; the laughter and the food somehow lent an air of hope to a discussion of the plainly wrong.

'It's the law,' she said. 'Since 1938. Just like the law that says my father and I can't work in any profession.'

'Because you're Jews?'

'Now you are starting to understand.' Then her face fell from joy to despair. 'They tell me I started speaking at a very early age, that they could hardly shut me up. I don't take any credit for that; it was just the way I was. And when I started learning English it was just the same. Before I knew it I was reading English books.'

'The ones down in your cellar?' I suggested.

'*Your* cellar,' she said, leaning forward with a certain intimacy. It was said with feeling, and was such a kind gesture to make to someone who was still virtually a stranger.

'Actually, no,' she said. 'Not the books in the cellar. I started on *The Wind in the Willows*, *Swallows and Amazons*, *The Secret Garden*. Many more. It seemed natural for me to study English and become a teacher.' Then she sighed and said, 'I only did the job for eight or nine months, but it felt natural – like I was born to do it.'

'I don't understand,' I said. 'Did they just tell you one day, "You're Jewish so I'm afraid you have to leave"?'

She glanced up as she thought, then nodded. 'I also had a letter, but yes, much like you say. The head of the school told me he wanted to keep me on, and held out as long as he could, but it was the law and the school had to obey the law.'

'Blimey,' I said. 'Just like that?'

She nodded again. 'And the same happened to Papa on the same day.'

'And Lorenzo?'

'Ah, my big bad brother.' She stared wistfully into space. 'Oh, he had lost his job as an architect long before then. He worked when he could – doing whatever he could find, but it's hard to be a freedom fighter and a fruit picker at the same time. He tried – he had to because he had children to feed. But when Donna was killed something died inside him too. He . . . has a temper now that he never used to have.'

'So where is he now?'

She shrugged her faintly bronzed shoulders, and I struggled to shake the image from my mind.

'Who knows?' she said. 'It's probably best I don't know. Mama and Papa and I agreed to look after Lorenzo Junior and Anna for him. In return he fights for us.'

'So he's lost his wife and . . .'

'And his children, yes.'

'This must all be very difficult for you,' I said. 'Having to look after them on top of everything else.'

'Oh, there are good days when one of them laughs and makes me laugh too, and it reminds me of when life was better. And there are bad days when I feel like I've lost everything too. I even lost those children's books I loved to read.'

I gave her a puzzled look.

'We weren't allowed to bring everything from the farmhouse,' she said. 'The new owners just burned the rest.'

'That's terrible,' I said, knowing the words were trite under the circumstances.

We carried on eating for a few minutes. It was one of the few silences between us.

Then I said, 'It must be hard for your mother and father to take after all they've worked for.'

'Mama and Papa? Oh, yes. Mama is strong. *Molto forte*. Things can make her cry but nothing will break her. But Papa? Some days I cannot even talk to him.'

'And on the days you can?'

She thought for a moment, then said, 'I tell him the same as Mama does, that you have to learn to cope with your losses and always hope for something better. Do that and laugh when you can, like you and I have been doing today.'

'I'm glad I made you laugh,' I said. 'It's a way I can pay you back for your kindness.'

'Ha!' she said, and dismissed my words with a wave of her hand. 'You risk your life in a foreign country to help me. You owe me nothing.'

I stalled at that. I'd never thought of it the way she had. To me I was fighting for king and country, but it opened my eyes. Rosa opened my eyes in lots of ways.

'Your farm,' I said. 'Is it the one where you work now, where you saw me yesterday by the vines?'

'That's right.' She smiled, pursing her lips to hold in emotion. 'Isn't that good of the new owners to employ me? And a very convenient source of labour for them after Papa and I lost our jobs.'

'Does your papa work there too?' I asked.

She shook her head. 'He's too proud, too angry. He says he would burn the farmhouse down if he had to set foot in it. Of course, he wouldn't actually do that; he has too many happy memories of the place.'

This was all a revelation to me, and I wondered why we hadn't been told of these things back home.

'So . . . you lost your jobs and home because of Mussolini,' I said. 'God, I hate him *even more* now.'

'Oh, it's not completely his doing. He was a good leader for many years. He sent children to school, promoted industry, construction and farming. There was a time when people thought he would make Italy great again. I have to be honest even though it hurts me to admit these things. But now the man is Hitler's puppet, nothing more, enacting German laws in Italy. We can lose our jobs.

We can have property just taken away. And there are more laws. I am no longer a citizen of the country I've lived in all my life. And I couldn't marry a Gentile if I wanted to.'

'What's a Gentile?' I said.

Then she started giggling again, her petite nose twitching as she did so. She was making fun of me, but being ignorant was a price worth paying to see happiness dance across her face.

'You know something, Mac? I haven't laughed so much for a long time. I have to thank you for that.'

'If I can be the butt of your jokes,' I said, 'it's fine by me.'

We carried on talking – I have no idea how long for – but I know that as she told me more it felt like blinkers were being taken off me. I learned how the government had systematically destroyed the lives of many other families too. Papa was permanently angry, seeing everything he had worked for taken away at the stroke of someone's pen. Lorenzo was widowed and on the run, possibly dead by now. Lorenzo Junior and Anna were as good as orphans. Rosa and Mama struggled to keep the whole thing together. I was only eighteen and uneducated in these matters, but I knew it stank.

I also learned how the political changes had damaged the country on another level. The government had split the community. Many neighbours quietly supported Rosa's family and others in their situation by donating food or clothing, but some blamed them for Hitler's rise to power and his apparent control over Mussolini, and yet more simply hated Jews – like the family next door who wouldn't speak to them and spat when they were in the street together.

I was dumbstruck throughout her talk, and when I eventually did speak I must have sounded like a child to her adult, even though she was only a year older than me. I said I didn't know anything about Jews, just that Hitler was invading every country around Germany, and Britain had to stop him taking over the entire continent. All of that was true. It was why I'd joined up.

As we talked on, the laughter lessened. That was understandable, but even as a young man I was always a glass half-full type. I tried to change the subject.

'It must be enjoyable having your niece and nephew around,' I said.

'They can be naughty,' she said. 'And they are two more mouths to feed. But yes, I love them as if they are my own.'

By now we'd finished eating. I wondered whether Rosa was going to suggest I returned to the cellar. I didn't want that, and started thinking what else I could do in there apart from read books. As I thought about it a question came to me.

'What's in the chest down there?' I asked, pointing towards the cellar, trying to be as casual as possible.

For a few seconds she was flustered by the question.

'Oh, it doesn't matter,' I said. 'Excuse my rudeness.'

'Mac, there are private things in there,' she said. 'Family things. Please don't open the chest.'

'Of course not,' I said.

She was clearly embarrassed about something, so I started telling her how I'd enjoyed the food we'd just eaten, and that I'd never tasted bread as good as that.

For the first few days I kept thinking about how I could rejoin my unit. Rosa convinced me this would have been futile and very dangerous. She pointed out that I had absolutely no idea where they were, and that my shoulder was still recovering. Then I considered writing to my parents to tell them I was still alive, because I knew how worried they would be. Again this was clearly too risky. My British Army clothes were also a risk because if I'd been found it wouldn't only have been me who got killed. So we got rid of them and I dressed as a civilian.

A couple of weeks passed by. I think. Being confined to the cellar,

I was never quite sure what day it was. But in that time I became quite at home in 'my cellar'. I often heard Lorenzo Junior and Anna through the internal door, talking or giggling. Occasionally they rattled the doorknob and I would hear them grunting as they tried to push it open by force. I didn't understand what they were saying, but I could hear their whispers and arguments about what might be on the other side of the door. It must have been an exciting – as well as a dangerous – time to be a child. What I heard endeared them to me, so I felt it was such a shame we could never meet.

They broke up the boredom because most of the time I had nothing to do except read. Often, when Mama and Papa took the children out for a few hours, Rosa and I would sit and eat at the kitchen table. A few times I even cooked for her, trying to make something nice for when she'd had a hard day working on the farm. Of course, I was hopeless. She just laughed when she saw what I was doing and took charge, leaving me to do the chopping and washing up afterwards.

There was pleasure, and yes, fun. But the fear of being found and shot at any hour of the day or night was always there. And there were long periods of soul-destroying boredom, at a time in my young life when I felt I should be getting out there and achieving things. And yes, in those hours of boredom I did wonder what was in the wooden chest, although I never considered trying to open it. So I kept telling myself I was merely recuperating, letting my shoulder recover. Behind those thoughts, however, I knew I hadn't joined the war effort to be safe. That wasn't helping anyone but myself.

One cool afternoon we were cooking together. I'd chopped some freshly picked tomatoes and onions and Rosa was frying them in a pan with oregano. I was slicing a little cold cured meat to go with it – a rare treat in those war days – and I stopped and sighed, deep in thought. I must have been behaving like a disinterested teenager – which, I suppose, I was.

'What is the matter?' she said.

'Nothing,' I answered quickly.

She nodded, but knew me well by now because she was a very perceptive woman. She showed me a pitying smile.

'Oh, I just feel so useless,' I said. 'I don't know what to do with myself most of the time. You know I'm grateful for what you're doing for me, but I can't sit the war out here, Rosa, I just can't.'

She stepped towards me and held my hand. She said nothing, but her warm, brown eyes met mine, then she put her arms around me and laid her head on my chest.

Then the tomatoes, frying in the pan, started spitting. She laughed and went back to stirring them.

'I'm sorry,' I said. 'I must sound so selfish.'

'No,' she said with lightness. 'This is natural. You want to help. That's good.'

'But how can I do that? I mean, how do I get out of here? Where could I go?'

'You just have to wait for an opportunity. In the meantime you can eat.'

'Thank you,' I said. 'And I'm sorry.'

'Don't apologize,' she said. 'You are a man. You can't cook. This is only natural.'

We both laughed, but my laughter was brief and superficial this time. 'I mean it,' I said. 'I owe you everything – for helping me. I know it's a big risk for you and your family. I . . . I don't know what would have happened if you hadn't found me.'

Of course, I *did* have a good idea: the blunt fact is I'd have either died from exposure or been shot.

'Thank you. And I'm sorry you get bored. I try my best to—'

'Stop, Rosa. Don't apologize, please. I'm not complaining. I'm just telling you how I feel. It's not your fault, really it isn't.'

She stepped towards me and put her arms around me again.

This time I held her too and ran my fingers through her long brown hair, breathing her in. We stayed like that for a few minutes, neither of us speaking, but both understanding, and separated only when the food was ready.

As on most days, it was pasta and a simple tomato sauce. It was something I'd never eaten in Britain but had got a taste for from the first time I'd tried it.

We sat down together. I twirled my spoon in my fingers and edged closer to her. 'Incidentally,' I said, 'do you understand Shakespeare?'

She stopped for a moment and gave me a strange look. 'Yes, I read Shakespeare.'

'Yes, but . . . do you . . . do you actually understand any of it?'

She giggled, grunting laughter through her nose, which I found unladylike but at the same time very alluring.

'What?' I said, starting to laugh at her reaction. 'What is it?'

'You are so funny,' she said. Then she leaned across and kissed me full on the lips. I couldn't smell any perfume, only woman – strong and beautiful woman.

'Now eat,' she said.

I did, but I found it difficult to concentrate. I'm sure the food was as delicious as always, but my mind was elsewhere.

∽

At this point I feel I have to detail something of my life after the war. It's probably fair to say that I've only ever been in love with three women. The other two were my wives.

My two wives were very different women, but I loved them both more than I loved myself – although nobody would believe that. They were both warm, lovely women. And the marriages were happy for a few years, but both, sadly, were completely messed up by me being rotten. I had a feeling at the time that my wartime experiences might make it difficult for a marriage to work. I never thought that was an excuse for my behaviour, and I still don't, but hindsight proves me right.

I met Glenda at a dance. She gave me the eye, I asked her to dance. Eight months later we were married. Yes, things really were that simple in those days. She was confident and outgoing almost to the point of brashness, always making the first move. I liked that aspect of her – at first. Soon after our first anniversary something happened to me, and I don't know what – if anything – triggered it. I started to have bad thoughts, and for many months I kept them to myself. The thoughts were that Glenda was seeing another man. I know she wasn't. In fact, I knew it at the time. But eventually it became an urge I couldn't hold back; it was either going to turn me mad or control me. Sadly it was the latter. I simply had to tell her to stop talking to other men – it was a compulsion. She was understanding at first and largely did as I asked. Then I told her to stop going anywhere without me.

Fortunately for Glenda, she wasn't the sort of woman to be dominated like that.

At the time I hated the way she was – not doing what I told her to. Of course, now I know it was for the best, that it was good for both of us that she was strong-willed. We argued, but she was emotionally much too strong for me, which was something else I couldn't cope with. It came to a head when I locked her in the house. I went to rowing practice, but I don't think I said a word for the entire time. And it turned out she'd broken a window and escaped. When I caught up with her I had every intention of apologizing, telling her it wouldn't happen again. Instead I found myself telling her it was for her own good, that she shouldn't be seeing other men. I kept telling her I loved her, but it even sounded hollow to me at the time. It might have sounded hollow, but it was true. We divorced.

For years I believed I'd made a mistake, that perhaps I wasn't the marrying kind.

Patricia was much more reserved, timid even. We'd worked together at the council for over two years and we'd shared lots of jokes and conversations, so I thought I knew her well. I also knew she hadn't had a single boyfriend for those two years.

When I asked her out to the cinema she asked whether I meant just the two of us. That sounded good to me, the fact that she was a little naïve, as if it made me feel more powerful. It felt like she was a better match than Glenda had been. We went out a few more times, and when I eventually made my move, in the darkness of the back row, she didn't need much persuading. As we'd known each other for two years I thought this was it – that I'd found my soul mate and we would be together forever. Within a blissful week I'd asked her to marry me and we couldn't get to the registry office quickly enough. I was convinced this was real love and I could put the disaster of Glenda behind me. In hindsight I should have put more thought into exactly why my first marriage had been such a disaster. At that time they'd just started talking about providing counselling for people like myself – people who'd gone through trauma during the war. But I simply didn't consider it as an option; that sort of thing was for weak-minded individuals, I was stronger than that, and was confident that after marrying Patricia my life would be perfect.

When we'd been married for a few months we talked about having a family. I wanted to start trying straight away; she thought it better to wait until we had more money. The disagreement turned into a regular argument, and that was when those bad thoughts started spreading through my mind again. I convinced myself Patricia had an ulterior motive for not wanting to start a family, and could almost see myself tearing the marriage apart – like I was back at the cinema watching some horrible, painful drama unfolding before my eyes but was unable to affect the outcome in any way.

I'm ashamed to say I ended up treating Patricia just as I had Glenda – controlling her, stopping her even speaking to other men. We still worked at the same council offices, and I found myself following her around the building, checking on her movements and who she was talking to. Word got around. I knew what people thought of me but didn't care; I was obsessed with finding out who Patricia was having an affair with. But I was being an idiot again, and, of course, it ended in divorce. Patricia was understanding up to a point, but she simply couldn't put up with me when I was like that. No woman could have.

Either of those women could have given me children, lifelong companionship, somebody to love and somebody to be loved by. At the time I just concluded that I wasn't the marrying type and suppressed the urge to get involved with other women, even though I longed for female company. Instead I threw myself into my hobby, rowing up and down the Thames when my damaged shoulder allowed it, and later in life – when I couldn't row so much – coaching others.

Only in recent years have I accepted the causes of my behaviour towards my wives. Yes, it really has taken that long for me to fully understand myself. There were really two reasons.

One was that I was almost scared to commit myself totally – scared to love unconditionally and be loved in return – because of the fear that one day it would all be ruined and I wouldn't be able to cope with the loss. Better to have never loved than to lose love, to paraphrase.

The other reason? Simply that neither of those women was Rosa.

And, by God, my heart sinks to write those words.

If I'd have known these things earlier I could have done something about it – or, at least, tried to. Either way, now I feel a fool for doing nothing.

But I'm not bitter. Whatever else happened to me – the nightmares, the loneliness, my broken marriages – I always knew that although life was far from perfect it could have been much, much worse. I still think of my time spent with Rosa all those years ago and I have the same positive outlook on those thoughts: that it was a privilege to share those times with her, that I simply can't be bitter about the way my life turned out.

Even now, in my seventh decade, I still wake up with the same thought: every day I'm alive and a free man just has to be a sunny day.

CHAPTER THIRTEEN

Nicole set out along the river towards the college at the far edge of town.

She'd told Mum it was a waste of time – that she could look the course details up on the internet. But it might be useful to feel the vibe of the place, and also she could bring back course booklets and leave them lying around the house, so Mum would see she was doing *something*. And as long as Mum was happy she was doing at least *something*, then it would make life easier for both of them.

The air was a little fresher today along the river, carried on the breeze that fluttered the leaves of the willow trees lining the riverside path. Nicole stopped for a minute to admire the river traffic chugging up and down, and the ducks and geese harassing the tourists for bread. The sun was so bright and solid above her that she had to hold the edge of her flat hand up against her forehead as a makeshift visor.

It wasn't London, but perhaps there was a certain something here.

She walked on.

The college was a modern building – what Dad would call a glass-and-metal-poking-out-everywhere building. But it seemed an informal, friendly sort of place, an impression reinforced by the assistant at the reception, who smiled warmly and asked whether she could help.

Ten minutes later, Nicole left the building with a handful of leaflets and headed back home. A stone's throw from the college she heard her name being shouted. She turned. It was Shaun in an athletics top, all shiny teeth and bare shoulders.

The corner shop budgie had escaped from its cage.

'Small world,' he said.

'Small town more like.'

He smiled. Even though he was already smiling he seemed to smile on top of the first one. '*Nice* town,' he said.

'Nice?' She grunted a laugh.

He walked alongside her for a few minutes, neither of them speaking.

'You going to the shop?' Nicole asked eventually.

'Yeah.'

That meant she was going to have the pleasure of his company for pretty much all the way home.

Great.

'What course are you on, then?' he said.

'I'm not.'

There was more silence. But he was still here. He was trying.

'What about you?' she said. 'What course are you on?'

'Sports Science.'

'Like, how to row?'

'Bit of all sorts, really. Every sport you can think of, bit of biology, bit of nutrition. But I know how to row already, I *really* know how to row.'

'Did Mac teach you?'

He laughed. She stopped walking.

So did he. Then he apologized.

Obviously she looked offended. But she wasn't offended, just puzzled. Puzzled at herself.

Why did she ask him about Mac?

Her question had been instinctive.

'Wasn't making fun of you,' Shaun said. 'Honest. It's just that Mac was a coach from the sixties to the eighties. He taught *my dad* to row, not me.'

They started walking again.

So why did she ask him about Mac? Probably because it was something to say. And he did seem an interesting guy from his notepad scribbles.

'You ever meet him?' she said.

'Who? Mac?'

'No, Winston Churchill.'

This time Shaun spluttered into uncontrollable laughter, his shoulders dropping as he almost collapsed into a crouch. 'Oh, you kill me,' he said. 'You really do.'

Yeah, nice choice of words there, budgie man.

'Did you ever meet Mac?' Nicole said, this time slowly and clearly.

Shaun straightened himself out. 'Mac? Yeah, sure. He used to pop in the shop a lot.'

Nicole thought about that for a moment. 'Oh, yeah. Of course.'

'He'd given up coaching by then – got too old for it. Sad really. My dad used to tell me stories about him. He used to organize trips to rowing regattas, a lot of them abroad. Seemed to be his life.'

'Was he a good rower himself?'

Shaun shook his head. 'Supposed to be when he was a lad, apparently. Suffered with a gammy shoulder when he was older, though. It was obvious he had the physique and the technique. At the club they say even when he was only coasting along, not breathing heavily, he was going pretty fast – for an old guy, like.'

Nicole went to speak again, but Shaun got there first. 'Anyway, why are you so interested in him?'

'Oh . . . you know, just 'cos we're living in his house and all that. And he was a legend after all, you said so yourself.'

'That's true.'

'Did he ever win anything?'

Shaun shook his head. 'Nah. According to my dad he couldn't cut it when there was any pressure on him – when it got competitive. He seemed to enjoy rowing for the sake of rowing rather than racing.'

Nicole screwed her face up. 'What does that mean?'

'Try it and you'll find out. Come on. I told you, you'd be good at it.'

'I know. You said.'

He smiled that broad white smile again. 'You're hard work, you are, Nicole. Good fun, but hard work.'

A few minutes later they reached the corner shop. Shaun faced her, stood up straight, and put his hands on his hips. 'Sorry. Look, I know I'm a bit of a rowing nut, but I really think you'd be good with a bit of help. And yeah, I'm club secretary, so I'm sellin' it, but really, you'd enjoy it.'

Nicole nodded. 'I'll think about it.'

'We meet down at Danver's Shed – just over the bridge and turn right – Mondays, Wednesdays and Fridays, five till seven all summer, when the evenings are light.' He pointed a finger at her face, then wagged it in time with his words. 'And that's the last time I'm inviting you, all right?'

She huffed a laugh. 'Good.'

'So you'll be there?'

'No.'

He almost creased up. 'You're hard work, you are. You know that? Did I tell you that?'

He was still laughing as he went into the shop, leaving Nicole and her leaflets to go home.

When she got to the front door she stood there for a few seconds, key in hand, and thought about Shaun. Perhaps he wasn't such a bad budgie after all. He had a certain charm, and she needed friends. Of course, she already had friends, from school. She told them all they could visit, posted it on Facebook, told them her address and directions.

Please feel free to come up and see me in Henley. It's the third town on the right after Windsor Castle, you can't miss it.

But obviously you could.

Yeah, perhaps Shaun wasn't such a bad budgie after all.

She went inside and put the leaflets on the kitchen table – where they would be seen. Then she made a large mug of tea, took it to her bedroom, and opened the old notebook.

CHAPTER FOURTEEN

After Rosa and I shared that first kiss it didn't take long for us to become closer.

Who knows whether the danger evoked the passion between us, or whether sometimes – just sometimes – the basic human pleasures are heightened when people feel desperate and fearful of the future. All I know is that for many weeks there was never a bad word between us, always love and humour, and any sadness was shared. Rosa spent her days working on the farm, and I spent my days incarcerated, usually reading, and we spent every minute we could together.

One cool afternoon in September 1943, when I was lying with Rosa on the matting, with her head resting on my chest, we talked like we had for months – as if the rest of the world didn't matter. But things were changing outside our cosy and secure cellar, and I feared for our future.

In July of that year Mussolini had been replaced as Italy's leader, and was now in prison. The new leader publicly appeared to be in the same mould as his predecessor, as if he, too, might turn out to be a puppet of Hitler. But then, in the first days of September, clearly swayed by the Allied advances in southern Italy and by the bombing of Rome, he had negotiated a ceasefire with the Allies.

The rest of the world really did matter.

'Rosa?' I said.

I sensed her stir, felt the warmth of her torso pressing against mine as she let out a long and relaxed sigh.

'What do you hope to do?' I said. 'After the war, I mean.'

'Who says the war will end?' she answered.

'But surely . . . all wars end.'

'I hope you are right. You are like my brother. He kept talking about these things. He said that if the people keep fighting back the authorities will be forced to turn the country back to the way it was ten years ago.'

'Surely that would be a good thing?'

'It would, but . . . it's unlikely to happen.'

'Why not?' I asked.

She thought for a few seconds, tracing patterns on my chest with her finger, then said, 'The problem is that many people think of social progress as whatever is happening – good or bad – and that going back to the old ways would be like going backward, that it would be negative. Anyone who complains is told, "You should move with the times" or "You have to accept progress."'

It took a while, but I understood how those simple words made so much sense. And it was typical of Rosa and her beautiful, insightful mind. But something else was puzzling me, and now I felt close enough to Rosa to pose the question. I hadn't dared raise the subject before out of respect for the political situation, and, if I'm honest, because of my feelings of ignorance. But now, with the ceasefire, there seemed to be a realistic chance of better treatment for Italian Jews, so I asked.

'There's one thing I don't understand,' I said.

'About what?'

'Well, the whole war. I mean, what exactly have the Germans got against the Jews anyway?'

She composed herself before answering, her clear hazel eyes looking up to me. 'You shouldn't think it's *all* Germans,' she said. 'It's really only the Nazis and their followers. And they aren't only in Germany. Many people in Austria, Poland, Russia, Czechoslovakia too – even here in Italy – they feel the same. Yes, a lot of people in Europe.'

'But that makes it even more . . . well . . . confusing. I mean, if that many people want to . . .'

'To close down our businesses, to take our jobs and property away by force?'

'But . . .' I shook my head. 'I'm sorry,' I said. 'Forget I asked.'

She looked up to me. 'No, no. Go on, please. It's good that we talk. Everybody should talk about these things.'

I composed myself, then said, 'Well, all right. But if that many people – not that I agree with them – but if that many people feel that way about the Jews, then there must be *some* reason for it.'

'Must there?' she said, and left the words hanging there.

Sometimes I feel like the words have been hanging over me ever since.

I tried to smile, but it was forced and came out crooked. Then I apologized for being stupid.

She flung her arms around me, squeezed, and said, 'Lorenzo used to say one day we are sure to get the farm and our jobs back, and when that happens we can just carry on as if nothing ever happened.'

'Is that how you see yourself after the war?' I said. 'Just working on the farm?'

She shrugged. 'Mmm . . . also to be married with a family.'

'Really?' I said.

She opened one of my shirt buttons and slipped a hand inside.

'Oh, yes,' she said. 'As long as he was tall and handsome, brave and kind.'

'And English?' I asked with a smirk.

Her hand left my chest, travelled up to my face, and pinched my nose. 'Don't be cheeky,' she said.

I felt her fingers brush through my hair, then she reached up and kissed me. To this day I swear I can sometimes sense her lips pressing against mine.

I pulled her on top of me, making her shriek with laughter, and we rolled together off the matting and onto the cold stone floor. Not that we cared.

I looked deep into her eyes again, pushed my fingers through her hair, then the veneer of pretence fell from our faces. We both knew this was temporary.

'Let's make a pact,' I said. 'I'll come to Valleverde after the war. If you want to see me you have to tie ribbons around the olive tree.'

She kissed me again. 'In that case I'll buy all the ribbons in Rome. We can run the farm together, me and my big, strong Englishman.'

'And Mama and Papa can live with us,' I added. 'They can see out their autumn years pottering around the farmhouse.'

'I like that idea,' she said. Then she placed her face right up against mine and frowned. 'But what is "autumn years pottering"?'

I held a forefinger up to her face and gently tapped that perfect nose of hers. 'At last,' I said. 'Something Mac knows that Rosa doesn't.'

Love is always such a precious thing, but more so in desperate times; somehow it's more intense because of the fear it displaces for a few minutes or hours. Even now I still look upon those times in that cramped cellar as the sweetest days of my life. There, I felt insulated from most of the evils occurring in the world outside, and sensed a little hope.

My hopes were dashed, however, days later when the political situation took a sinister turn. German forces had already been stationed in northern areas of Italy for a long time in support of the Italians, but during September, as a direct riposte to the new government's ceasefire with the Allies, Hitler's army essentially took control of northern Italy. So, for us, it was a race between the Allies coming up from the south versus the Germans coming down from the north. My geography of Italy wasn't great, but I soon learned we were roughly halfway between those two extremes of fate.

And fate did not deal us a winning hand. Mussolini was freed from prison and reinstalled as a puppet leader of northern Italy, and very soon Rome fell to the German forces. We were under Nazi control, directly or indirectly.

But worse was to come.

In October the authorities started rounding up Jews and taking them away. It was a development Rosa and her family had been expecting for some time, and when it started she knew where they were being taken to – internment camps in the north of the country. They were so sure it was going to happen they'd arranged for Mama's sister to take Lorenzo Junior and Anna abroad – to the USA, I think. I knew I would miss their chattering and whispered arguments broadcast from the other side of the locked door. They were too young to understand what was happening, but their innocence was something of a tonic to me in those long, lonely days. I saw them only once, but for Rosa – aware that children's tongues can be hard to control – even once was too often, so I never told a soul about it.

It happened on one of those all too common days I was alone in the cellar and thought the day would never end. Rosa and I had taken breakfast together sitting on the trunk in the cellar, then she'd gone to work on the farm, leaving me to pace my cell, read its library, and try to write a few scribbled notes of my own. But then the boredom got to me and I lay down and fell asleep with an open book on my chest.

I woke to find both of them standing over me. They were still whispering to each other in Italian. I didn't understand the words but I knew they were asking each other who I was. When I opened my eyes they gasped and stepped away.

I sat up, pointed to the door and told them to leave. They looked where I was pointing but didn't leave – didn't even understand me, I suppose.

Then Lorenzo Junior nervously asked me the question directly – who I was. Again, I can't say what words he used, but I understood the meaning at the time.

'Go back into the house,' I said, my pulse thumping. I sometimes wonder if they'd have left if I'd shouted, but they were such sweet things I just didn't have the heart.

Lorenzo looked at the book next to me. '*Inglese?*' he said, pointing at me.

I gave in. I nodded to him, then stood up and tried to usher them towards the door to the house. He spoke again, I think he was asking if I was a soldier, and I ignored the question. But he wouldn't stop. He prodded his chest with his finger and pronounced his name. He pointed to Anna and told me her name. There was more but I didn't understand at first. After a few moments I realized the boy was asking for my name.

I pointed to the door again and started pushing them both towards it.

Lorenzo asked me my name again. I figured there was no harm – it wasn't my real name anyway, and by all accounts they would be leaving very soon. So, partly to get them to leave, I said, 'All right. My name is "Mac".'

He repeated it, though it came out as 'Mmmmacca!'

Anna did the same and giggled.

I shooed them away and told them never to tell anyone about me.

They both giggled at this. I assumed they didn't understand, so I repeated it – this time with a stern edge to my voice.

I grabbed Lorenzo and held my forefinger up to his lips, making a shushing noise, then did the same with Anna. They nodded and ran through the doorway.

I assumed Mama or Papa had forgotten to lock it just that once, and it was never left unlocked again.

A couple of days later I stopped hearing their voices, so asked Rosa about them, and she told me that with the worsening political situation their great-aunt had indeed taken them out of the country. I was secretly disappointed but told her it was for the best. She agreed, telling me that the rounding up of Jews was gathering pace.

I missed them, even though I'd only met them once. But on the positive side it made it safer for me to go into the rest of the house every day and eat with Mama and Papa. Mama was a smaller version of Rosa, just as beautiful in spite of the odd grey hair, and seemed to have an apron permanently tied around her waist. Papa was a fairly short but barrel-chested brute of a man with a solid mass of black hair, which belied his years. Mama said that now the children had gone they were both free to work on the farm. Papa wasn't having any of it at first – insisting it was still his farm – and they argued strongly about this in front of Rosa and me. They did, however, always make up in the end, and even at my young age I found it touching that they were arguing about what to do together rather than each doing what they wanted. I could easily see them arguing – and making up – for another forty years.

Mama had just about brought Papa around to the idea of working on the farm when the issue became immaterial, and proving what good timing the departure of Lorenzo Junior and Anna had been. Their leaving had also spurred me on. I told Rosa I'd got itchy feet – a phrase she hadn't heard before, which gave us both a moment of levity I still treasure. I said that although I was torn, I had to leave. I said I hadn't joined the army to hide like a coward, and my shoulder was now healed.

That was the day before the soldiers paid us a visit.

It was sometime in November 1943. We were woken just after dawn by a hammering on the front door of the house and shouting that filled me with fear. I was still sleeping alone in the cellar and rushed to the door that led to the street. I looked through the cracks in the wood to try to see what was happening, but all I saw were lights and uniforms flashing by. But I *heard* plenty of aggressive shouts and purposeful footsteps, so I knew what was happening. Then I heard the main front door – the white-painted one right next to the one I was standing behind – being smashed in and boots running through the house. I rushed to the internal door and was horrified at what I heard. I still understood little Italian, but heard loud and clear what was happening: Rosa, Mama and Papa were being shouted at, ordered to leave and bring as much as they could carry. Minutes later they all rushed out of the house, and I returned to the door leading to the street. What I glimpsed through the crack in the door confirmed what I already knew. The three of them, each holding a bundle of clothes, each in tears, were being forced at gunpoint into the back of a truck.

I felt so helpless. Even if I did have the key to the door I was now pressing my head against in anguish, would I have used it? Would I have gone to help?

As I was wrestling with my conscience there was more shouting, this time what sounded like an old woman to the side of me. The shouts came closer to the door. Then I almost choked in fear as the woman – whoever she was – started rapping her knuckles on the very door I was leaning on. I heard a soldier's boots stamping on the ground outside, getting closer. Then there was talk between him and the old woman – both mere inches from my face. '*Un altro Ebreo!*' she was shouting. '*Un altro Ebreo!*'

I was close enough to smell her breath, but couldn't understand what she was saying as she knocked angrily on the door. A few days later, however, I found out: she was telling the soldiers where there was 'another Jew'.

I've never forgotten those words. They still occasionally wake me up in the early hours.

There was more shouting – I assumed it was the soldier ordering me to open the door – then the crashes on the door started. It bent inwards a couple of inches with every blow. I ran to the other door. I knew it was locked but desperately tried it anyway. I knew I might be killed for hiding but I was also worried that Rosa and her family would get punished for harbouring me.

Then the door flew off its hinges in a cacophony of splinters, and a red-faced soldier stood in its place. All I saw for a few seconds was a pistol being waved around the cellar, quickly homing in on me. I put my hands up and prayed; it was all I could do. I felt my heart thumping away, but the man's shoulders relaxed ever so slightly and so did I. He looked back through the door to the truck, as if asking for a second opinion on the nature of what stood before him, and as I braced myself for the shot, he relented and reeled off some Italian to me.

I'd seen what had gone before so took a guess at what he was saying. I gathered all the clothes I could carry and went outside. The soldier pointed to a truck – not the same one as the others had got into – but at first I ignored him.

I couldn't take my eyes off the woman who had told the soldiers where I was. She was small and dumpy, but she held her head up high and the scowl on her face was big and brave – proud, even. She muttered the word '*Ebreo*' and spat on the ground at my feet.

Then the soldier repeated his order and rammed his rifle into my back. A surge of pain hit me. I don't know how I kept hold of the clothes I was holding, but I did, and obeyed the order.

The old woman nodded and then even applauded as I did this. I couldn't work out how she knew I was hiding in the cellar. I hadn't been outside the house in all of those weeks, and hadn't spoken to anyone but Rosa and her family.

The truck I was driven off in was similar to the one used when I'd been captured the first time. In other words, it had obviously been used for transporting animals. The difference this time was that I didn't know anyone. I asked if anyone there spoke English but nobody even understood the question, and I got a slap on the head from one of the soldiers for my trouble. I felt more alone there than I had been even when incarcerated in my cellar.

At least in the cellar I knew I could look forward to seeing Rosa. Now I had no idea whether we were even heading for the same place.

The journey north from Rome hit me harder than the one from Sicily. In Sicily I'd been captured in action and spared, so my overwhelming feeling was one of relief, and also I'd had Burt and Devendra to keep me company. But here there was nobody with whom I could discuss where we were all going, nobody to share my worst fears with. The people with me weren't unfriendly in the slightest, but we all knew I was different, and for two days I hardly spoke and felt very lonely.

The fact that I didn't speak any Italian was also a stumbling block when we got to the internment camp. It was in northern Italy, noticeably colder than Rome, and in a place I now know to be Fossoli. My lack of language skills wasn't immediately important because as we all queued nobody dared speak in front of the armed guard anyway. When I got to the front of the queue I was asked something – presumably my name, age and occupation. I didn't know what to say at first, not until they asked more loudly.

'I'm English,' I said. 'I'm a British soldier and I don't speak Italian.'

It was a brave – or stupid – thing to say, but I had no choice and had to tense my body to control my trembling.

The man shrugged, made a point of looking at my civilian clothes, and gave a puzzled frown.

'*Inglese*,' I said, pointing to myself.

He carried on speaking Italian and I carried on saying '*Inglese*'. There were more Italian words, this time between themselves, and a gun was pointed at me. By now my nerves appeared to have hit a ceiling, and I felt I had nothing to lose.

'I am *not* a Jew,' I said very firmly. 'I am a *British soldier*. I am a prisoner of war so please treat me like one.'

Of course, they continued to speak Italian, but I stuck to my guns, so to speak, and kept telling them I wasn't an Italian or a Jew.

But we made no progress, so I was dragged away from the others and taken to a tiny concrete hut. There was absolutely nothing in the room – bare walls, no windows, a dirt floor. It was also freezing cold in there – colder than it had been on the truck. I sat down in one corner and hugged myself to keep warm.

I don't know how long I was kept in there, but I could hear shouts and calls from outside every few minutes. I was also hungry, but especially thirsty.

I was confused by what happened next. I thought I might have been hallucinating.

The door opened and two German guards came into the cell.

German guards? I thought.

Then one of them spoke – in very good English. I was still confused but at least I could communicate now.

'You say you are English?'

'British,' I said. 'A soldier in the British Army.'

They looked me up and down, the blue-grey trousers, the off-white shirt, the brown jacket. All of these said casual Italian labourer.

I explained to him how I was captured in Sicily, then escaped from the truck and ended up living with a family of Italian Jews near Rome, where I disguised myself as a civilian.

The guard thought before replying. 'Yes. That would explain why you have no uniform. But any one of those prisoners out there could say the same thing. Why should we believe you? You have no uniform, no identity tag around your neck.'

I felt around my neck, but I'd taken my tag off along with my uniform. The plan had been that if I was seen or found nobody could prove I was an escaped British soldier. At the time it seemed safer to pretend I was an Italian civilian. Now it seemed an unfortunate mistake.

'Can't you tell I'm English from my accent?' I asked, now feeling desperate.

The answer was a simple 'No'. It made sense; the guard understood English but clearly couldn't distinguish accents.

I got even more desperate. 'Have you heard of the Geneva Convention?' I said.

He turned to his comrade and spluttered a laugh. Then he stepped closer to me, our faces inches apart. 'That applies to enemy soldiers, not to civilians. And especially not to *Jews*.'

I felt a spray of spittle on my face on his last word.

He stared at my face for a few seconds and said very sternly, '*Il tuo nome?*'

By now I understood that he was simply asking for my name. But I wasn't going to play. I just shrugged and told him I didn't speak Italian.

He repeated the question, this time shouting it in my face. I could feel the anger in his hot breath.

His face trembled with anger, he muttered what I assumed were German curses. I didn't budge, didn't speak. It was stalemate.

He turned his head to one side and shouted out something in

Italian I didn't understand. Then the door opened and an Italian guard holding a metal mug stepped inside. He completely ignored me, and handed the mug to the German guard. As he did so he said casually, but quite clearly, '*Attenzione, è veleno.*'

I understood the first word, but not the rest.

Then the Italian left the room.

'Are you thirsty?' the German guard asked me in English.

'Very,' I said.

'So drink.'

He handed me the cup. I wasn't sure at first, but took it and sniffed it; it was clear and colourless. I looked back to him. He gave me an encouraging but slightly manic smile and his eyes enlarged momentarily.

'Go on,' he said, as if speaking to a child. 'Drink. It is good for you.'

I did, at first taking the slightest sip. A part of me wondered whether this would be the last ever liquid to pass my lips, but after the first dribbles hit my arid tongue I couldn't stop myself and poured the rest down me, holding the mug above me, resting its edge on my tongue.

I gasped and swallowed again, then looked at the guard. I could see his top lip twitching. Then he suddenly turned to the other guard, barked out, '*Englander!*' and left the room.

It was only much later that I learned what '*Attenzione, è veleno*' means – what the man was saying for my benefit. The words translate as 'Careful, it's poison'. Only then did I know what they were trying to do; the drink was water, but if I'd understood the Italian guard I probably wouldn't have drunk it.

Later I also realized the significance of the German guards: now Italy wasn't only dancing to Germany's tune, the northern part was actually being run by German soldiers.

I was taken to barracks where I met some other British troops.

In spite of not knowing what was going to happen to me I was relieved simply to have someone to talk to.

And then, early one morning just before dawn, everyone in our hut was woken up by the guards. They told us to get up and gather our belongings.

We were leaving the camp.

What was happening? Were we being freed? Was the war over? Or were we going to our deaths?

The possibilities genuinely were that extreme, and my mind was in a mess. We were told to grab as much clothing as we could hold because it was cold where we were going. That was the only clue we had.

One of the prisoners asked the guard where we were being taken, what was to become of us. He got a rifle butt on the side of his head for his enquiry, but immediately scrambled up and followed the rest of us outside. Again we were shoved onto cattle trucks, which were then locked from the outside. Just like those on which I'd spent so many dull and tiresome hours travelling from Sicily to Rome and, later, from Rome to Fossoli, it was cold and noisy and only fit for animals.

But at least I could talk to people on this journey. We agreed that as we had all been told to bring as much clothing as possible, it was unlikely we were being driven to our deaths.

Eventually we stopped and were all put on a train. It was little better and we were still locked inside with no water or food, and no way of relieving ourselves.

However, I'd convinced the Germans I was a British POW, and had to be grateful for that. There were a few people in our carriage who were obviously not British POWs – Jews. Over the next few hours I got used to their faces – the young and bright, the older and more worldly – and wondered what was to become of them. And I knew in all likelihood I was going to be treated better than they were. If it hadn't been for my persistence and a little luck, I too would be just another one of them.

I felt guilt and confusion over their future. I was a soldier, I had actually been trying to *kill* enemy soldiers, and had been caught red-handed. But these weary figures sitting around me on that train had done absolutely nothing wrong as far as I could tell apart from being Jewish. And yet I had been assured I would be treated as a POW, so would get better treatment.

I tried not to think whether Rosa and her family were in one of the other carriages, and didn't dwell on the possible fate that awaited them wherever they were.

CHAPTER FIFTEEN

Nicole heard her name being called, so she closed the notebook, put it back under her bed, and left her bedroom.

'You sure you'll be all right on your own?' she heard her mother say from the hallway as she went downstairs. Nicole was too stunned to answer, and could do nothing more than stare at her mother, who was preening herself in front of the mirror.

'Mum?'

Yes, it was hard to believe it was her. There were heels Nicole hadn't seen before, a skirt that was at least ten years too short for her, and the full works on her face.

'It's Mum, Jim, but not as we know it,' Nicole mumbled.

'You what, love?'

'Oh, nothing.'

'Okay, so don't tell me.' Her mother turned around and glanced behind her at the mirror. 'Anyway, I'm going out. As long as you're going to be all right on your own this evening.'

Nicole thought about that for a couple of seconds, then grunted, 'What?'

'Hell-oo! Whatever you've been doing up there hasn't done you any good. I said, *I'm going out for the evening.*'

'But where?'

'Just into town.' The last word was pronounced 'tone' as she pursed her lips and dabbed on even more bright red lipstick. 'A friend from work. Just a drink. Nothing important.'

'Is it, like, a date?'

Her mother thought for a moment. 'Not sure whether you'd call it that.' She leaned into the mirror and fluttered her eyelashes like it was a test run. 'All Derek said was—'

'*Derek?*' Nicole blurted out.

'Just a guy I met at the coffee machine. We got chatting. I said I was single. He said if I was lonely . . .'

Nicole edged towards the front door. 'But . . . but you can't.'

'Can't what? Go for a drink?'

'Oh, Mum.' Nicole could feel the waver in her voice. 'You're still married.'

Her mother let out a long sigh and faced Nicole. 'Oh, love.' She held her arms out, and Nicole fell into that place that was both safe and, of late, distant.

They hugged, and Nicole was rocked as her mother spoke again, this time with softness – a softness edged with regret.

'I've been so down lately, Nicole. I *need* some enjoyment. I've got to . . . to move on in life. I'm single now, and I know that idea must be a shock to you. I can hardly get used to it myself.' She gave Nicole's back a gentle rub. 'But don't worry; I won't be inviting him back here.'

'I hope not.'

'Not yet, anyway.'

'What?' Nicole pulled herself out of the embrace.

'I'm just saying not *yet*. It might happen one day, but it might not.'

'Oh, God. I really, *really* don't want to hear this, Mum.'

Nicole's mother went to speak, but just held back, then put on her coat and grabbed a small handbag (which, like the shoes, Nicole hadn't seen before), slinging it over her shoulder. She laid a hand on her daughter's arm and tried to firm up a smile. 'It'll be all right, Nicole. Just . . . just don't worry about me.'

She gave Nicole a kiss on the cheek and left.

Nicole let out a few hard-fought breaths and sat down on the stairs.

Was this what life was going to be like from now on?

Was there going to be a succession of 'Dereks'? And if there was, then what the hell was she going to tell Dad?

And in the meantime how was she going to spend her evenings? Perhaps joining college was a good idea after all. The thought was nauseating, telling people she had no qualifications, having to 'mix' again, trying to elbow her way into some sort of group. But it was something – something better than hanging around waiting for Mum to bring back the latest 'Derek'.

She got up, went into the living room and switched on the TV.

The couch made an explosion of air as she dropped onto it.

She spent a few minutes flicking through the channels, and kept glancing – not really being sure why – at the clock on the wall above the TV.

The clock wasn't the one they'd been given by Dad's parents for their twentieth wedding anniversary. No, *that* one was in the bin. It was a cheap thing Mum had bought for—

Then she realized why she kept glancing at the clock: it was twenty to seven.

She jumped up from the couch.

Right. TV off. Run upstairs. Coolest jeans on. Killers or Bruno Mars T-shirt? Neither, just plain white. Run back downstairs. Grab coat. Key? Check. Ten-quid note? Check. Then outside, to the end of the street and round the corner towards the river.

But where the hell was Danver's Yard or Shed or whatever it was called? Why hadn't she checked before? *Duh!*

Hold on. Yes. *Now she remembered.* Over the bridge and turn right. She checked her watch. It was now just after a quarter to. They were probably still on the water. She headed for the bridge; she could find Danver's whatever it was when she got to the other side.

She walked briskly for the first few hundred yards, then broke into a trot once the river was in sight. She slowed to a brisk walk, worried it might bring on a headache.

'Don't stop!'

The voice seemed to come from the heavens.

'You're not even trying!'

There it was again. She turned and looked behind her, but there were only a few dog-walkers minding their own business.

'Hey! Nicole!'

She turned towards the water and her eyes fell onto that toothy grin that was now becoming familiar. Shaun and another guy – more thickset than him – were gliding by on a two-seater rowing boat. There was probably a name for it, but it was a two-seater rowing boat.

Shaun let the other guy pull on his own for a stroke as he yelled out, 'Race you to the yard!'

For a split second Nicole almost started running again. But no. She wasn't going to dance to his tune. She watched the duo disappear under the bridge. Even though they looked like they were putting no effort into their strokes, they were pulling away quickly.

As Nicole crossed the bridge she saw them turn and pass back underneath her. By the time she reached Danver's Shed, Shaun and his fellow rower had the boat upside down over their heads and were manoeuvring the thing into the storage shed. She waited patiently for them to complete the task, and stood out of the way as five or six other boats were likewise put to bed for the night. One of them was being carried by four women.

'Changed your mind about joining us?' Shaun said as he

waddled towards her in a Lycra contraption that looked like a gymnast's leotard. He stopped, squirted liquid from a plastic bottle into his mouth, and stood tall and wide, legs apart.

'Might have,' she said. 'If the offer's still on.'

He nodded slowly. 'Sure.'

'Cool.'

'You know when we meet?'

'Mondays, Wednesdays and Fridays at five.'

'Correct.' He moved out of the way and gestured towards the women who were gathered just along the launch area, their boat now put away. 'Look, I'll introduce you to the girls when you come again. And we'll make sure you get a go, yeah?'

Nicole looked at the girls, all professionally kitted out, all looking like they took their rowing pretty seriously. 'Isn't it worth having a go with you first? Just me and you in one of the two-seater boats?'

Shaun laughed, then grabbed a small towel and wiped the sea of sweat from his ruddy face. 'Double sculls. That's what they are. And . . . Mmm . . .' He shook his head from side to side a few times, as if weighing up something not very important. 'Yeah, can't see why not. Guess it might help if I show you the basics first.'

She nodded to his chest – a chest wide and taut but still puffing a little from his exertions. 'I haven't got one of those things, though.'

'No worries, just wear something loose. T-shirt, tracksuit, trainers. Yeah?'

'Sure.' She nodded excitedly. Perhaps a little too excitedly. 'What . . . erm . . . what are you up to now?'

'Me? I'm off to my girlfriend's place, get all this kit off me and get showered.'

'Oh.' Nicole tried a smile but it just wouldn't come. 'Oh, okay.'

'Really pleased you're coming along,' Shaun said, with an effortless grin that seemed designed to rub it in that little bit more. Then he backed off, and shouted from a few yards away, 'Catch you later, yeah?'

'Yeah,' Nicole shouted back.

The other guy, the one Shaun had been rowing with, gave her a polite smile. She smiled back and he looked away, blushing a little. He put on a pair of tan deck shoes, gave her another brief smile, then left.

Nicole turned and went home.

CHAPTER SIXTEEN

It was so cold on the train I hardly slept. We travelled for a day and a night before it stopped.

Thank God, I thought. *We've got to wherever we're going.*

I thought wrongly.

We were given some bread and jam, and told to eat the snow that lay around us if we were thirsty. Then we were herded back onto the train. I tried to sleep just to take myself away from the cold and the jostling from other prisoners, but I couldn't. It was torture, and for the first time in my life I questioned whether I actually wanted this life. Only when darkness returned did I drift off to sleep.

We must have spent three or four days in that freezing, cramped train carriage. I could see outside through the large gaps in the wooden panels, and when we plunged into a forest the train slowed and the carriage stopped jostling us around so much. Then it halted completely. I don't know how long we were kept waiting on the train but it was the first peace we'd had for a day or two and I fell asleep. Eventually the big wooden doors of the carriage rattled and opened, and we were told to get off. We were in the middle of a forest, but it wasn't pretty or scenic. And it didn't smell of fresh pine.

There seemed to be barbed wire everywhere I looked, broken only by wooden cabins, lookout towers and some huge brick buildings with chimneys stretching up as high as the trees surrounding us. I assumed the smell came from them; it was disgusting – like frying food but with a coppery tang to it that stuck in the back of my throat and clung to the hairs in my nostrils. It took me a long time to get that smell out of my system; in fact, I'm not sure I ever completely did.

We were all kept in check by large dogs and soldiers with their fingers on triggers of rifles. A guard shouted for the POWs to follow him. We did, and as we gathered around him to have our papers checked I watched what was happening to the other prisoners. They all lined up, shuffling forward like a dishevelled and drunken centipede. As far as I could see they were being separated into two groups: the elderly, women and children went one way; the fit men came towards us.

And then I thought I recognized one of those men as he looked up. I wasn't sure where from; he just seemed familiar. He was small but powerful looking, and the top half of his body rocked from side to side as he trudged on. I tried to catch another glimpse of his face, but he disappeared into the crowd, and all I could do was stand there, trying to think where I'd seen him before.

Then a guard shouted for us all to follow him. We marched along a dirt track, still with no idea what was happening. Marching was agony after spending all that time confined like a battery hen in a crate. My legs just wouldn't work properly, my joints felt like they needed oiling.

Thankfully it was only a short journey. The POWs and the Jews were separated and we were pointed in the direction of a series of wooden cabins. It was then that I took the opportunity to look at the scene before me.

It seemed to be a huge building site – the size of a small town.

Wherever I looked I saw concrete foundations, piles of bricks, half-erected buildings, pipes and drums of cable. I was looking at all of those but still wondering what the horrible smell was. It didn't seem to be coming from anywhere specifically, but was just an invisible cloud that hung all around us, seeping into skin and clothes.

Once we were inside the cabin, one of the men mentioned the smell. Another nodded and said, 'Bloody repulsive. What the hell is it?'

'Burning meat?' another said, grimacing at his own suggestion.

The rest of us nodded, not really wanting to agree.

The beds were basic affairs – material packed with sawdust that rested on rickety wooden frames. It was still very cold – much colder than it had been in Italy – but I slept like a newborn baby that night. I didn't know where I was and didn't care. I just needed rest.

The next day I was woken up by a strident but not aggressive voice. I was still cold, but was now more interested in where we were. The person with the strident voice, who turned out to be a sergeant from another cabin, answered my questions.

His official briefing told us we were essentially in a labour camp – known as Auschwitz-III or, alternatively, Auschwitz-Monowitz. He said that apart from the cold and the smell the camp was quite bearable. We would get Red Cross parcels with cake and bully beef and the like, and would have our ranks respected and relative freedom of movement as long as we did as we were told. That essentially meant staying away from the barbed wire along the perimeter boundary and not talking to the Jewish labourers who we would come into contact with during the working day. The POW camp was mostly full of Brits, with the occasional Canadian or Australian.

Then he asked us all for our ranks, and Jimmy Banks, a corporal from Australia, was chosen as our leader.

As soon as he left, we all looked to Jimmy. Only a minute into the job, he already had questions to answer.

'Working day?' one chap said.

'But we're POWs,' another added.

Jimmy cleared his throat, but then just shrugged. He tried again:

'I don't know, chaps, I really don't. But I'll take it up with the authorities here.'

We were fed a pretty awful breakfast of biscuits, tiny chunks of beef, and water, and then found ourselves being marched to the administration offices. We had our details taken, and the men at the front were asked what skills they had. A few of them said they were tradesmen – plumbers or bricklayers or woodworkers – and there were approving nods and grunts from the officers in charge. Others asked why that mattered. They were just told to answer the question.

I didn't dare say a word unless spoken to, but a few of our men mumbled concerns and Jimmy Banks barged his way to the front. He was met with a guard and a rifle, the bayonet blade inches from his chest.

'I'm the appointed leader of these men,' Banks said. 'Could you remove the bayonet please?'

We all looked at the guard – a young, sullen-faced youth – and could almost see the beads of sweat forming on his brow as he stood firm.

But Banks matched him. 'I have a legitimate question to ask,' he said. 'You can't threaten me.'

I was so impressed with his courage I nearly cursed there and then, but I think my throat was too dry to speak.

Another guard – an officer, I think – said something in German, and the younger guard slowly withdrew his bayonet and stood aside, never taking his eyes off Banks.

'I need to know what's going on,' Banks said to the officer. 'Why are you asking my men their trades?'

'We have work for you,' the man replied in good English. 'We have a factory that needs building.'

Banks was incredulous at first. 'But . . . we're prisoners of war. We are *not* here to work for your war effort.'

The officer touched his peaked cap, repositioning it slightly. 'You have to pay your way, that's all. You will work for food and lodgings.'

'I'm afraid that won't be possible,' Banks replied.

The man smiled a broad and confident smile. 'And why is that?'

'A little thing called the Geneva Convention.'

The man nodded, but didn't say anything else. He just shrugged as if to say, *So what?*

Banks was now getting flustered, his face twitching and his voice wavering. But he persevered.

'The Geneva Convention, to which Germany is a party, strictly forbids prisoners of war from helping their enemy with the war effort. It would be like German prisoners of war in Britain helping to build bomber aircraft.'

'I can assure you there are no bombers here, just a construction project.'

'But nevertheless, the Geneva—'

The man held up his hand, gloved in tight-fitting black leather, to silence the protestation. He barked out something in German to the young guard, who stepped forward again and placed his bayonet so its blade was almost touching Banks's belly. We could all see the guard's knuckles whitening as he gripped his rifle, with no doubt as to his intent.

'Inside Monowitz *this* is our Geneva Convention,' the officer now said, wafting a hand towards his compatriot. 'Do you understand?'

Banks didn't need to reply. He stepped back from the blade and turned to us, his face pallid. Then he slowly and unsteadily walked to the back of the crowd. He did, however, have the presence of mind to mutter something else to the men, which got to me eventually. He said everyone should say they had a trade, even if they hadn't. I decided to say I was an apprentice bricklayer; my guess was that as soon as I said the word 'bricklayer' that was all that would matter, and if it turned out I was no good at it I could always say I'd told them *apprentice* bricklayer.

Over the next few hours we were all allocated jobs in what turned out to be a vast construction project, from bricklaying to welding to pipe layout to electrical connections, and when we got back to the cabin we all rallied round Banks, told him he'd tried and couldn't have done any more.

Soon we learned more from other POWs about the Auschwitz complex of concentration camps. In our section, which we simply called Monowitz, we had a right hotchpotch of people. In charge were the SS and the Wehrmacht – almost fighting between each other for superiority. Then there were the managers who had been appointed by the factory owners – a private company. There were civilian workers from Poland – not prisoners, but here as paid workers. Then there were the POWs from all over Europe, America and the Empire. Finally, at the bottom of the pile, there were the Jewish workers – essentially treated as slaves. We POWs worked for nothing, but we weren't often ill-treated. The Jewish workers appeared to do all the back-breaking, dirty and dangerous work, like carrying bags of cement, shovelling earth and gravel, and pulling wagons.

Conditions for us weren't as good as in the Italian camp, but they could have been a lot worse. I was still recovering from the truck journey, and however warm I became, my bones still felt the cold of those days on the road. Over the next week, however, days when I was always on the move, always generating heat, I started to feel better.

Something else that made me feel better was being able to write to my mother and father. I'd considered writing from Valleverde but dismissed the idea as too risky. Now I wrote every day in the knowledge that my letter would get home. Much later, Mother was to tell me that receiving that first letter – the first one she'd received since Sicily – was one of the most joyful days of her life.

We all worked diligently for those first few weeks, just keen to settle in, not wanting to cause trouble. My bricklaying was awful, but I told everyone I was learning, and getting better every day, learning the correct mix of sand with cement and water, how long I could use it for before it went off, how to keep the lines straight and so on.

Soon winter had set in, but we were still reasonably comfortable. It was freezing outside but we just worked harder, and we had a stove inside the cabin to provide a bare minimum of heat.

One evening – I think it must have been late in December 1943 – Jimmy Banks called me to the corner of the cabin, where he was sitting with the sergeant who had originally briefed us.

'Need a word, Mac,' he said. I was suspicious, but not in a frightened way; I would have trusted this man with my life.

He continued: 'Getting pretty nifty at this bricklaying work, aren't we?'

'I'm certainly getting enough practice,' I said with a smile.

He grimaced – like I was doing something wrong. I asked what the matter was, told him I was getting more and more skilled from practice as the weeks went by.

'That's not the way things work,' he said. 'I've been talking with the heads of the POWs, talking about all the work we're doing.'

I told him I didn't understand what he was talking about.

He looked to the sergeant, who then put a hand on my shoulder and leaned in to whisper. 'Do you really want to help the Germans?' he said.

I said I didn't realize I had any choice.

He whispered more. 'The pipe layers, they make sure there are always leaks in the pipe-joins, the electricians wire things up the wrong way, so fuses will blow or motors won't work when the power is switched on.' Then he raised his eyebrows and just stared at me for a few seconds.

'You see,' he continued, 'just supposing there were to be too much sand or water in the mortar mix. That could make for a very weak wall. Of course, it would look good to a passing inspection, so you wouldn't be getting yourself into any trouble.'

I looked at Banks, who nodded suggestively.

I nodded too, then told them I completely understood. They both gave me encouraging, almost proud, smiles. I shook hands with both of them, then saluted and left.

I'd got used to the cold now I was being active rather than being cooped up, but was still struggling to accept the stench in the air, and over the winter months I learned more about the other two Auschwitz camps. Auschwitz I was the main administrative centre, where all the processing of documents was carried out. Auschwitz II – also known as Auschwitz-Birkenau – held the vast majority of the prisoners. We often used to see them being marched past, very thin and dirty sorts in what looked like striped pyjamas. It was a sight that was hard to take your eyes off.

There were always rumours as to what was really happening, but I had no idea how much truth was in them. I simply preferred to get on with my job, and enjoy what little time off we had, when we'd play football or cards or just talk. The standard food was quite inedible, but those Red Cross food parcels made up for it – cake, chocolate, tins of bully beef, all like nectar in a place like that.

One day Jimmy Banks gathered us all around and said we had to try to get some of the food we had to the Jewish prisoners.

There were grunts of discontent, but Banks told us it was an order, not a request, although it was up to us how we carried the order out.

I agreed with the men; I didn't want to give food away. I'd already lost weight because I was doing physical work, and I didn't want to lose more. Looking back it's something I'm ashamed of, but I was young and only trying to keep up my hopes of getting back home. Also, being into sport, I wanted to look after myself, and that meant keeping myself well fed.

A few of us voiced such concerns, but we were told orders were orders.

Looking back on how I behaved then and what I said, I feel the guilt deep in my belly. At the time I possessed the selfishness of youth – the misplaced and short-sighted concern about how the situation would affect me. Yes, Rosa and her family had been Jews, but I didn't actually think of them as Jews; I thought of them as Rosa, Mama and Papa. It was a convenient distinction; it was a time when I feared for my own survival, which tends to crystallize a person's priorities.

It took one sickening experience at the camp to change my mind about helping the Jews.

It happened when we were all hard at work outside, and out of the corner of my eye I spotted two young girls running along the outside of the fence. All hell broke loose among the guards, and I stopped working to watch, as did everyone. The guards shouted and screamed as if the two girls were threatening the future of the Third Reich. Guns were aimed at them, shots were fired over their heads, and they stopped running. They held their hands up, and four guards ran through the gates towards them. They knocked them to the floor, dragged them by their arms inside the camp, and forced them into a corner. They were surrounded on two sides by an electrified fence, and on the other two sides by four guards.

These girls can't have been more than nine or ten. The guards shouted at them to remove their striped tops, which they did, and one of the guards inspected the inside of the girls' forearms. By now I knew that was where the tattoo was.

'*Juden!*' he shouted, as if he had found the devil.

What I saw next blurred in my mind and still makes me shiver to this day. Two of the guards pulled out whips and started to lash them. The girls, dirty, skinny and shaven-headed, screamed – at first for mercy, then in pain. I assumed they would get a few lashes and be told to return. But no. It was relentless. The girls fell to the ground and curled up, foetus-like. Their backs started to glisten like red snakes squirming for release. They flinched as they yelped, and soon their torsos were skinless carcasses.

This must have been witnessed by fifteen or twenty POWs, a few of whom started walking towards the commotion. They were stopped by fellow POWs – the ones who had been there longer.

One of the girls suddenly sprang up and jumped onto the electric fence. Her torso jittered, she let out a final – almost soothing – grunt, then fell lifeless to the ground.

That left the other girl to suffer the full fury of two whips, while the other two guards stood watching.

It was then that I ran. I didn't have a clue what I was going to do, just that I couldn't bear to watch it any longer and do nothing. Then I felt an impact on my ankle and all I could see was the sky spinning past me. When it stopped I was dragged to my feet by two POWs who held onto me tightly.

'You can't,' one of them said. 'What's the point?'

I started arguing with them, so they frogmarched me to a cabin and sat me down. They explained that this was how it worked, that there was far worse happening, and that we had to choose our moment to get revenge. But I vowed to do the right thing as much as I could from then on, even if it meant that I went a little hungry.

If that experience changed my mind about helping the Jews, another event was a perfect lesson in exactly how to orchestrate revenge. Again, I was outside, working on a wall.

At the far side of the camp there was a furnace of sorts, a large metal brazier about four yards by four yards. It was used to burn waste such as paper from bags of cement and wooden pallets. The complex was so huge that this was burning day and night.

The guards kept close to it in the cold weather.

Eli was one of the Jewish prisoners who kept us bricklayers supplied with sand and cement. He was skinny, as they all were due to the poor diet. Some of the other bricklayers used to leave a square of chocolate or a chunk of cake in his wheelbarrow when nobody was looking. The man spoke broken English and always greeted us politely. It was obvious he didn't hold any grudge against us, and was a good worker.

One day, Eli gathered up the empty cement bags and took them to the brazier. On the steps leading up to the platform he slipped, letting out a yelp as he fell. He stood up and rubbed his shin, which he'd obviously cracked on the step. A nearby guard shouted at him, and pointed at his own knee. I could see from where I was standing that a gob of cement had found its way onto the guard's uniform. Eli apologized and used his hands to scrape the cement off the man's uniform.

The guard smiled. Then, as Eli turned towards the brazier and threw the bags onto the fire, the guard rammed the butt of the rifle into the middle of Eli's back. I watched, unable to blink or swallow, as Eli fell, then grabbed the edge of the brazier at the last second. I could just see his arms and the top of his head as he tried to drag himself out. His feet must have already been on fire. The guard stamped on Eli's hand and kicked his head, and the screams of this man, burning alive in the furnace, stopped all work until the guards came and told us to carry on. I think even a couple of the German guards had been shocked at what they'd seen, and showed us some leniency as we struggled to get going again.

By then, of course, I knew I just had to accept these disgusting events and get on with my duties. That isn't to say my mind wasn't twisted and confused; I was still torn between my overriding will for self-preservation and my feelings of concern for these people, but I had an urge to do something more for them. Leaving them the odd square of chocolate or chunk of corned beef almost seemed an insult.

After a very difficult hour struggling with my own emotions, I noticed two POWs talking together on the blind side of a newly built wall. There was something going on, as stopping work to talk was risking the wrath of the guards. I didn't fully understand, but watched with great interest.

As they returned to work, one of them – a big brute of a man as tall as me but far stronger – picked up a small length of waste wood and headed for the brazier. The first man started to climb the scaffolding.

I watched one, then the other, hopping my gaze between the two. Waiting.

The one who was on the scaffolding was looking over towards the brazier. I saw him make a quick prayer, then throw himself off the top, down towards a solid concrete base. I gasped, fearing for the man's life, but then, at the last moment, he reached out with one hand and grabbed a piece of scaffolding. He started shouting, screaming for help. Then I looked towards the brazier just in time to see his accomplice – who was now approaching the brazier – swing the length of wood at the guard whose uniform still had that smudge from the gob of cement. The guard was busy looking over to where the shouting was coming from, so didn't stand a chance. The blow to his head knocked him clean over, and as he hit the deck the POW smashed the length of wood onto his head again and dragged him to the edge of the brazier. Within seconds the guard's body had disappeared over the edge, to lie with Eli's. Then the POW tossed the wood in and ran away, back to where everyone else had gathered, where a man was dangling precariously from the scaffolding.

Of course, the man quickly managed to pull himself up, and after rubbing his shoulder as if it was hurt, assured everyone he was feeling better. And over the next few minutes there seemed to be a rush to gather rubbish and dispose of it in the brazier. We had no illusions about our immunity; the Germans would assume the missing soldier had deserted, but we knew there would be serious – probably deadly – repercussions if there was a scrap of evidence to the contrary.

When I read the above words now, the cruelty and brutality of those events is hard to stomach. But for me, at a little over nineteen years old, life was only just starting to spiral down into hell.

CHAPTER SEVENTEEN

Nicole heard footsteps outside her bedroom, so closed the notebook and quickly shoved it under the covers.

The door opened and her mother's head appeared around it.

'So, are you going?'

Nicole just looked up without answering.

Her mother sat down on the bed next to her. 'Are you all right?' she said. 'You look upset.'

Nicole swallowed, cleared her throat, and ran her fingers across her face to check for tears.

'Actually, you look *very* upset.' Her mother put her arm out to one side, beckoning her daughter in. Nicole bounced her bottom along towards her and felt the comforting arm pull her in. The two of them rocked back and forth a few times.

'I miss Darren,' Nicole eventually said.

Her mother paused, staring ahead vacantly, before saying, 'My baby boy.'

'You remember when Gran died?' Nicole said.

Her mother frowned and said, 'Why are you thinking of Gran?'

'Well . . . thing is . . . when she died, I didn't really understand it.'

'You were eleven, darling.'

'I know, but . . .' Nicole took her mother's arm from around her and the two of them held hands. 'At the time I just thought she'd be away for a while . . . like somehow I'd see her again. But with Darren I didn't have that feeling. I knew it was forever.'

Her mother brought a hand up to her own face and rubbed her eyes gently. 'I know, love. It was a hellish time.' She squeezed Nicole again. 'You know, I've lost count of the people who've told me I have to move on, that one of these days I'll feel better about losing my baby.'

'And do you believe them?'

Her mother sighed, then said. 'No, but maybe I will one of these days.'

'I'm not sure I even want to move on,' Nicole said.

'Me neither. But I know what people mean.'

'Really?'

'It's all about working out a future without people you've lost, imagining for a moment what *they* would want for you.'

'I don't understand,' Nicole said.

'Well, what do you think Darren would want his big sister to be doing – moping around and feeling sorry for herself, or getting on with her life and achieving something?'

Nicole twirled the gold ring on her finger.

'Talking of which,' her mother said, 'are you going to this rowing club thing?'

Nicole looked into her mother's red-rimmed eyes, smiled flatly, and nodded.

'Good girl. Know where all your stuff is?'

'I'll find it.'

'And I'll have something cooked for when you get back.'

After her mother had left, Nicole moved over to the cardboard boxes on the far side of the room. She opened one and pulled out a pair of jogging bottoms. She gave them a sniff, then nodded to herself. She found a T-shirt and did the same test, and opened a few more boxes and rummaged around inside them.

Then she stepped outside her bedroom and shouted downstairs, 'Have you seen my trainers, Mum?'

'Which ones?'

'Any.'

'Have you looked in the cellar?'

Of course. If in doubt try the cellar.

Nicole pulled on the tracksuit bottoms and a baggy T-shirt and thundered downstairs.

She thundered slightly more carefully downstairs again into the cellar.

She checked her watch, then quickly found the large vinyl bag containing all her sports kit. She picked out the newest-looking pair of trainers and pulled them on.

As she was tying the laces her eyes fell upon the gold ring, now starting to look at home on the second finger of her right hand.

She twirled the ring around her finger a few times, its edges twinkling by the light of the unshaded bulb, and glanced to the old briefcase. Then she twirled the ring right off her finger and dropped it into the briefcase.

Perhaps it belonged there.

Minutes later she was stepping out of the front door, looking up. Today the skies were a dull grey rather than bright blue as they had been on the last rowing evening.

'Be careful,' her mother shouted out behind her.

'What?' Nicole screwed her face up. 'It's rowing, Mum. It's not dangerous.'

Her mother came to the door. 'I could come and watch you if you want?'

Nicole bared her teeth. 'Eek! No thanks.'

'If you're sure, but perhaps if you start competing.'

'Er . . . yeah, right.'

She left, turned right at the corner shop where the big chirpy budgie hung out, followed the road to the river, and ten minutes later reached Danver's Shed.

Boats were half out of the shed, or half in the water, or resting on the path. Lycra-clad bodies lifted boats or twisted their bodies this way and that by way of a warm-up.

Oh, God. Nightmare situation alert.

Like when you enter a room full of people who are all best buddies with each other, who are all smiling and laughing and chatting to each other, and you're Billy No-Mates because you haven't a clue who they are and they've never seen you before.

But she did know one of them. Sort of.

Shaun was on the far side of the group, clearly jostling for the alpha-male position with two other guys. She lifted a hand and made a half-hearted attempt to attract his attention. Failing.

Oh, well. She could just stand there for . . . for as long as it took.

Then she heard a voice say, 'Hi.'

She turned. It was the 'other' rower, Shaun's partner.

'You were here last time, weren't you?' he said. He nodded over to Shaun. 'Did he rope you in?'

'Something like that.'

'He's like that. Always on the lookout for new members. He thinks he'll earn commission.' He held a hand out. 'I'm Austin, by the way.'

Very formal.

'Nicole.' She placed her hand in his. His hand was large but held hers like a valuable china ornament.

'He doesn't really earn commission. I was joking.'

'I got that.'

'Right.' He forced a smile. 'You're a complete beginner, right?'

'Right.'

'So you don't know what to do?'

Nicole shook her head, then leaned over and took a good look inside the boat alongside them. Two sliding seats, four oars. Nothing else.

No room for anything else.

'Have you ever rowed on a machine?'

'Nope.'

His eyes bounced upwards and he rested his fists onto the side of his very taut midriff.

'Sorry,' Nicole said.

'Only kidding. Everyone has to start somewhere.' Then he smiled in a peculiar way, pulling the edges of his lips down rather than up. 'So, do you want a quick lesson?'

'Oh . . . erm . . . I think I should go out with Shaun first.'

Austin peered over past Nicole's shoulder, searching. 'It's up to you, but I think he's hoping for a run-out with the head of the women's team. Or something like that.'

Nicole looked over too. They stood in silence for a few moments, both smiling politely, fiddling with their hands, and occasionally glancing at Shaun, who showed no signs of stopping talking.

'We can either wait for Captain Bullshit,' Austin said, 'which might take forever, or I can show you the basics.'

Nicole snorted a laugh. 'Okay then,' she said. 'If you don't mind.'

'Cool.' He rubbed the dark pepper of stubble on his chin as he thought. 'So you don't know anything?'

Nicole nodded down. 'I know that's a rowing boat. That's about it.'

'Sort of.' He held a finger up and smiled warmly. 'We like to think of this as a scull.'

'Oh, yes. I knew that.'

'A double scull.'

'Double 'cos it's got two seats. Right?'

'Correct. And scull because it's got four oars. So. First thing is to get you seated properly.'

Telling Nicole 'the basics' took about ten minutes, but knowing them didn't seem to help. Blades, oarlocks, outriggers, the catch, the recovery phase. It was too much, but then Austin said, 'Look, forget all that crap and just row,' and a minute later they were off and Nicole watched the riverbank drifting away from them.

She didn't feel as if she was doing much, but with Austin in the back seat effortlessly pulling his oars back, the scull was slicing through the water quite nicely. She was trying to follow the same timing but was mostly pulling her oars through the section of fresh air just above the water.

After a few minutes she watched the verdant riverside scenery fly past them both – silently save for the rub of the wooden oar against its holder and the splash of blade entering water. There was some noise from each riverbank, but it all somehow seemed to be coming from a different world.

Yes. There was something in this rowing thing. It wasn't exciting, it wasn't cool, it wasn't a hobby her school friends would have taken up in a million years.

But there was definitely something.

Austin's thoughtful silence also helped. Shaun the chirpy budgie might have spoiled the moment by talking all the way.

And then, just as the background noises of the town had disappeared and Nicole's mind was getting ferried away in a soulful trance, the scull gently slowed down.

'We're getting close to the weir,' Austin said. 'I usually stop here for a bit. That okay?'

'Sure,' she said over her shoulder.

He dragged an oar into the water, keeping the other out, and the scull gradually turned around.

'We can just take five here,' he said. Nicole turned just enough to see him reach down and pick up a plastic bottle. He tapped it on her shoulder and said, 'You want a drink first?'

She shook her head, then turned sideways on her seat. It seemed rude to face away from him. She turned just in time to see him unclip the cover with his teeth and shoot a stream of liquid into his mouth. He put the bottle back and looked left and right, gazing out over the fields in the distance.

'I can see why you're a good pairing,' Nicole said.

'Mmm?' It looked an effort for Austin to drag himself back from his daydream.

'You and Shaun. He's, like, a golden-tongued charmer; you don't say much.'

He gave his head a quick shake and frowned. 'Oh, no. Sorry. Must seem rude.'

'Not really,' Nicole said. 'He can be a bit too much.'

'Tell me about it. He can't even stop when we're in lectures.'

'You're on the same course as him?'

He nodded, then bounced his eyes to the sky. 'Worse luck.'

'What? Sports Science?'

'He told you? Good course, though – if you like sport.'

'You're kidding,' Nicole said.

Now his wide mouth grinned. 'Well, yes, obviously. But yeah, it's a great course – even better if you can steer clear of Captain Bullshit. Anyway, enough about me and him. What about you? You new around here? I mean, to Henley?'

'Moved into Mac's old place.'

'Mac?' Austin's eyes widened, he seemed to wake up another notch. 'You mean *rowing* Mac?'

'Apparently that's the one.'

'Ah. Shaun told you all about him.'

'You know he coached Shaun's dad?'

Austin laughed. 'I think Mac coached pretty much everyone in Henley who grabbed an oar from the sixties to the nineties. My dad wouldn't stop talking about him.'

'Shaun said he's a bit of a legend.'

'I guess he is to some people. Well, yeah, he is.'

'You don't seem sure?'

Austin paused, and his voice became quieter, more serious. 'It's probably unfair, but I'm thinking about the stuff my dad told me about him. Not very nice, some of it.'

Nicole waited for some explanation, but all she heard was the distant quacking of a lone duck at the riverbank. She was about to ask what Austin meant when he spoke again.

'Right.' He rotated his shoulders a little by way of a warm-up, then grabbed his oars. 'You ready for the return run?'

Nicole nodded, and then they pulled away back towards Danver's Shed.

CHAPTER EIGHTEEN

I t was now spring 1944. I'd survived the many cold and dreary weeks of winter, and become hardened to the realities of life in Auschwitz-Monowitz.

Winter had been an arduous time for me but my body had responded like an athlete's. I was thin and sinewy, and had got used to having no feeling in my toes and fingers. But we POWs had luxuries other inmates didn't have and I never took them for granted. There were many around us in much worse positions, and by now we had a system of sorts in place to help them.

Each cabin tended to do their own thing, but we all talked and swapped ideas. The POWs in my cabin had a daily whip-round of food, which was secreted in various locations around the construction site, which basically meant anywhere out of sight of prying eyes – a hut or the inside corner of a wall, or perhaps inside a metal tank. The location was varied each time to avoid raising suspicion.

Whenever Jewish labourers dropped off a delivery of construction items we would tell them where to put it, but would often end the instruction with 'Jude' at the end, pronounced *Juder*. We would say something like, 'Put it behind the wall, Jude.' They knew from that to keep their eyes peeled for a piece of bread or cake or meat.

Both parties found it amusing that we were mocking the German treatment of their captors. Should there have been humour in such a hellish place? In hindsight perhaps not, but we all took our levity where we could. We liked to think it helped morale among the Jews. They had precious little else to find pleasurable in that wretched place.

But now I realize the whole experience was a lot for a young man of nineteen to bear. I withdrew inside myself whenever I could for the sake of my own sanity. Although I'd sworn to help the Jews whenever I could, I myself continued to lose weight, and had started to consider my own well-being as the only thing that truly mattered.

To that end, I dismissed thoughts of Rosa and her family. In fact, I consciously tried to banish any memories of them from my mind. They were all in the past, and I had to consider my future. During those slightly warmer spring months of 1944 I started to reconsider my decision to help the Jews at every opportunity. Instead of leaving four squares of chocolate I left one or sometimes none at all. The pieces of cake or meat got smaller. And if anything became mouldy and I couldn't stomach it, then they would get it. *Better for Jews*, I thought. I was following orders, but on my terms.

I still hate myself for adopting that attitude; I've always told myself I was simply being human, that it was the survival instinct kicking in when there was so much death and suffering around me. I was working hard so needed the food myself. I saw many Jews come and go. I witnessed a lot of them die – usually collapsing on the ground from exhaustion and malnutrition, their cadaverous bodies being dragged away by the guards. By then we all knew why the smoke from the chimneys smelled so repulsive.

In my private moments I'd argued with myself for weeks. One part of me was convinced that food given to people who were going to die anyway was wasted food. They were being worked to death, and a few morsels more would merely prolong their agony. It was better in my stomach because I was likely to survive the war.

Then, one morning in the summer of 1944, something happened that changed my outlook forever. I was outside, enjoying a rare warm and sunny day, when I noticed a new Jewish labourer pushing a wheelbarrow of sand towards a wall being built forty or fifty yards to my left by Colin Cooper – a Londoner I knew from my cabin. I stopped working for a moment and shaded my eyes with my trowel to see better. Yes, it looked like him. Was this new labourer the man I'd noticed in the queue on arrival here? Whether he was or not, I felt like I recognized him – even *knew* him. I just didn't know where from.

I kept my eye on him until he disappeared to get more sand, then I continued with my brickwork. But my mind wasn't on the job. I stopped occasionally, deep in thought, thinking where I might have seen him. He appeared again, and I walked closer to get a better look. It didn't help, so I returned to my work.

A few minutes later it hit me why he looked familiar, even though I'd never seen him before. I wasn't certain, but I was sure enough that I hardly put a brick on straight for the rest of that shift.

Later that day, when we were in the cabin eating, I went over to Colin's bunk and asked if he minded if I sat down next to him. He shrugged, so I did.

'The new worker you have,' I said.

He just grunted at this, as if he didn't understand the question.

'You had a new worker this morning,' I said. 'Not very tall but very sturdy. Bringing sand and cement to your wall.'

He shrugged again and said, 'So?'

'Do you know his name?'

'Why would I know his name?' he said, frowning.

'I just thought you might have talked.'

He shook his head. 'Not worth the trouble.'

I didn't know what to say after that; it seemed pointless. I told him it didn't matter and returned to my bunk. Then I had an idea. We all got cigarettes in our Red Cross parcels – not many, but too many if, like me, you didn't smoke. Even back then I never thought they were good for your lungs, so I used to barter with mine – swap them for more cake or chunks of meat.

I grabbed two of them and went back to Colin, who, by this time, had got some cake in his hand and was carefully biting chunks off, making sure not one crumb fell to the floor.

This time he kept his eyes on me, as if he thought I was going to do something to him. He even flinched slightly as I pulled the cigarettes out of my pocket.

'These are for you,' I said.

He looked around. He still obviously thought it was some sort of trick.

'If we can swap walls,' I added.

The stiffness in his shoulders eased off a little. 'Oh,' he said. 'I see.' He carried on chewing, then swallowed the piece of cake in his mouth. 'Your wall a bit harder is it?'

'Yes,' I said. 'It's in the sun most of the day. Straight ahead of me. In my eyes.'

He glanced at the two cigarettes I held out, then looked me in the eye and said, 'If you're offering two it must be worth four.'

I almost told him he had a bloody cheek, but he must have been about ten years older than me, and that counted for a lot. I went back to my bunk, got two more cigarettes, and the deal was done.

The next day I couldn't wait. I was absolutely exhausted – and it takes a lot to exhaust a nineteen-year-old lad accustomed to hard work – but I'd been a jangle of nerves the previous night and had hardly slept. My nerves were stopping me settle even at breakfast, which was just coffee, watery soup, and a bit more cake from my own stash.

I started on the other wall, and when the Jewish labourer brought the first wheelbarrow of sand I wasn't quite so sure. I took a good look at him and became more certain: his small, squat frame, the angle of his eyes, the small, straight nose, the squareness of his jaw. It could have been anyone, but I didn't think it was, and I had to know for sure.

That first time a guard was looking, so I said nothing. But when he came again I took my chance. I took a piece of cake out of my pocket and offered it to him.

He kept his head low, then looked left and right, his sunken eyes darting around. Then he looked straight at me, suspicion etched on his features. He took the cake and crammed it into his mouth like a starving rat.

'What's your name?' I said.

He stopped eating for a second, but ignored my question.

'Speak English?' I asked.

Again, nothing. But now I was this close to his face I was more certain. Either I was going mad or he had the eyes and chin of his father and the nose of his sister.

He gobbled down the cake, then turned and started wheeling his barrow away towards the truck of sand.

'Is your name Lorenzo?' I said to his back.

He stopped and hooked a glance at me. I knew the answer from the stormy expression on his face. But he carried on.

It was only much later in the morning, when we were both that little bit more sweaty and dirty, that I got the chance to talk to him again. I followed him to the truck of sand.

'You *do* understand English,' I said. 'I know you do.'

He ignored me again and just carried on shovelling sand. I had one last roll of the dice – one way I could be sure.

'Were you married to a woman called Donna?' I said.

He turned to face me directly. I saw hatred in the red of his eyes as he ran towards me and grasped me by the throat. He must have been six inches smaller than me, but I couldn't have been more scared of him if he'd had a knife in his hand. I pulled myself away and said I was sorry, but he wouldn't leave me alone. Then we both heard a gunshot and he stepped back. A guard ran towards us and raised his rifle to Lorenzo.

'No!' I stood in front of Lorenzo, and for a second I thought it was going to be the last mistake I would ever make.

But Lorenzo bowed his head in apology and backed away towards the truck of sand. The guard pointed the rifle at Lorenzo, then back at me. He was as clueless as I was – and looked as young too. If it had been an older, more experienced man the outcome might have been different. But he eventually lowered his rifle and stood away, just observing us.

Of course, neither Lorenzo nor I uttered another word for the rest of that morning. The guard stayed there, watching both of us until lunchtime, when we all left to go our own ways.

When Lorenzo and I returned, and we were alone, I tried to continue our conversation.

'I'm sorry,' I said. 'I didn't mean to upset you.'

He said nothing for ten or twenty minutes, just carried on shovelling sand into his wheelbarrow and pushing it to various places.

Then he returned and stared into my eyes for a few seconds. 'I speak a little English,' he said in a soft, cultured tone, which was at odds with his appearance. 'How do you know these things about me?'

Bracing myself for his reaction, I said, 'You look so much like your sister.'

He looked shocked all over again. 'My sister?'

'Rosa Di Vito,' I said. 'From Rome, from Valleverde.'

Now he looked like he was being accused of something.

'It's all right,' I said quietly. 'I'm on your side.'

He spoke with difficulty, or, more likely, with mistrust: 'Who are you? What do you want?'

I swallowed hard, drew breath and said, 'I . . . I want to know where Rosa is.'

His stare dropped to the muddy earth below us.

'Lorenzo?' I said, conscious I now sounded like I was interrogating him. 'Do you know where Rosa is? Or what happened to her?'

He gave his head a doleful shake and said he didn't know. But then he looked to the heavens – or rather to the plumes of sweet but acrid smoke that filled the skies around us.

I followed his gaze and felt weak and sick. I thought I was going to faint.

'Oh, no,' I said. 'Oh, please, God, no.'

Then he stepped over to me and put a hand on my shoulder. 'Now I remember. You are her English soldier, yes?'

Her English soldier.

I felt tears welling up and wiped my eyes. I nodded and said, 'Do you really think she's . . . ?'

He hesitated to answer, then said, 'I don't know – not for certain.'

Was he lying just for my benefit?

I was just about to ask him when he'd last seen her, when a guard appeared from around the corner and we had to separate and carry on working in silence.

But over the next few days Lorenzo and I talked more whenever we had the opportunity. I felt guilty about giving him mouldy food that first time and swore to myself I would do better. All these years later when I think of this I hate myself, but the truth is that I was only treating him so well because he might have been able to lead me to Rosa.

We talked about his work with the Italian underground movement, about how he'd been happily married for a few years before the political climate changed. He said he didn't know exactly where Lorenzo Junior and Anna had been taken and missed them so badly it kept him awake some nights, but he thought they were safe. He also said he felt guilty, that he thought he'd betrayed them by going off to work with the underground movement, putting his beliefs before his family. I should have reassured him, told him I was sure they would understand, but I was too young to express such feelings.

He wouldn't tell me much more at that stage and I didn't want to badger him, but I had some sort of answer. He had clearly spoken to Rosa at some point – whether in Fossoli or here in Auschwitz or elsewhere – and she had told him what had happened in Rome. The question I asked myself was whether he knew they were all alive or knew they were all dead.

And whether he would tell me.

Over the next few days I took more food to him – mostly of good quality. You could almost see the improvement in him that a few extra calories brought.

And yes, it took a few days, but eventually he did talk more about what had happened. He spoke with his nostrils flaring and his lip curling in hatred.

As soon as the Germans had overrun the north of the country he'd been arrested as a political agitator and sent to the internment camp at Fossoli. He spent months there with fellow political activists, but then, when a new delivery of prisoners arrived, he spotted his papa in the crowd and ran towards him. Papa cried to see his son again, and told him what had happened in Rome. It wasn't long before Mama and Rosa were found in the masses there, and the family were reunited. Sadly it was to last only for a brief period. Within days all four of them were herded onto the same train, but in the panic Lorenzo got separated, and he hadn't seen them since.

He'd tried his best to look for them while queuing at the entrance to Auschwitz. He told me he knew the rumours but tried to blot them from his mind.

We all had our own rumours in there, some more based on fact than others. So I asked him what he thought the rumours were.

Apparently the people in the queue were separated into two groups. One contained the young men like him who could be of use labouring on the building site, and the other contained everyone else.

I asked him what they did with everyone else.

Again, he looked up to the black clouds of smoke, which cloaked the whole area day and night.

I didn't believe him. I told him that if they were burning bodies, then surely it would be only those of people who had perished from disease or starvation, and that Mama, Papa and Rosa all seemed to be in relatively robust health.

He grimaced, then said, 'I hope so.'

We left the conversation there.

We did, however, talk at length over the next few months, and I got to know him well. There was always an undercurrent of unease, the fear that one or other of us would mention Rosa, which might lead on to theories of what might have become of her.

Instead we whiled away the boredom with talk of science, philosophy and politics. It turned out he was being modest when he'd said he spoke little English. He was merely a little rusty, and came to enjoy learning one or two words he hadn't heard before. In fact, he was much cleverer than me on every subject you care to mention, which wasn't surprising considering he was an educated man and a qualified architect. Sometimes I would watch his ill-nourished frame – broad of bone but scrawny of flesh – lugging around wood and pipe and wheelbarrows of sand, and would almost cry at the waste of a great mind.

He was also one of the bravest people I've ever met in my life.

CHAPTER NINETEEN

I t was a warm, still evening. Perfect for rowing.

Again, Nicole had been lying on her bed reading the notebook; again, her mother had disturbed her, asked if she was going to rowing practice – hinted that *she should* go to rowing practice.

So she'd got ready, tried to pull her mind back to the present, and hurried out around the corner shop, straight to the river, and across the bridge to Danver's Shed.

'You want to try rowing with some of the women?' Austin said as they all carried out a few stretching exercises.

'Don't mind.'

Austin said nothing.

'Not rowing with Shaun tonight?' she asked him.

'He's with the fours. I've got a bit of a thigh strain, taking it easy.'

'So why don't I go out with you again?'

He swung his arm around like windmills a few times, then again the opposite way, before saying, 'Sure.'

He held the boat steady as she got in, and in no time they were skimming along the water. They rowed smoothly, quietly and serenely for ten or fifteen minutes, passing one or two chugging boats, the odd swan, numerous dog-walkers and the timeless willows guarding the waterside.

Nicole's timing – if not the strength of her stroke – was coming together. For the first time she could sense a little teamwork, that she was actually making a contribution. And with Austin behind and out of sight (and not speaking), she could almost imagine she was out there on her own, that the powerful strokes were from *her* arms and *her* legs, that she was pulling the scull through the water under her own steam.

Well, at least until Austin stopped rowing and the whole thing quickly fell to no pace at all.

It was time for a break, but Austin didn't say that; he just stopped rowing. Nicole was getting to like the silence of his style but just occasionally a little more information would have been welcome. She felt the tap of the bottle on her shoulder. She squirted a little of the energy drink into her mouth and handed it back, then heard Austin do the same.

'You know we were talking about Mac the other day?' she said without turning around.

'Uh-huh.'

'Well, did you ever, like, meet him?'

Austin squinted up to the sun. 'Mmm . . . Once or twice. Even in his early eighties he used to pop down and see us once in a blue moon. He couldn't get into one of these things but he like to shout encouragement as I remember. I think that stopped when he had his first stroke.'

'What was he like?'

'Erm . . . Big guy for his age. Must have shrunk in the wash as time went on. My granddad says that always happens. Bet he was a good rower when he was younger, though. You could tell from the shape of his frame.'

'But did you ever get to know him?'

'God, no. Well before my time. And anyway I'm not sure I'd have wanted to.'

Nicole hooked her head around, almost disapproving of the reply.

'I told you before. I heard some . . . stuff about him.'

'You mean, just rumours?'

He shook his head. 'I wish they were, but it's stuff my dad told me.'

'So . . . like what?'

'Oh, a few things. There was this time he was at rowing practice. Apparently halfway through the cops turned up, wanted a word with him. He was too ashamed to talk about it, but word got around, and my old man knew one of the cops so got the story straight. Turned out he'd locked his wife in one of the bedrooms and gone rowing, just leaving her there. She escaped through a window, though. What a bastard, eh? Locking her up like that.'

Nicole gulped. 'Yeah. Bastard.'

'Also Dad said when his second wife left him he used to trawl around the pubs in Henley looking for her. She'd moved out of the area but he still believed she was seeing some local guy.'

'That's spooky.'

'Just weird to me.' Austin thought for a moment, then said, 'But perhaps that's being a bit unfair. They reckon he had a rough time in the war, but I don't think he ever really talked about it. Guess he was a good guy overall, though. Never actually harmed anyone. Just a bit, like, twisted.'

Nicole nodded, but said nothing.

'Course, he didn't have any kids. They reckon that's why he put so much effort into coaching rowers, as if Shaun's dad and my dad and a hundred others were like substitute kids for him.'

'You make him sound a bit . . .'

'What? Tragic?'

'Sort of.'

'Bad war experiences, two broken marriages, no kids. Guess he was a bit. Not that you'd know. Few times I met him he seemed a happy old dude – always smiling, cheering us on. I think he just enjoyed what he did. Never unhappy or down. At least, if he was he hid it well.'

'You think he was content after all that had happened to him?'

'Oh, yeah. Reckon he still is too.'

Nicole looked up to the blue skies, spoiled only by the scars of a few vapour trails.

She hoped Mac was still happy.

'Anyway,' Austin said, 'why are you so interested in him?'

'Oh, nothing. He just left some random stuff in the house.'

'Don't think he could have taken it where he was going.'

Nicole smiled sadly. 'No.'

'If it's important you want to ask Shaun; his dad could talk about old Mac all day. You could even arrange to meet up with him if you fancy the idea.'

Nicole shook her head. 'Oh, no. Not crucial. I'm just, like, making conversation.'

'Sure. So what about you? Working or studying?'

'Uh-uh.'

'What? Neither?'

'You're as bad as my mum and dad.'

'Sorry. It's just . . . you seem, like, pretty switched on. Thought you'd be sortin' out college or a job.'

'Yeah, well, I'll probably do that at some stage.'

'Good. Shouldn't waste time. Life's too short an' all that.'

Nicole heard and felt the clunk of oars being readied for action.

'Talking of which,' Austin said, 'we'd better get back. They'll be sending a search party out for us.'

The boat turned as Austin pulled with his right arm only. Soon they were slicing their way through the water back towards Danver's Shed.

CHAPTER TWENTY

Auschwitz-Monowitz could never have been anything but a wretched place, but I'd almost started to depend upon the small but welcome amount of enjoyment I got from the thought of working in the fresh air. *The thought*, that is. Actually carrying out the work was hard, but it was a relief from lying on my bunk.

Lorenzo had become someone I called a friend and would be proud to describe as such to anyone. He was also a link to Rosa, to a better life in another world, a world I felt I'd betrayed by forcing memories of her behind me. But the link to Rosa had now become secondary; I liked the man for himself.

I knew, however, that I had to be careful about talking with him, to choose my moments when nobody was looking.

I wasn't careful enough.

One morning, as we were filing out of the cabin to go to work, Jimmy Banks told me to hang back, said he needed to have a word with me.

We sat across from each other at a small table used for playing cards.

'Mac,' he said. 'Tell me again how you came to be here.'

'What do you mean by that?' I said.

He held up a calming hand. 'Just tell me the truth. Please.'

So I told him exactly what I'd told the others, which was half of the truth. I said I'd been involved in the assault on Sicily, had been captured and sent to Fossoli and from there to Auschwitz-Monowitz to work. As I spoke the last of the POWs left. Now we were alone.

'The thing is, Mac' – Banks shifted uncomfortably on his stool – 'you've been seen talking.'

'Talking?'

'To the Jew. Quite a lot.'

'The Jew?'

'The Jew you work with.'

'And?'

'Do you know him?'

'Not really,' I said. 'I'd never met him until a few days ago.'

'So why do you spend so much time talking to him?'

I'd told Banks the truth – that I'd met 'the Jew' only a few days before. I didn't think it wise to tell him any more than that.

'I'm . . . just trying to get on,' I said. 'You know how boring it is if you never speak to anyone. Why? What's the problem?'

'You know it's forbidden, don't you? Forbidden to talk to Jews any more than is strictly necessary to carry out your work?'

I said nothing. I knew he was right but couldn't see the harm, and we'd been careful not to be seen – or, at least, tried to.

He leaned into me. I could sense the tremble in his voice. 'You see, I was called to see one of the Kommandant's deputies earlier today.'

On hearing that word I felt my hairs bristle.

'There's no easy way to say this, Mac,' he said. 'They think something's not right.'

'Not right?' I said. 'Not right in what way?'

A sickly smile appeared on his face, which turned into a

grimace. He was squirming around now, and I saw a little sympathy in his expression. 'He . . . he told me you were caught living with a Jewish family in Rome.'

Any words I wanted to say stuck in the back of my throat.

'And it was hard to argue with him,' he added.

'Did you . . . try?'

'Of course I tried. But look at yourself, man.' He wafted the back of his hand in the direction of my clothes. 'You're even dressed like an Italian civilian.'

'But I told you. I escaped from the Italian soldiers and found some civilian clothes. I changed into them to avoid capture.'

'Really?'

'Yes, *really.*'

'You didn't barter your uniform for cigarettes in Fossoli?'

'Well . . .'

'Like you told Ray Thomas?'

I held my head in my hands. That was the explanation I'd given for my appearance. Now I cursed myself for changing my story.

'And you bribed Colin Cooper to be with this Jew. It all looks suspicious.'

'Look,' I said. 'If you want to know the truth—'

'But, Mac.' He frowned and gave me his sternest look. 'I asked you for the truth a few minutes ago.'

'Yes. Okay.' I had to stand and take a few paces up and down the centre of the cabin before I spoke. 'It's true what they say.'

'I see,' he said.

'But it's hardly like I joined the enemy,' I said, now struggling to keep my voice low. 'I was captured in Sicily. The truck was involved in an accident. I escaped and got taken in by a Jewish family in a place called Valleverde on the edge of Rome. I spent the back end of last year hiding in their cellar.'

'Is that why you joined the army? To hide in a cellar?'

I bore down on him at that. He didn't flinch. 'They were being persecuted by the authorities,' I said. 'And they were trying to help me – to help the British war effort.'

There wasn't much light in the cabin, but I could see his face drop with disappointment.

'It was behind enemy lines,' I said. 'What else could I do?'

'But think about it, Mac. With that story, and with you talking so much to the Jew . . .'

Then I snapped words to him: 'They have *names*, you know, just like us.'

'I didn't mean it like that,' he said.

I pointed at him. 'And don't forget people like that are the reason we're fighting this war.'

'Are they?' he said. He let out a hint of a laugh. I almost hit him.

'Well, I think so,' I said. 'The man you call "the Jew" has had his life turned upside down by Mussolini and Hitler – they've killed or imprisoned his whole family apart from his children, who he might never see again. He's got more brains than you and I put together and he's lugging sand around just to put stinking morsels of food in his belly.'

Banks gave a look of surprise. 'I must say, Mac, you're not really helping yourself with any of this. The issue in question is your identity as the Germans see it. You're wearing Italian civilian clothes. If you'd even kept your identity tag around your neck—'

'But I'm telling you the truth, Banks. I'm a British soldier. And I told you, I got rid of my uniform and tag to look like a civilian. You must have . . . records and photographs somewhere. *Surely.*' My fist hit the table and the whole thing jolted.

'Listen, Mac. I believe you. And if you can convince the Kommandant—'

'*Hold on, hold on.*' I paused, struggling to control my breathing. 'I don't understand. I have to meet the Kommandant?'

160

'I did all I could. But it's been forced on me. The safety of the whole cabin is at risk here, I had to agree to it. I mean, I couldn't do anything else.'

'Banks. Sir. Just tell me what's happening.'

'They think you're a Jew – a Jew trying to pass yourself off as a British POW.'

Again I choked instead of speaking.

'You know if they think the rest of us are colluding they might execute all of us.'

'For God's sake,' I said. '*There's nothing to collude in.*'

'You and I know that, Mac.' He sighed. 'But I think I know what's at the bottom of this.'

'Well, I'd be grateful if you told me, sir.'

'I think they're still jumpy about their missing soldier – the one whose ashes are lying at the bottom of that brazier.'

'But that's not my fault. It had nothing to do with me.'

'Oh, come on, Mac. You know it doesn't work like that. In here it's an eye for an eye.'

'But . . . what about the Geneva Convention?'

'Oh, forget the bloody Geneva Convention, Mac. Don't you realize that's immaterial inside these fences? Surely you've worked that out?'

'But you must have put that to them in your meeting?'

'Of course I did.' He gave his head an apologetic shake. 'But it's a game. They just say that doesn't apply to Jews. And they're right; technically they aren't prisoners of war.'

'Oh,' I said. I was running out of words as I was running out of arguments.

'Also,' he continued, 'there have been uprisings by the Jews in some camps, and it's made them very suspicious of anything that looks out of place.'

'Like me?' I said.

'I'm sorry, Mac. I argued and argued; as God is my judge I really did, but . . .'

Then I told him to look me in the eye. He wouldn't.

'So what's going to happen to me?'

'There was really nothing else I could do, Mac. I had to go along with it. They want to do some tests on you, that's all.'

'Tests? What kind of tests?'

He shrugged. 'I really don't know. I've got to take you to the administration block. They've agreed to keep me informed of your whereabouts.'

I stared at him for a few seconds, and saw the guilty eyes of a man who had, indeed, no choice – although I couldn't bring myself to accept that at the time. It was only much later that I came to understand his point of view. Yes, I had lied to a commanding officer. I wondered how different my life might have been had I been braver and simply told him the truth right from the start.

Even now he only flicked a glance at me, and said, 'You know I've got to consider the welfare of everyone here, don't you?'

I didn't answer, but walked over to the door and waited there in silence for him.

After that conversation I never spoke another word to Banks.

I didn't even say goodbye when he led me to the Monowitz administration block and left me there.

At the administration block a guard escorted me inside. I stopped, rooted to the floor for a second as I came face to face with Lorenzo, also accompanied by a guard. But now my friend chose to gaze over my shoulder rather than look at me. I felt a strong shove in my shoulder blade, the hint to carry on. I ended up at the opposite end of the room to Lorenzo. Nobody spoke, and I didn't dare break the silence, but I kept looking in Lorenzo's direction, trying to catch his eye. Any facial expression from him might have made me feel better, less wretched about landing us both in trouble, but he wasn't entertaining the idea.

The silence was so eerie, and continued until more guards came into the room and talked among themselves, occasionally pointing and glancing in our direction. When they pointed at Lorenzo they would wave a dismissive hand, but with me they were less certain. I got the feeling their plans for him and me were quite different.

Then, with the bare minimum of words, we were forced into a jeep and driven away from Monowitz. I didn't know where we were being taken, and I'd guess that Lorenzo, my alleged partner in crime, didn't either. I have absolutely no recollection of what was running through my mind because my head was a jumble of senseless fear. The journey itself only heightened my fears. Through the fences I saw thousands of those figures clad in dirty, striped suits. The scenes were nothing like Monowitz; at Monowitz there had been motion – people mingled, walked, gesticulated as they talked. These figures merely stood still and stared out.

It wasn't long before we were driven through the main gates of what I later knew to be Auschwitz I, the administrative centre for the whole complex. There I looked up and saw some words in German pass me by – large letters in blackened iron. I thought at the time it must have been the name of the sub-camp.

It wasn't.

It was guidance, the ethos of the camp to which everyone had to subscribe. '*Arbeit Macht Frei*,' it said in those letters, large and dominant above us all. They later became famous, but at the time I had absolutely no idea what they meant. Only many years later did I find out the English translation: 'Work makes you free,' or words to that effect.

As I was to find out, the work inside there definitely didn't bring with it any sense of freedom whatsoever; I survived, but feel a prisoner to this day.

I remember the jeep being driven very gently because it seemed so unreal and out of keeping with everything else there – the barking dogs, the guns, the shouting of orders. It came to a halt outside in a large courtyard near what looked like an office complex.

My guard got out and beckoned me to follow. I did, and then Lorenzo eased himself as if to get out. His guard held him in place, back onto the seat. Words were exchanged between the guards, which neither I nor Lorenzo understood. Then Lorenzo's guard turned to the driver of the jeep and uttered the word we both understood and feared. The word was 'Birkenau', and he pronounced it with a lack of emotion that made me feel queasy.

Lorenzo immediately tried to get up again, but the guard repeated the word and had to hold a rifle down against him. He struggled against it nonetheless.

At first Lorenzo spoke in Italian. Even if I understood Italian his words would have been too fast and frantic for me to make out, but I got the gist of his protestations; we'd all heard the rumours of Auschwitz-Birkenau and what happened to the people who were sent there.

Then Lorenzo switched to English in the desperate hope the guards might understand.

'No!' he shouted. 'Please! Take me back to Monowitz.' He dropped to his knees on the floor of the jeep. 'I won't talk and I'll work twice as hard,' he said. 'You can take my tongue out. I'll never talk again. *Please!*'

The two guards glanced at each other and cracked a smile. Lorenzo's guard grabbed him by the arm and pulled him back onto his seat. He barked out something very quick and sharp to the driver, pressing his rifle ever more roughly onto Lorenzo's chest. A second later the jeep drove off with Lorenzo still arguing through his tears.

It was a pathetic sight; this brave freedom fighter now reduced to grovelling for his life. I thought he would have been more resolute and principled, but which of us truly knows how we would behave when faced with almost certain death?

Before the jeep disappeared from the courtyard I was prodded with a rifle. The guard pointed to the door of what could have been the offices of a very ordinary, but functional, office block, and we went inside.

CHAPTER TWENTY-ONE

Nicole and her father were back in Benton's, the same nondescript greasy spoon café reached via the nondescript staircase jammed between nondescript shops.

Yes, it was that time again. *Another one of Dad's official visits. And another cheese and ham toastie.*

Nicole shifted uneasily in the straightjacket of the plastic bucket seat.

Dad was once again going on about what a fool he'd been, how it didn't mean anything to him and nothing really happened anyway, but that it was all his fault for neglecting Mum when she needed him most, and also for driving when he really shouldn't have.

Nicole wanted to say that Mum had overreacted, that what happened to them happens to thousands – no, *millions* – of couples. But as the first words formed on her tongue she felt a blade of guilt pierce her, so fell silent.

The silence continued for a few minutes – apart from Dad crunching his toasted cheese and ham sandwich.

'Anyway,' he said after a few bites, 'are you sorting yourself out in Henley?'

'As in . . . ?'

'You know, arranging a course or a job or something.'

She could say she was going to look for a job, but then he would say she deserved better because she was clever, and she would say she didn't want better, and then it would be clear he was getting angry with her even though he'd think it didn't show.

'I've been to the college,' she said. 'Looked at a few courses.'

'Good. I just don't want you to end up one of those people who do nothing but stay in the house all day.'

'Or like one of those people who live on cheese and ham toasties in cheap cafés.'

He stopped chewing for a second, one cheek bulging out like a big bald hamster with tomato sauce all around its mouth. He gave her a glare and carried on.

Well, *that* was new one. Nicole had been on the verge of making him angry but trying not to show it; now he was trying to show anger even though they both knew it was false.

He hurriedly chewed and swallowed, then said, 'Stop being so cheeky.' He pointed the remainder of the toasted sandwich at her. 'You're not too old to . . .'

Nicole snorted a giggle. 'Oh, I think I am, Dad.'

'Mmm. Yes. I guess you are. But seriously. Please. I know it's a new town and all that and you've got to settle in, but all I want is for you to . . .'

'To do something constructive?'

He nodded. 'Exactly. Like I said, *anything* would be a start.'

Nicole saw creases in her father's brow. And yes, they'd definitely grown a little in the last couple of months.

'I've joined a rowing club,' she said.

Yes. Awesome. His face lit up like a baby given a shiny piece of paper. *Result.*

'Oh, that's really great. I'm pleased.' He nodded encouragement. 'Enjoying it?'

167

'I think I will when I learn to row properly.'

'And what does your mum think about it?'

'Oh, she's really pleased too.'

'And how's she coping?' he said, replacing the elation with calm concern. 'I mean, with the new house, town, job?'

'She's good.'

He drew breath and tilted his head to one side.

There was something coming. It was that look.

'You said she talks about me?'

Serious face. 'Oh yes. All the time.'

'What sort of stuff does she say?'

Then he continued before Nicole could reply, 'I mean, do you think . . . like, theoretically . . . if the possibility were there . . . would she see me again?'

This time Dad fell silent, wanting her to answer, but she couldn't. It looked like she was only ever going to be seeing him a couple of afternoons a week in this same greasy café. She just had to give him – and herself – a little hope that things would get better, that there would be days out and evenings together, that perhaps he might even come around to the house at some stage. The truthful answer to his question was *No.* Actually, the truth according to Mum was *When hell gets a colony of penguins living on its roof.* But the answer she desperately wanted to give was *Yes, of course,* because if she was only going to see him a couple of afternoons a week they just *had* to be happy ones.

As Nicole dithered even more, her father leaned in, hardly blinking.

'No, no,' he blurted out, holding a hand up to stop an answer that was probably never going to come anyway. 'Forget what I said. It's nothing to do with you, poppet. I mean, it's not your fault, any of it, not a bit. But she's all right, you say?'

Nicole nodded as coolly as she could manage. 'Bit stressed, but—'

'New house, new job. You'd expect that.'

'Of course.'

'Is she . . .' He shrugged and waved his hands around casually. 'Is she . . . seeing anyone?'

Panic. Panic.

That would be a big lie. A proper one.

Can't lie. But definitely can't tell the truth.

Think. Think. Think.

'Dad . . . I'm pretty sure . . .'

'Yes?'

'I'm pretty sure she'll come round to the idea of seeing you. She just needs time.'

Oh, his eyes smiled. Dad's eyes smiled.

'But . . . she still hasn't got over Darren,' she added.

God, how adult was she being? *Mum hasn't got over losing her son.* Never mind *Nicole hasn't got over losing her brother.*

'You know she never will, don't you, poppet?'

Nicole nodded.

'Sorry. I've just *got* to stop calling you that.'

'I do get it, Dad. Darren was her baby.'

He nodded. 'Exactly.'

'But what happened wasn't your fault, Dad.'

Her father squirmed in his seat. Then he looked left and right, sighed, and said, 'That's just it, Nicole. It was. I'd been . . . you know . . . at lunchtime.'

'I know that, and I know it was wrong, but it's not like you were over the limit.'

Nicole looked at him, really looked at the red threads in the whites of his eyes as his wounded face stared back at her.

'What?' she said. She moved closer to him and lowered her voice. 'Dad? What is it?'

He took a sip of coffee, then said, 'I think you need to know, Nicole. You're seventeen and you can't be my poppet forever.'

She waited, hardly daring to breathe.

'About the woman,' he said.

'The woman?'

'The woman I daren't tell you the name of in case your mum finds out and thinks I'm poisoning you.'

Nicole nodded, unblinking.

'On that lunchtime I'd gone out for a drink with her – just one. We were . . . you know, just colleagues. And friends. And I was a bit annoyed at having to leave work early, and . . .' He gulped and took a shallow breath. 'You see, I was driving a little too fast. And . . . well . . . just as we hit the bend my phone went off, and I reached out for it. I knew who it was, and I wanted to answer it.' He shook his head. 'I never got there. But if I'd ignored it, like I always do. If I hadn't been driving so fast. If I hadn't been drinking . . .'

As her father shrugged, Nicole struggled to force words out. 'Oh, God. *Da-ad*,' was all she could manage.

'When I went to hospital they handed my belongings over to your mum – including the phone. They'd checked the records and knew there was a call, but I didn't answer it so they couldn't charge me with anything. But, you see, the caller left a message, and your mum listened to it. It was from my friend, saying thanks for the lunchtime drink and how much she'd enjoyed our chat and how she'd like to do it again sometime. Your mum put two and two together. And that's why she still blames me for the accident. And you know what? She's right.'

Nicole felt queasy, and took a few deep breaths. Her father said nothing, but just stared into his coffee, slowly swirling it around. She cleared her throat.

'So, nothing was going on between you and this woman? You weren't having . . . ?'

'An affair?' He shook his head firmly. 'And your mum knows it.'

'But why does she think . . . ?'

'Oh, that came afterwards. We found it so hard after the accident – both of us. We didn't tell you at the time but she desperately wanted to move house.'

'Really?' Nicole said.

Her father nodded. 'She said everything in the house reminded her of Darren and she had to get away from it. I was the opposite. Everything reminded me of him and I wanted to stay. We had lots of arguments over that.'

'But Mum got her way eventually.'

'Oh, Nicole.' He sighed. 'I shouldn't have let it get that far. I should have agreed with her. But Darren was my baby as well as hers, people forget that. And your mum was cold. I couldn't talk to her. She was angry whatever I said, whatever I suggested. But I needed someone to talk to, someone who wasn't going to bite my head off.'

'The woman?'

He nodded. 'And after what happened I was an idiot to do that. I know that now.'

Nicole braced herself and said, 'So . . . you just talked? Nothing else?'

He shook his head. 'Promise. But your mum found out and I guess that's why she's like she is. She blames me for the accident, but she knows I didn't have an affair or anything.'

Nicole put her hand on her forehead, and said, 'Oh, Dad.'

'So, you see, neither of us is perfect,' her father said. He looked at Nicole, startled. 'Nicole? Are you all right?'

She didn't move.

'Nicole? It's not your headache is it?'

She let her hand fall and showed her father a flat smile. 'No,' she said. 'I'm good. But you're right, you have been an idiot.'

'Just like I told you,' he said. 'You should listen to your dad more often.'

And then Nicole's smile grew just a little.

'Anyway, that's it,' he continued. 'That's my dirty secret.' He let out a long breath.

'Look.' Nicole paused for a couple of seconds. 'Whatever you've done, you're still my dad.'

He opened his mouth but struggled to speak.

'And you can still call me "poppet" if you want.' She leaned in more closely. 'If you say it quietly.'

'Good.'

'And as long as nobody else is around.'

Now Dad gave her a proper smile again, one that showed off those wrinkles, and finished his toasted sandwich in silence.

'Anyway,' he said as he wiped the crumbs from his mouth a couple of minutes later, 'you didn't tell me.'

'Tell you what?'

'Whether your mum's seeing anyone.'

Panic. Panic. Think. Think. Think.

She let out a nervous laugh. It bought her a few seconds. 'Erm . . . well . . . Oh, give her a chance, Dad. She's only been here a few days.'

Her father now looked straight at her, much how a detective inspector might eye up a suspect. His gaze eventually dropped, and he said, 'Sorry. Of course.'

Nicole tried to disguise her heavy sigh of relief, then said, 'Are you going to have anything else?' and pointed to the counter.

'Ice cream?'

She nodded. 'Me too please.'

CHAPTER TWENTY-TWO

In this 'office block' that was the Auschwitz administration complex I was taken to a waiting room full of strange sorts; among them were four or five sets of twins, three dwarves, a little blind girl who appeared just perfect in every other way, and a boy with deformed legs straggling behind him whenever he moved. None of them were strange in themselves, you understand, but the variety lent a very unnerving atmosphere to the gathering – especially as none of them uttered a word for what must have been well over an hour.

I wish I could say I feared for them all; in truth my mind was too tense and full of thoughts of my own situation to care for others. I suppose I was in some sort of trance, so at first I hardly noticed the woman in the SS uniform entering the room with a clipboard clasped under her arm. I definitely noticed when she called out my name. All I could do was look at her. I didn't dare speak as she walked over to me.

'Are you John MacDonald?' she said, stumbling over the 'Mac'.

I nodded, and she told me to follow her. She led me out of the room across a brightly lit corridor – which hurt my eyes after the dimness of the waiting room – and into a small room right at the end. The woman pointed to a chair and left. I sat.

This was a change. The room was clean and bright and shiny, with chrome instruments and glass cabinets with chrome handles. I looked further and saw a huge ceramic sink, anatomical charts, many rows of books and a table with some chemical apparatus on it. Also, just behind me, was a full-size skeleton.

Most worrying of all, on one side of the room, resting innocently against the wall, was some sort of portable operating table, with thick leather straps at each corner.

So what had seemed from the outside to be an office block was more like a laboratory block. My throat was so sticky with dryness I was struggling to swallow, and I didn't know what to do with my arms – to fold them or leave them out in front, hands resting on knees. Then a door on the far side opened and a man in a brown civilian suit walked in.

He smiled, and I started hyperventilating. I didn't know why at the time, it just wasn't like me; then again, I'd never been in a situation even approaching this one. In the past I'd pushed myself so hard with physical work my muscles had gone numb, I'd been punched and kicked in the odd scrap until my ribs were tender to the touch, and I'd suffered hunger and thirst I wouldn't inflict on an animal. I could take all of those things – the *physical* things – but sitting here alone was different. I was as frightened as a lost child because I had absolutely no idea what was happening or what was planned for me.

The female guard came back in and exchanged a few words with the man in the suit. I heard my name, saw them glance in my direction, and felt my heartbeat telling me to run. My head said that wouldn't be wise even if I could regain control of my faculties enough to try.

My breathing worsened. I felt a tightness in my chest as if someone were standing on it. Then my vision blurred. All of this must have shown because the man in the suit crouched down beside me. He spoke good English in a sensitive, cultured voice.

'Are you all right?' he said. 'Would you like a drink of water?'

His words, so unexpected I didn't understand them for a few moments, echoed in my mind.

Did I want a drink of water? I had a flashback to the trick they'd played on me at Fossoli with the poison that wasn't. I was tired, confused, halfway through a nightmare for all I knew. I said and did nothing, but within seconds the man was handing me a glass of clear liquid.

Dare I?

The temptation was too great. I took it and drank it. It was clean and cold and tasted of being brought back from the dead. I finished every drop and placed the empty glass in his outstretched hand.

'Don't worry,' he said with a very slight and kindly smile. 'I'm not going to hurt you.' He turned to go, then checked himself, adding, 'But I will need a blood sample.'

All of his words were delivered like he was a trained and very sympathetic medical man. He exchanged a few more words with the female guard and she left.

I stayed silent. I must have looked like a pet on an examination table. I know I felt like one. He took his jacket off and hung it up, then looked at me straight on, rubbing his chin and saying, 'Mmm . . .'

He seemed to be taking an unnerving interest in each of my facial features in turn. He grabbed a white coat from the stand and put it on.

'Could you stand up please?' he said.

I did, and he pointed to a height-measuring device on the wall. I walked across to it.

'You are very tall, aren't you?' he said as he noted down my height on the clipboard the female guard had given him.

Still I didn't speak.

He told me to sit down again. No – he *asked* me to sit down, even saying 'please' again. I remember wishing he wouldn't use that word; every time he was polite and civil it unsettled me that little bit more.

Then he crouched down in front of me, his face inches from mine. He held my chin and gently turned my face left and right, examining it from every angle – examining what, I had no idea.

He turned away, opened a drawer of the desk, and pulled out a brown leather case. He placed it on the small table next to me, and slid a tongue of leather from the eyelet with a flick of his little finger. I flinched as he went to open the case, starting to hyperventilate again.

'Look,' he said to me, his smile now faltering. 'I've told you I'm not going to hurt you, so stop behaving like this.'

But I couldn't relax, and he sighed and shook his head. He showed me the contents of the case. It was full of precision measuring devices, the kind with a thumb-roll adjustment, like a model maker or a small-scale engineer might use.

'You see?' he said. 'There's nothing in here to hurt you, so stop being so weak-minded.'

But I flinched again as he took one of the devices out and brought it up to my face. Now he held my head firmly, as if the kid gloves were off.

But he was absolutely right; there was no pain. I did, however, feel very uncomfortable, as if I was merely an object being prodded and examined with no respect.

Only years later did I put my finger on how I felt; it was like being measured up for your own coffin.

The man spent twenty-three minutes taking measurements. I know because I stared straight ahead for all this time at the clock. He measured the distance between my eyes, the distance from my nose's tip to its bridge, the height and curvature of my forehead, the distance from the tip of each ear to the point of my chin, and many more measurements that seemed utterly pointless to me. He even double-checked a lot of them.

Then he took a blood sample from the inside of my elbow. It might have been the adrenaline pumping through me or his skill, but I hardly felt a thing. He pressed a tiny piece of material to the bloody pinprick and lifted my arm up with a gentleness that did nothing to put me at my ease.

He sat down, scribbled a few notes, then put the pen down and turned to me.

'MacDonald,' he said. 'Was that really your father's name?'

I nodded, and he said, 'Hmm . . .' and squeezed his eyes almost shut.

Then he said, 'So, what was your mother's maiden name?'

'White,' I answered.

'Not Weiss?'

'No.'

'Or Wiesel?'

'No.'

'Are you certain?'

'Yes.'

'Hmm . . .'

He paused, sat back, and read the notes he'd written.

A few minutes later he went to speak, but held his tongue. Then he rubbed his chin again before speaking.

'You are one hundred and eighty-six centimetres tall,' he said.

I said nothing.

'That's quite tall,' he said, nodding to himself. 'But Jews can be tall sometimes.'

He scribbled down some more notes, and a wave of nausea engulfed me as the point of this whole examination dawned on me. I couldn't speak – not that anything I could have said would have made any difference. The room started floating before my eyes. I really had fallen into a nightmare.

Confirmation came within minutes.

The man – a qualified doctor of some sort, I assumed by now – shouted for the guard to return. She did and strode over to the desk. She looked at the clipboard with my notes on it and her eyes fell to the bottom of the page. '*Jude?*' she asked.

The man nodded.

She spoke again. And again it was only one word.

'Birkenau?'

The man nodded again, briefly closing his eyes.

The moment I heard them casually conclude that I was a '*Jude*', I understood the true meaning of the word 'powerless'. Every element of self-determination evaporates in the space of a few words, and you might as well be a newborn baby among lions.

There was something else I learned in those dark times that followed. I know the feeling of being captured – of having the muzzle of an enemy rifle press against your flesh. It's the feeling that the call of death isn't too far away. I also know the feeling of being less than human in the minds of those who have total control over your destiny. Of those two, I know which is the more terrifying.

So ever since that day I've had immense sympathy for any prisoner of any sort whatsoever – whether deserving mercy or not: those who need detaining to protect the rest of society, those merely defying authority, or those harmlessly breaking society's taboos. And yes, even those Nazi officials in post-war trials. All are human, even those who have committed inhuman acts.

My next few hours in Auschwitz were a blur of fear and apprehension. For many months I'd watched columns of those soulless, striped figures shuffling along with heads bowed – being led to their deaths, I strongly suspected. Now it would be different; now I would be watching from the inside.

I was taken into another room, discussed in detail as if I wasn't there, and finally led outside and marched to Birkenau.

I passed those monstrous chimneys, which reached to the heavens and belched out the devil's breath, and I passed thousands of those living cadavers.

Was I now going to be one of them?

Finally the guard accompanying me pointed to the cabin that would be my new home, and left.

It was a wooden hut – like those in the POW camp but much more basic. I learned very quickly that it had no heating whatsoever and more cramped bunks. The mattresses were essentially sawdust or sand covered in material that was filthy and stank of every horrible bodily fluid imaginable. We slept two men to a mattress, top to tail. Insects crawled everywhere, like this was their territory.

I didn't speak for hours; I just curled up on a filthy mattress and closed my eyes. I saw no point in trying to communicate – or even finding out who spoke English. I saw little point in anything for a while.

The optimist in me had now deserted his post.

But as I drifted in and out of a light, troubled sleep, I couldn't help but hear that the voices jabbering on all around me were a concoction of every language but English. But the more I listened, the more I made out one that was familiar.

I eased myself off my bunk and headed for the far end of the cabin. A group of men were sitting on the bare wooden floor – there were no chairs in the cabin. Two of them were talking with their backs to me. I waited to hear the one on the left speak again. Then I interrupted.

'Lorenzo?' I said.

He turned. For a second his eyes widened in surprise. Then his stare turned into a sneer.

'What do you want?' he said.

I wanted someone – anyone – to be on my side, but I couldn't put that into words so I said nothing.

He pointed a wagging finger at me while he spoke in Italian to the man next to him.

And it didn't sound pleasant.

The other man frowned and stared at my face. His eyes flicked to my feet, then back to my face.

'What is it?' I said. 'What's happening here?' There was no answer, so I moved a couple of paces closer to Lorenzo and tried again. 'Why are we in here together?' I said.

His friend stood up, then started spitting out words and poking his fingers into my chest, forcing me away. But the man was smaller, older and definitely skinnier than me, so I stood my ground and turned to Lorenzo.

'What have you told him?' I said.

'Only the truth,' Lorenzo replied. 'That I had hope while I was working at Monowitz, and now I am here because of you and will probably die here.'

I hesitated to answer. It wasn't what I expected of Lorenzo, but his words weren't too far from the truth. And he blurted out more.

'You know what it's like to beg for your life with these people? I feel sick, disgusted with myself. I should have fought them, made them shoot me.'

And it was true. I had felt wretched watching this proud, intelligent man plead with the guard – to even offer his tongue in exchange for his life.

'I'm sorry,' I said after a few seconds. 'Perhaps I should never have talked to you . . . but when I thought I recognized you I . . . I couldn't stop thinking about Rosa. Perhaps I should have forgotten about her, but I want to . . .'

I left it there because I didn't know what I wanted to do now. To find her? To free her? Just to know she was still alive?

Then it was Lorenzo's turn to hesitate. I could see him struggling with his emotions, his swarthy, dirty face starting to crack. Eventually he drew a hand back through his hair and huffed heavily to the floor. He stayed with his head bowed down, then muttered some more words in Italian.

The man who had been threatening me now seemed to look at me in a different light too. I like to think Lorenzo had told him how I wasn't such a bad soul after all; it certainly seemed that way because the man sidled away to leave the two of us alone.

'Oh, it's not your fault,' Lorenzo said. 'None of this is your fault.'

'You seem better,' I said. 'And I'm glad you didn't attack the guard in the jeep.'

'I thought I was going to the chambers. I didn't know I was going to be a Sonderkommando.'

'A what?'

He shook his head and spluttered. I thought perhaps he was crying again. I didn't understand what was happening. Then I realized he was laughing, and I understood even less.

He patted the floor next to him and I sat down. Now I was closer I could see the redness around his eyes, evidence of his tears of rage.

'What's a Sonderkommando?' I asked again.

'You and me,' he said. In a second, all traces of humour dropped from his face. 'And everyone in this cabin.'

I didn't ask again, but I suspect my frown told Lorenzo I still didn't understand.

'We are slaves,' he said. 'Not called slaves but we are. And slaves of the worst kind.' He pointed to the man who had just left. 'Paulo was telling me what we have to do in return for these better cabins.'

I looked around us at the filthy beds, the dirt floor, windows that invited wind as well as light.

'These are *better* cabins?'

He nodded. 'I am told that. There is a good reason to keep us alive, so we have better rations too because of the heavy work we have to do.'

'Heavy work?'

Lorenzo just shrugged. 'I don't know what that means; I've only been here a few hours.'

We talked about what that work might be, fearing to ask the other, more experienced inmates. Soon we went to eat. And there was no cake or bully beef – just lukewarm, watery soup and bread as hard and tasteless as cardboard.

Then I spent a lonely, apprehensive night sleeping in the cold, daring to ease my toes into the armpits of the man I shared a bunk with, and allowing him to do the same to me. The blanket was as filthy and dust-ridden as the mattress.

I thought I had fallen into hell, and everything in there was horrible – the harshness, the inedible food, the cold, and yes, even some of the people. However, it was only on the next day, when I started my first day of work as a Sonderkommando, that I found out what true horror was. I've spent half of my adult life trying to forget the work I had to carry out there, and the other half accepting that I will always feel disgusted with myself for going ahead with it rather than choosing to be shot for disobeying orders.

CHAPTER TWENTY-THREE

Nicole heard her mother running up the stairs.

She closed the notebook and flapped the bedcover over it just as the door opened.

'What are you up to?' her mother asked.

'Oh, nothing. Chillin', y'know.'

Nicole could almost feel her mother giving her a thorough visual examination. And, to be fair, it did look odd, her just lying there on the bed, fully clothed, no iPod, phone or tablet.

Better answer needed.

'I mean, I was just reading a book.'

Her mother looked again, making a point of staring at Nicole's empty hands.

'I just put it down. Don't want one of my headaches to start.'

'Oh, I see.' Her mother tried a smile.

'So what did you want?'

Her mother drew her eyebrows up sharply. 'What d'you mean? Do I need an appointment to see you now?'

'No. Sorry.'

'You know you've missed rowing practice?'

Nicole glanced at her watch. She must have got carried away reading.

'Didn't you fancy it tonight?' her mother asked.

Nicole shrugged. 'Not really. But I can go next time.'

Her mother smiled. It was that sickly, sympathetic smile. 'Doing anything tonight?'

'Bit of TV. Reading my book.'

'In that case why don't I cook your favourite?'

'What?'

'Sweet and sour chicken. Won't take long. On the table in half an hour. Okay?'

Nicole eyed her suspiciously.

Her favourite?

What was she up to? What could—?

No, she was being too cynical. Mum was just making up for being a bit horrible about Dad the other day. Yes, that was it.

'You all right?' her mother asked, peering at her.

'Yes. Awesome. Sorry. Yeah. Sweet and sour. I'd like that. Thanks, Mum.'

'Good. Good.' She lingered at the door. 'I'll, erm, leave you to . . .'

'Read my book?'

'Yes. Oh, and erm . . . do you think you could do the washing up tonight?'

Nicole nodded. 'Cool.'

'Only . . . I'm going out.'

Before she knew it Nicole had let out an *I didn't expect that* sort of 'oh'. Then she said, 'Are you seeing Derek again?'

Her mother nodded casually. 'Just for a drink.' She looked into space for a moment, then said, 'Well, a few drinks. Maybe a movie.'

Nicole took a deep breath, but said nothing.

Her mother huffed out a laugh. 'Not really right, is it?'

'What do you mean?' Nicole said. 'What's not right?'

'I mean, it should be the other way round, shouldn't it? At our ages it should be you going out enjoying yourself and me staying in and doing something boring.'

'Boring?'

'Reading this book of yours. Sorry. Not *boring*, but you know what I mean. I'm going out drinking and you'll be in bed when I get back. Which one is it anyway?'

Nicole chewed her lip for a moment, then said, 'Mmm?'

'The book you're reading? Anything I've heard of?'

Nicole shook her head. 'Like you said, boring. Wouldn't be your thing.'

'No. Probably not.'

Probably not. But she was looking around the bedcover just to be sure anyway.

Change of subject required.

'I saw Dad again today,' she said, blurting the words out.

'Oh, yes?' her mother replied flatly.

'He was asking about you.'

'Asking what?'

'Oh. Just . . . how you were.'

'Tell him I'm fine.'

'I did.'

'Good.'

They nodded to each other. 'Right,' Nicole's mother said.

'Right,' Nicole said.

'Anyway. I'll see you downstairs in half an hour.'

She left, and Nicole reached for the notebook.

CHAPTER TWENTY-FOUR

I was woken at dawn after my first cold, lonely night in the hell that was Auschwitz-Birkenau, and we were all lined up outside the cabin in that stinking smog for roll call. Then we were told where to report for the day's work.

I ended up in a team of four. I felt lucky that Lorenzo was one of them; I thought having someone to talk to might stop me feeling so isolated. It didn't work out like that in practice, but I'm sure having another beginner around helped – someone who shared my shock and horror in the company of others who had become hardened to it all. The other two men in our team simply got on with it as if they were digging up roads or painting walls. Later I was to realize they had formed a mental barrier between their sensibilities and what they saw and did.

The first day we were at one of the crematoria. Our job was to take bodies that were delivered to us, place them onto racks, and drive the racks deep into the furnace. The image of the skeleton I'd seen in the laboratory kept flashing in my mind, but some of these bodies were still warm; not long before they'd been living, breathing humans. All were shaven-headed, most had diseased skin, some had wounds. To think, a little over a year before, I'd never even *seen* a dead body, and now here I was, manhandling them with no respect or dignity for them or me. There were no prayers or moments of quiet reflection. I remember thinking about the coal fire we had in the house back at Henley, and the great chunks of anthracite coal that were delivered by a white-haired old man and his pony and trap. My mother would place the pieces of coal onto that fire with more care and consideration than we afforded the dead people we were now shoving into the furnace.

I was in a daze for the whole day. The possibility of talking to Lorenzo was forgotten – I don't think I uttered a word to him. I think he felt the same way as I did – like a butcher hurling hunks of meat around some abattoir.

I couldn't eat at midday, and – in spite of feeling exhausted and nauseous, in spite of having a stomach in knots with pangs of hunger – I couldn't eat in the evening either. And there was no way I could sleep that night. The faces of those who had passed through my hands now passed through my mind, clawing me back from slumber every time I threatened to nod off. I'm not sure to this day whether I did eventually sleep – whether those obscene images were whirling around in my conscious mind or inculcating themselves in my nightmares.

All I know is that it didn't get any better on the second day. I was separated from Lorenzo and taken to the storage area. Bodies upon bodies, perhaps ten deep, were stacked up lengthways like logs, feet pointing towards us, running the whole length of the room. My job was to drag them onto trolleys, which I pushed towards those whose turn it was to operate the furnaces on that particular day.

By the end of the second day I'd succumbed to emotional numbness and ate, albeit in silence. I think I'd started to get used to it, to accept that I had no control over what I was doing and that my own survival depended upon me eating. But I didn't sleep any better that night; whenever I closed my eyes I was in hell and had to open them again and seek out light of some sort to trace the grain of the wood or follow the fold of a blanket or just see *anything* other than what I had witnessed. Only on the third night, when I was starting to hallucinate, did I finally find relief in sleep.

On the fourth day, however, just as I was coming to terms with what I was doing, the ante was upped again. I was taken to a place even worse than the furnaces, even worse than the storage area.

We'd all seen the columns of 'stripeys' being marched towards those inconspicuous bunker-style buildings. And, of course, everyone realized there were no columns marching away from them. We didn't know the details, but we had a good idea what was happening. We just didn't talk about it. On that day at Birkenau, however, all of the detail imprinted itself on my mind.

And it's still there.

After roll call we were all marched to the bunkers. They were concrete affairs, half underground, half overground, and hence much bigger than they looked from the outside. We were told to wait in the small anteroom, that we mustn't utter a word, but that we must ensure all prisoners were forced through the solid metal doorway into the next room.

Then we heard the trudging noises – no voices. There were something in the region of a hundred and fifty of them, mostly women, children and old men. They all took off their clothes, spectacles, shoes and false teeth. One old man took off a false leg.

All of these articles were placed on the floor.

I didn't understand why these people seemed so willing. Lorenzo gave me a puzzled look, and later told me he was thinking the same. That evening another Sonderkommando – a Czech who also spoke a little Italian – explained it to Lorenzo, who passed it on to me. These people had been told they were going into the shower block to be deloused and washed. They were also told they would get an extra portion of food for their trouble. The next day I watched more closely and saw the guards hand a few people what looked like bars of soap. Then I noticed signs about disinfection. I could hardly believe how well orchestrated the whole exercise was.

Once the people had filed into the room and the door was tightly shut, we were all told to leave. As we walked away, a guard called the Czech Sonderkommando over and handed him a small package. He casually climbed up to the top of the bunker and dropped it into what looked (to the unaware) like a ventilation shaft.

Then we all had to leave the vicinity for a few hours. We spent the time chopping wood in the forest nearby. That happened every time. Oh, how I both loved and hated chopping down those trees. It was an escape from reality and respite from the misery of my own guilt and self-loathing. For those few hours I could tell myself I was nowhere near the evils that were being perpetrated, and my hands felt clean for a while. I've never been able to do any of that work since those days, and I can't even bear seeing or hearing trees being felled.

When we returned from the forest, the fans were running full blast, blowing air through the bunker and up out of the ventilation shafts. When the fans stopped we had to go in.

The first time this happened I thought I couldn't be more nervous or scared than I'd already been. I tried to calm myself down, to tell myself I'd handled so many dead bodies by then it shouldn't have been difficult.

But when they opened the door it felt like a hot, clammy pair of hands had grabbed my head and was forcing me to look at the scene. The room was full of corpses, all lying across one another, so many that the floor wasn't visible. There was also blood and vomit among the mess. Corpses were piled up around the ventilation shaft. Prisoners had clearly clambered up on top of each other, like rats desperate to reach those last pockets of air, all the better to claim those extra few seconds of life. Some bones – and the occasional skull – had been broken by those desperate enough.

The job I was being ordered to do hardly needed explaining to me, but at first I turned away. A guard started shouting at me and pointing at the bodies. I shook my head again and so he nudged me with the end of his rifle. I pushed it away, and he lifted it up, pointed it directly at my forehead and cocked the trigger.

I could hardly breathe with the tension as well as the stench, but I managed to hold my hands up to him and nod obediently.

I've often wondered whether I should have just let him pull the trigger.

But I held my senses in limbo and got on with the job. We had to manhandle bodies out of there by attaching leather straps around necks or torsos and dragging them out. Then we heaved them onto carts and wheeled the carts to the crematoria or storage areas.

And while we were carrying out this wretched task there were other men, picking their way through the bodies, ripping off ear-rings and pulling rings from fingers. They would also examine the teeth of those still-warm corpses. Every so often the pliers would come out and be forced into the mouth of some poor resting soul. There would be a crack, a crunch, and then a gold, but bloody, tooth or filling would be plucked out. The gains were handed to a guard.

There was worse still, if there ever could be a barometer of wickedness on this lunatic's carousel. I can barely bring myself to put the actions into words. We were told that every one of those men, women and children could be hiding gold or jewellery, and we Sonderkommandos had to search them. How do you search a naked dead body for small items? I leave that to your imagination.

Thus there was no dignity for the deceased – absolutely none. Of course, there was none for us either, but we each adapted in our own ways. Some accepted the self-loathing, the feelings of disgust for the whole human race. Personally, in the back of my mind, I convinced myself I had been taken over in some strange spiritual way and it wasn't me who was doing these things. Of course, as

I read these words in the cold reflections afforded by decades of distance, it sounds stupid. But that was how I felt – how I coped.

At first I couldn't take my eyes off their faces – vacant and expressionless – as I tied the leather straps around them. I wondered whether they were really dead, and let go of the strap once or twice in shock when an arm or leg moved. On each occasion a guard started shouting at me, so from then on I tried to close my eyes as I dragged the corpses along, and made damn sure I didn't look at their faces whenever I had to open my eyes.

Physically I had no problem with the heaving of bodies onto carts. I'd lost a lot of weight since being captured, but I was nowhere near as thin as Lorenzo or the others, who were also smaller than me. That cake and bully beef was a distant memory but the benefits of it were still there in my flesh.

The visions of those first few days working at the gas chambers have always haunted me – disturbing my sleep, occasionally causing my heart to skip a beat when I saw someone lying still and prone. The tendency occasionally caused friction in my marriages. In the middle of the night I would turn in bed, see either Glenda or Patricia sleeping peacefully, and feel my whole body lock up momentarily, sometimes making me retch, always preventing me from getting back to sleep.

Not all prisoners accepted their fate willingly. After stripping and while being funnelled into the chamber, there was the occasional moment of lucid realization from the more astute prisoners. Anyone who resisted at this stage was relatively easily forced into the chamber at the point of a guard's bayonet. Occasionally the bayonet would have to be used, and the person – as good as dead already – would simply be flung in.

After my first few days as a Sonderkommando I thought I would never cope, and half a dozen times I refused orders until faced with a guard's rifle. On every occasion I thought, *Next time, next time I'll take the bullet rather than do this*. Of course, I never did push back that far, but the idea almost became some kind of perverted fantasy.

As the weeks rolled by I became accustomed to those foul sights and smells. And the disgusting things I had to do.

And then, as before, just when I was thinking I was becoming desensitized to the horror of it all, I saw something worse.

On the way to the chamber, as they were opening the door, I saw it on the wall.

It was at knee height, and as clear as a photograph: the tiny, bloodied handprint of a young child.

I didn't sleep or eat that night.

I don't know how many weeks passed because I'd stopped counting or caring; I just concentrated on making it through to the end of each day. I didn't speak much – even to Lorenzo – and if I got any spare time I left the cabin and sat down alone near the perimeter. Through the endless fence I could see the camp prisoners – thousands and thousands of them dragging themselves around the yard. Their bodies were sapling thin, their gait sluggish and leaden through lack of energy.

In addition to those who died in the chambers there were many who died of thirst, disease or starvation in their cabins and in the muddy yard outside. The dirty job of clearing those bodies up also fell to the Sonderkommandos. The first time I was called to do the job, I'd already been clearing bodies out of the chambers and shoving them into the furnaces for a month or more, and so was numbed to the horror of lifeless corpses. Somehow using a leather strap around the neck to drag bodies across the dirt didn't seem quite as revolting when they had died peacefully in their sleep. Although I knew full well that the starvation and disease had been more or less forced upon them, it wasn't quite as sickening as dealing with a room crammed with people who had been gassed an hour or so before and who appeared frozen in their death throes.

I also found out that although our Sonderkommando cabins were worse than those in the POW camp, they were palatial compared to the standard Birkenau prisoners' cabins. Bodies were everywhere – all skeletal whether alive or dead – on the bare earth floor as well as on the bunks.

There was little communication in those cabins. I'm sure there were Poles, Hungarians, Czechs, Belgians, Dutch and more in there, but they all knew who we were and why we were there, and pointing to a dead body is the same in any language. We dragged the bodies away and hoisted them onto carts; at least the remaining prisoners got a little more space. I did wonder at first what they thought of us Sonderkommandos. We were privileged compared to them, destined or chosen to be allowed to live while they must have worked out their fates, but we also removed the dead bodies and so made their lives a tiny bit more tolerable. Did they hate us? I'll never know. Did they hate me personally? I don't think so. I hope not.

Even now, when it shouldn't matter, I hope not. Because it matters to me.

In 1944, when summer was waving its goodbyes to the already vulnerable, a group of three of us were told to go to the women's camp. Once there, we separated, and I had to clear the dead bodies of four young women from near the perimeter fence. It seemed a routine job. I hooked the leather belt around the first one's neck, leaned back and started to pull it along the ground towards the cart. It was raining lightly, and the mud made dragging the corpse a little easier on my leg muscles.

I was cold and wet but my face tingled with heat when I heard my name mentioned from behind me. I let go of the belt and turned to see where the voice was coming from. Was I imagining it? A hallucination was quite possible given my deteriorating state of mind. I didn't notice at first; there were many young women – all bones and dirty striped rags, all shaven-headed. I stared, scaring a few of them so they turned and scurried away.

Then one of them took a step closer.

'Mac?' she said. 'It's you, isn't it?'

I spluttered for a few seconds, hardly able to breathe, tears of confusion and rage clouding my vision and mingling with the rain on my face. I rubbed my eyes, stepped over to her, and had to rub them again.

'Rosa?' I said.

In Rome she had been a full-figured woman with flowing chestnut hair and a flawless complexion. She had been beautiful, and still was to me. But the incarceration had taken its toll on her. Like the rest, she was thin, but there was so much more. Her eyes were grey and sunken like craters; her jawline was more prominent, with skin tightening over its sharp features; stubble poked out from underneath the rag tied over her head. She had a dirty plaster over the bridge of her nose and sores on her cheeks and forehead.

'Dear God,' I said. 'What have they done to you?'

Then she said the words that still haunt me to this day. Her eyes dropped to my feet and back up again, then to the corpse I'd been dragging just moments before, and finally to the leather belt lying in the mud, pointing in my direction.

'What have they done to *you*?' she said.

I, too, looked to the corpse, and it took a second for me to realize what she meant. 'But I . . . I don't have any choice,' I said. 'It's this or be shot.'

She was about to speak, but I interrupted.

'Lorenzo is with me,' I said.

'Lorenzo?' She spoke slowly, as if confused. 'You've met Lorenzo?'

'I work with him. He's also a Sonderkommando.'

At these words her expression darkened even more. She tore her gaze from my face and turned away.

'Rosa, please,' I said, stepping forward and laying a hand on her shoulder. 'What else can we do?'

She said nothing, but gave a despondent nod and laid her hand on mine.

It was all the answer I needed. I held her gently in my arms and was shocked at how little of her there was.

'I'll get you out of here,' I said. 'Once the war is over I'll come to Rome. We can be together.'

If I'd thought about that – the hopelessness of our situation – I wouldn't have said it, but it was my deepest desire talking. For months I'd been missing Rosa so much it hurt. With the passing of those months, and with them the passing of so many horrors in front of my eyes, my will to live had waned. But now I saw something to look forward to.

She went to answer, but something caught her eye. I turned to look too and saw a guard in the distance walking towards us.

We talked more about the farmhouse and her family; after all these years I forget exactly what we said. But I knew there was something wrong. Rosa's speech was slurred and confused. I think a lot of what she said was nonsense. They had ravaged her mind as well as her body.

Then we heard shouting, and the guard was upon us, waving his rifle. Neither Rosa nor I understood German, but we knew what he was saying to me: stop talking and get on with your job.

Rosa slowly turned and walked away, stumbling and falling twice within the first few steps.

Under the gaze of the guard I did indeed get on with my job. I can't actually remember doing it, but I must have dragged all four of those dead women by my leather belt and heaved them onto the cart. I can't remember because my mind was far, far away. But I took the bodies to the storage area and returned to my cabin.

CHAPTER TWENTY-FIVE

Nicole and her mother were eating at the kitchen table.

It was sweet and sour chicken.

Nicole's favourite.

Apparently.

They were eating in silence. Nicole trying to keep her mouth full – trying to contain the question bouncing around inside her head.

But it bounced out.

'So, you and Derek, are you . . . ?'

'What? Dating?'

Nicole shook her head. 'Never mind. On second thoughts I don't think I want to know.'

There was a long pause, then Nicole's mother laid her fork to rest and said, 'Darling, can I please ask you something?'

Nicole looked at her expectantly.

'If I do bring Derek back here . . . I mean, if we carry on seeing each other . . . ?'

Her mother left the question there.

'What?' Nicole said.

'You . . . you won't mess it up for me, will you, sweetheart?'

'What d'you mean? Mess what up?'

'Nicole. Darling. I need you to accept that things . . . well . . . they change. I'm not the person I was and I don't think I ever will be. Everybody needs a little love sometimes and I'm no different.'

Nicole said nothing. They both carried on eating.

'Derek's a nice man,' her mother said. 'I think you'd really like him.'

Then Nicole looked up, and said, 'I don't understand what you mean. Why would I mess things up for you?'

Her mother beamed a smile – the sort Nicole hadn't seen for a long time – then reached over and held her hand tightly. 'It's going to be all right, Nicole. I promise. We're going to be happy together.'

Nicole tried hard to return the smile.

So, *we're going to be happy together*? Was that 'we' as in *Mum and Nicole* or 'we' as in *Mum and Derek*?

'Nicole?'

Nicole was now shoving the last few scraps of food around her plate, rearranging them rather than eating them. It was like being out of ammunition. 'What?'

'Promise me you'll think about it, sweetheart.'

'Yes, Mum. I will. I'll try.'

'Good.'

After dinner they watched TV together for half an hour, then Nicole's mother announced she was going upstairs to get ready.

Nicole had almost finished the washing up by the time her mother came down, and thankfully was facing the sink – facing away – while her mother completed her preening exercise and applied those last-minute touches of make-up in the mirror.

There was a brief embrace for Nicole from her mother, an apology for not giving her a kiss as she'd just put her 'lippy' on, and a few seconds later Nicole was alone.

She finished the washing up, then listened to the emptiness of the house while she considered what to do next. She smiled sadly to herself as she remembered a house filled with the noise of Dad playing with Darren. Sometimes it had been indoor football with a foam ball, sometimes a duel with plastic swords, and long before that it had been very primitive (and blatantly one-sided) wrestling.

And her smile gave way to a tear.

No, Nicole. Stop it. Remember the *Sunny Day* thing.

She plucked a tissue from the box on the windowsill and dabbed her face.

Then she looked up. To her bedroom. *Yes.* A read would take her mind off her own problems. Also *no*. Mac's story was getting interesting now, but perhaps it might be better not to read on so soon after eating. She glanced at that bilious green door to the cellar, then went into the living room and switched the TV on.

But all she could think of was the cellar.

Thirty seconds later she was down there, with the dusty briefcase in front of her.

She shoved her hand inside it, fished around and eventually pulled out the gold ring. She tried it on again. This time it felt different. Not just a circle of metal. Somehow it seemed alive, like it had been worn by a real, living person – as if some of that life was still in it. But whose was it? Would the book tell her? It hadn't mentioned it yet.

She spent a few minutes admiring the ring, then looked around the grimy cellar – not at her stuff and her mother's stuff, but at the rows of tools lined up on the wall, at the glass jars full of nails and screws arranged roughly in size order, and at the ornate tin in the far corner with the rose embossed on the front. It was pretty in spite of the almost living rust clinging to its edges.

She sighed, put the ring back in the briefcase, and went up to her bedroom.

CHAPTER TWENTY-SIX

After I'd left the women's camp and put the bodies in the store I didn't give them a second's thought. I say that with shame, for they were people the same as Rosa, but it's the truth; my mind was too preoccupied running over the conversation I'd had with Rosa, occasionally wondering whether I'd really met her or whether the whole experience had been some sort of hallucination.

I returned to the cabin in shock and immediately sat on the floor. Lorenzo must have known something was wrong – whether from my slumped posture or the fact I hadn't uttered a word to anyone. Out of the corner of my eye I watched him edge over to me, and I looked up to see an expression that was asking me whether I was all right.

I stared at him and said, 'Rosa's alive.' His face went rigid. 'I've just seen her,' I said, 'talked with her.'

I thought he had a right to know. I also thought he might smile or show some small pleasure at the news his sister was still alive. But there was nothing. At first.

Then his dirty face trembled for a few seconds. He still said nothing, but in an instant he pounced and grabbed me by the collar.

I didn't resist. I just told him it was true, that I wasn't making it up.

His face dropped, twitching for a few seconds. He let go of me, his bulldog frame almost tossing me aside, and gave the wooden frame of a bunk bed such an almighty kick that a cloud of dust flew up from the mattress. The other Sonderkommandos stared. He barked out a few Italian words in quick succession, then turned back to me.

'Why today?' he said. He cursed the guards who had made him go to the chambers that day and started shouting again.

'The next time there are bodies to be collected from the women's camp *I* will be going, you understand?'

I nodded, everyone around us nodded too, even those who wouldn't have understood his heavily accented English.

But very soon they all knew, and for the next few weeks everyone else made their excuses of sickness and fever whenever they were ordered to fetch dead bodies from the camps. Often the guards didn't accept those excuses, often it wasn't the women's camp they ended up at, and whenever Lorenzo did engineer a visit to the women's camp he came back even more frustrated and cursing everybody and everything. I'd explained to him exactly where I'd seen Rosa, but it was no help. This continued for weeks, but he never did see her, so neither of us knew whether she was still alive.

As those weeks went by, Lorenzo retreated into his shell. As well as Rosa he had parents and two children somewhere, but perhaps he'd given up on them – or forgotten them because that was easier for him to cope with. Either way, I got the impression that what provoked such ill-feeling in him was the fact that his sister was within reach but at the same time unreachable.

I tried my best to support him, which somehow helped *me* cope. And although I'd seen Rosa in a terrible state and I didn't know about her current situation, there was a good chance she was still alive, and as long as that was true it was possible I would see her again. That slim hope gave me the will to survive.

After summer 1944, however, other events were overtaking any dreams and obsessions of mine. Hundreds of people were dying in the camps every day, and hundreds more – possibly thousands – arrived by train every day, many going straight to the chambers. The Nazi machine must have realized that the crematoria simply could not cope with the sheer volume of bodies that needed disposal.

Lorenzo and I became members of a team that had to create mass funeral pyres. With others we toiled for hours, chopping down trees in the forest both to make room and to act as firewood for the pyres, and digging out huge pits behind one of the crematoria. They were about the size of a small football pitch and about six feet deep. We fashioned gulleys at the edges of the pits.

Again, the chopping down of trees was both respite from the horror and its fuel, and I still both loved and hated the task.

Over the next few weeks we must have carted thousands of bodies to these pits and tipped them in. When each was full we added rags soaked in some sort of petrol or paraffin and set it alight. When the whole thing was on fire the gulleys syphoned off the molten human fat, which was then thrown back on to keep the whole thing burning strongly.

At first I checked every face, thinking one might belong to Rosa, putting me out of my misery. And yet, at the same time, I hoped and prayed I wouldn't find her. Where previously I'd cursed the lack of respect shown to the dead by the guards, now I found myself walking across this sea of corpses to see the faces of those closer to the centre, occasionally cracking the lifeless bones I trod on.

In time I actually forgot about trying to find Rosa, but the searching had become a habit – almost an unconscious act. Now I just didn't care that these were human beings we were dealing with; it was no more than a job for me. And I didn't think of myself as human. I'd stopped thinking about anything, in fact, apart from the mechanics of the task in hand.

I'm sure Lorenzo played the same mind games as I did, that there were only a few minutes of each day when he thought of loved ones. And any realistic thoughts of actually seeing her alive again drifted up and away from us with the smoke.

Then, in October 1944, the situation took another turn. There were rumours of revolt and sabotage by some Sonderkommandos. The rumours were confirmed when there was a pitched battle between some of them and the guards. Then someone blew up one of the crematoria and the whole Auschwitz exercise was in jeopardy. Many Sonderkommandos disappeared – we believed shot in revenge or as punishment.

We were marched to the offices and ordered at gunpoint to destroy all records. We didn't quite know why, but it was clear that the system was falling apart. The pits were ablaze with bodies night and day, yet still we couldn't keep up with the supply. Now bodies weren't even collected and stacked up in the storage areas as they had been. Food and water were scarce to non-existent; and we Sonderkommandos knew that the camp inmates were getting even less than us.

I'm sure some of them – more desperate than Lorenzo or I – turned to cannibalism.

Soon the harshness of winter was upon us. There was no organization, and we were all starving and freezing. A new rumour was circulating that the Russian army would be upon us within weeks. Rumour or not, it spurred on the Kommandant to act decisively.

Sometime in January 1945 we were told that we were leaving the camp, that food was available for those who joined the march, and that supplies would be carried by horses. We were told that those prisoners who stayed would starve, but we suspected that really meant they would be shot.

In spite of the arguments between myself and Lorenzo, by now we'd been through a lot together and felt like partners, so we talked about what to do. There was no possibility that one of us would go and one would stay. We were both exhausted. Beyond exhaustion, in fact. Past the state where our bodies would complain. We had no idea how long we would be expected to march for, much less how long we would last. It may have been the fear of what would happen to us if we stayed that made our minds up, but I don't think so. I think we both were desperate to get away from the sights, sounds and smells of that devil's prison – the cabins, the chambers, the crematoria and those pyres. And the bodies. This was as good a way as any to escape. And if we were going to die, doing so anywhere on earth would be better than in this madhouse.

So we left, with thousands of others. A convoy of barely-alives. Each of us was already thin and weak. As we were all being marshalled to leave, we scoured the camp for squares of material to wrap around our feet to supplement our poorly fitting shoes. We also knew our coats were insubstantial for a winter of marching on the road.

Once we bade good riddance to the camp and started walking there was little or no conversation; we just concentrated on keeping up with the pace dictated by the guards.

At first there was a murmur of optimism – or as close to it as I'd known for a year. If anyone had lameness or slipped on the ice, or even simply needed a moment's rest, others would help.

But that benevolent attitude didn't last long, and soon we felt less human than ever. But nevertheless we kept on, Lorenzo and I sticking together, each slowing when the other needed to rearrange his footwear or rest for a moment. But stopping was difficult, you were soon dragged along by the current of those thousands of drifting bodies.

In my more lucid moments I knew that I was better off than most there. I was skinny but not the living skeleton many were. Soon one or two bodies started dropping and were dragged to the side of the road.

By nightfall on the first day we had walked perhaps twenty miles, and were like zombies. The whole convoy stopped and sat down in the snow to rest. We were told to eat snow for fluid, and some food was taken off the bags carried by the horses and given to us, but it was a pitiful amount spread between so many.

Then, just as our muscles were starting to freeze stiff, we were told to get up and start marching again. My mind couldn't process the information and I could do little more than follow the hordes. We ended up at some disused warehouse that the guards had found and spent the night there. I slept more soundly on that floor than I had for months.

We started marching on the second day with no breakfast. We had all escaped Auschwitz alive, but on that second day there was a realization that this was an escape undeserving of the word. People limped on for mile after mile before succumbing to blisters, sores, the biting cold or simply lack of energy. They now started falling in much greater numbers, so much so that they were just left where they fell, huddled on the ground, for us to step over. There were one or two shootings, mostly of people who tried to make a grab for the food carried by the horses. Within a few hours there was simply no soul among us.

Even worse, scuffles broke out for the clothes of the fallen. I remember shoving aside a young woman in order to get to the rags of a man who had given up. It's quite likely he was still alive, but I pulled the shirt from his still-warm body, ripped it into pieces, and used the rags to line my shoes and those of Lorenzo, whose feet were now bleeding quite badly and turning black in parts.

I did this because we both knew – and had discussed at length – that looking after your feet was everything, and an extra layer of insulation against the bite of snow and ice, even if it was just a piece of cotton, was a potential lifesaver.

Towards the end of the second day we stopped again and were

given tiny amounts of food and told to eat snow again if thirsty. Then we were told to get up and carry on marching. The alternative was being shot or freezing to death, so we all followed the orders – at least, those who were able. For the others – the many who had simply given up – being shot must have been a merciful release.

It might have been on the third or fourth day that Lorenzo appeared to be one of those who had succumbed. We'd stopped for a rest and when we were told to get up I did, but he was motionless. He was sitting on a snowy mound of earth, his head bowed, his chest shrunken and heaving slowly.

I crouched down and told him to get up.

Still the only movement from his figure was that laborious breathing.

'Come on,' I said. 'We're marching on.'

He just looked up to me and I saw no spirit of life in his half-closed eyes.

Now I tried to shout at him. 'Lorenzo!' I said, but it was hardly a shout. I started talking to him about his parents and children, about Rosa. I can't remember exactly what we said, but I managed to get a few words out of him, which seemed to revive him for a minute or so.

A guard approached us and told Lorenzo to stand up. The guard didn't shout; I think even he was too exhausted for that.

Lorenzo just looked up to him and shook his head.

I stepped between them and said, 'I'll get him to stand up, just give me a minute.'

The soldier either didn't understand me or didn't listen, but used his rifle to push me aside. He told Lorenzo to stand up and pointed a rifle at his head.

Lorenzo's lifeless stare moved slowly from the soldier to the barrel of the rifle. Now there was no expression on his face – not even despair.

'Think of Anna,' I said. 'Think of Lorenzo Junior.'

Now his lips twitched.

'And think of Rosa and Mama and Papa. They could even be in this convoy.'

He gazed down the column of people marching past us, and then to me.

But he didn't move.

The soldier told him once more to stand. It seemed like Lorenzo's last chance. And as I saw the soldier's grip tighten on the rifle, I said, 'Stop!'

I don't know where I got the energy from but I grabbed Lorenzo's shoulder and started lifting. I feared the soldier would retaliate, but he simply moved on to the next target – a woman about my age. She was lying prone with her eyes shut, gasping her last.

As I lifted Lorenzo and we started walking on together a shot rang out behind us. I didn't turn to look; I simply didn't care.

The convoy walked on for another couple of hours without stopping for food or rest, Lorenzo and I blindly following those in front, seeing our breath in the moonlight with every step. Lorenzo could do no more than stagger all the way, his shoes now leaving red stains on the snow with every step he took. I suspect he couldn't even feel his feet.

And he didn't speak a word in that time. Once or twice I asked him how he was, but he didn't even acknowledge me. Whether his understanding of English had deserted him, or whether he had already given up in his mind, I don't know.

As we marched up a hill he stopped again, and his gaunt face turned to me. He leaned in and fell onto my shoulder. I struggled to hold him up, but his legs had collapsed. He fell to the snowy ground with a great thump, making no attempt whatsoever to break his fall.

I crouched down next to him and tried to lift him back up, but he was a dead weight. At the time I didn't understand why I couldn't lift him, because there was hardly any flesh on the man. Later I realized why: it was because at that stage my own physical state had deteriorated too, and I was as weak as a sickly kitten.

I held Lorenzo by his shoulder, pushed my face to within a few inches of his face, but again, there was nothing in his eyes. I talked to him once more about his family – I can't remember exactly what I said. Now he spoke, but he seemed delirious, struggling to make sense. I remembered the temper and passion in this man the first time we'd met, the fire in his eyes. Now there were only warm ashes.

And then, before my eyes, on that dark, cold roadside in Germany, those ashes were blown away.

CHAPTER TWENTY-SEVEN

Nicole was woken up by a noise. Was it the front door opening? It was hard to tell in her half-awake state.

Images of horror and degradation had festered in her mind long after she'd stopped reading, but she had eventually dropped off to sleep. So to be woken up again in the dark hours was doubly annoying.

Then she thought she heard the door close – like someone was trying to make up for the noise of opening the door by closing it extra quietly.

She looked across to the bedroom door, left slightly ajar, and saw no light coming from the hallway below.

And then she heard nothing.

Perhaps she had dreamed it.

She stilled her breathing and listened. But there was no more noise.

Yes, that was it. A bad dream.

But now it would be even harder to get back to sleep.

She closed her eyes, curled up and tried not to think bad thoughts.

*

She'd lost track of exactly how long she'd been trying to sleep – trying not to think bad thoughts. It could have been ten minutes; it could have been an hour.

In her clean bed. In her clean, warm, bug-free bed.

That was it. It was no good. She was never going to get back to sleep.

Maybe a glass of milk would help.

She pulled the covers off and sat on the edge of the bed, giving her eyes a rub, before venturing outside. She looked across the landing to Mum's room. Odd. The door was still open. Mum always slept with it closed. Surely she wasn't downstairs in the dark? Was she with Derek? Oh, no. She hadn't brought Derek back. For a 'coffee'. Oh, please, God, no.

An unpleasant taste developed in her mouth at the thought. She listened again – heard nothing again. If they were downstairs there would be talking, or at least some noise or other. The unpleasant taste started to overpower her. Perhaps she should just go back to bed.

But hold on. Don't be silly. Of course they wouldn't be doing anything in the living room. She shook her head at the idea and went downstairs.

She padded into the kitchen, turned the light on, and poured herself a small glass of milk.

A small glass of milk. She was about to bring it up to her lips but stopped and looked more closely at the pureness of what she held in her hand. The glass was clear and pristine. The milk was clean, fresh and chilled. And safe. She took a very small sip and let it settle in a pool on her tongue. She took some time to really taste it, to press her tongue against the roof of her mouth and savour it. At that moment it was almost as if she'd never tasted milk before; it had always pretty much gone down without touching the sides. She did the same with another sip.

Then she heard a cough.

She stopped and silently placed the glass on the kitchen table.

That was definitely a cough.

It had to be the living room.

But she'd passed the living room on her way to the kitchen and hadn't noticed anything.

And hadn't the light been out?

She turned to look again. The door was open wide. There was no light on, just a crack of street lamp shooting across the room. She swallowed. Her mouth was dry, the creamy oil of milk gone in an instant. She stepped over to the door and looked inside.

There was a figure, hunched on the couch.

'Mum?'

The figure's silhouette moved. 'Hello, love,' it said weakly.

Nicole let out a sharp sigh of relief. 'What are you doing, Mum?' She reached for the light switch but heard a 'Please, no' and drew her hand back.

'Mum? What is it?' Nicole sat down beside her. 'Are you okay?'

'I'm fine, darling. Honestly. Just feeling sorry for myself, I think.'

'Did your date go wrong?'

'No. I . . . I had a lovely evening.'

'Well, what's wrong? Did something . . . happen?'

'Not really. Nice drink, pleasant conversation, watched a good movie. Had a lovely stroll along the Thames afterwards.'

In what little light there was Nicole caught a certain shininess on her mother's cheeks.

'But you're upset,' she said. 'I know you are. Why are you upset? Did Derek do something?'

Her mother's shoulders shook slightly as she let out a short, soft laugh. 'You've nothing to worry about, darling. I couldn't ever wish to meet a nicer man than Derek.'

'But something must have happened?'

Her mother shook her head. 'Not really. Like I said, he's a very nice man. Very reserved. Very . . . *nice*.'

Nicole paused for thought, then said slowly and gently, 'Is that the problem?'

'God, no. It's . . .'

Her mother stumbled to find the words, then gave up. In the darkness Nicole felt her mother's arm snaking over her shoulder and giving her a tender squeeze.

After a few moments her mother turned to her and said quietly, 'You're growing up fast, my girl, aren't you?'

Nicole thought for a couple of seconds, then said, 'I don't think I understand.'

'Nicole. Darling. You're half right. But you should never underestimate the value of a man being . . . well . . . *nice*.' She squeezed Nicole's hand. 'Sometimes you want a little excitement, that's just natural, but sometimes – just sometimes – you have to learn to love with your head too, to know what will make you happy.'

Nicole said nothing.

She wanted to say, *You were happy with Dad*. She wanted to say, *And you know he didn't do anything with that woman from work*.

But she said nothing.

'Still,' her mother said, 'plenty more fish.'

'So . . . are you going to see Derek again?'

Her mother shook her head.

'I'm . . . I'm sorry, Mum.'

'Oh, that's all right, love. And please don't be angry.'

'Why would I be angry?'

Her mother hesitated.

Obviously this could be big.

'I've got another date lined up,' she said. 'Zac, his name is.'

'Oh.'

'You're not angry, are you?'

211

'Of course not,' Nicole lied. 'But . . . I don't understand?'

Her mother sighed. 'You know, I'm not sure I do. It's just . . . after so long with your dad it's hard. I'm not sure what I want anymore. I just feel a bit sad.'

Nicole felt herself being rocked back and forth for a few silent minutes, broken only by the occasional rumble of traffic outside.

'Oh, something else I didn't tell you,' Nicole's mother said. 'I met another man today.'

Nicole flinched slightly at the thought.

Another man? Dare she ask any more?

Her mother obviously read the flinch. 'It's all right,' she said. 'I'm allowed to meet people. It's all legal.'

'So who was he?'

Then her mother said in a mock theatrical manner, 'His name's Gerry. But relax, he's only a neighbour. I bumped into him on the way home from work.'

'Aah.'

That was *Aah* as in *Phew!*

'So what's he like, this Gerry?'

'Well, he's another old guy – old-*ish*. Still got his wife and his grown-up son living with him. Seemed pleased to meet me. Said it was a blessed relief living next door to someone normal after old Mac.'

Nicole struggled to speak at first, then said, '*Normal?* What did he mean by that?'

'Well, first I had to ask who he meant. It was the man who lived here before us, apparently everyone called him Mac.'

'But did you ask him what he meant by "normal"?'

'I didn't need to ask; he told me. Anyway, an old man living alone like that is hardly likely to be normal, is he?'

'So what did he say?'

'Oh, a few things.'

'Like what?'

Nicole's mother shrugged. 'Oh, I don't know, just the way he behaved, how he got upset at trivial things.'

Nicole waited, looking straight at her mother in the dimness. After a few seconds her mother continued.

'I mean, apparently there was this time when Gerry had to chop down some trees and asked Mac to help. Mac had a bit of a hissy fit, said he couldn't bear to chop down trees or even watch other people do it. Went a bit peculiar.'

Nicole thought for a moment, then swallowed and said, 'Guess he had his reasons.'

'And there was the digging. Whenever Gerry was digging in the front garden and Mac had to pass by he crossed the road and almost ran past. Strange man.'

'Yes,' Nicole said. 'But I guess things must have happened to him to make him like that.'

'Oh, I think so,' her mother replied. 'You never know what's happened to some people to send them strange.'

'Mmm,' Nicole said, not wanting to say more, aware her voice would waver.

'Anyway, talking of strange, it's nearly one o'clock. We need to get to bed. Are you rowing at the next session?'

Nicole nodded, hesitantly at first, then more confidently. 'Yeah. Sure.'

'Then you need your sleep, and I know I do.'

She stood up, pulling her daughter with her.

Nicole went into the kitchen, finished her milk, and they both went to bed.

CHAPTER TWENTY-EIGHT

On that roadside, in the frozen wilderness, I still held onto my friend, Lorenzo – even when his lifeless head had slumped forward, even when a guard came over and shouted at me to move on. The guard waited only a few seconds before shoving me away. I resisted as much as I could, then fell over with weakness, and for a moment was facing the muzzle of a rifle. I held a hand up to him to show I understood, then managed to plant a foot on the ground and push my knee to bring myself up slowly. I faltered and fell again.

The guard slung his rifle over his shoulder and grabbed me, helping me up onto my feet. I thanked him in English and he nodded back to me. It seemed a strange gesture from him, made even more absurd when he turned to Lorenzo's body, pointed his rifle at it, but didn't shoot. Later I heard rumours that they were short of bullets, which would have explained why he left Lorenzo. Why did he help me up? I like to think there was just a little humanity left in him.

I marched on alone – as alone as I could be in a walking dead of many thousands.

By daylight we'd reached a village – somewhere in southern Germany, I assume – and found a series of old barns to rest in. I found a space and settled down, at first instinctively leaving enough room for Lorenzo. It was cold and damp, but with straw and the sheer number of bodies it soon warmed up, and I fell asleep.

The next thing I knew I was being nudged awake. A golden block of daylight came from the doorway. Again, for a brief, half-waking moment I looked around for Lorenzo.

The guards dropped rations of bread and biscuits on the dirt floor, causing a minor scramble between a few of us. People pushed and shoved, but nobody had the energy for anything more than that. People who didn't even have the energy for that either went without or picked up the scraps at the end, caked in dirt and grit.

Then we were taken outside to troughs of stagnant water, where we drank and washed our faces indiscriminately. It was so cold it shocked my face and burned my throat.

But I needed waking; we were told we had twenty minutes before we had to start marching again.

In spite of the food – or possibly because of it – my stomach hurt all the more, and in spite of the night's rest my legs and feet ached so much I lost feeling in them. That morning I knew how Lorenzo had felt in his final few hours. I wondered how many miles it would be before I gave up too. Ten? Five? Only one?

I don't know how much longer we walked on for, but somewhere along the way, when the sun had started dipping in front of us, providing some much-needed warmth, we were ordered to halt.

There was furtive talk between the guards. There was frowning, there was nodding agreement. Then one of them approached one of the horses. These faithful creatures had been carrying supplies along with us. They had kept us alive without complaint or choice.

The soldier paused for only a second or two, then pointed his rifle between the glorious beast's eyes and pulled the trigger.

I heard a few more shots ahead of me and behind me, so it had obviously been a last resort agreed at a higher level. At first I was puzzled, but as the soldiers knelt down and attended to the horse near me, I realized. There were now no more food supplies for the horses to carry, so they themselves became the food supply.

Within minutes the horse next to me was a bloody hunk. The prisoners gathered round and were handed marbled slithers of raw meat with little or no coordination. Whether out of weakness or fear of the guards there was no jostling. People simply waited, staring and salivating, hoping to catch the eye of the guard carving up the carcass.

I got a few mouthfuls; it was like eating rubber covered in salt water, but also had that coppery aftertaste that almost made me vomit. In the back of my mind, however, I knew it was highly nutritious. If it hadn't been for that horse I might not be alive today.

After the carcasses had been stripped to their bones we continued walking until darkness enveloped us. We ended up at a railway station where we rested on the concrete floor. I passed in and out of sleep before being woken up to follow the herds onto a train.

We were packed into the carriage so tightly it seemed impossible for any of us to lie down, but we did – arms and legs across one another, just about able to breathe. I remember looking up at one point and thinking that the mass of writhing bodies looked like fishing maggots squirming in a pot. I did sleep, however – hemmed in by the bodies it was the warmest I'd been for days.

There was a change of trains – maybe two or three – before we arrived at a hellhole I now know to be Bergen-Belsen concentration camp.

In fact, hell could hardly have been worse. Corpses were strewn around the mud as if they had fallen from the heavens. Blood and faeces were splattered everywhere, and it was hard to tell whether the damage to the bodies was due to wild animals, disease or cannibalism. There was no food whatsoever, and the only water was from pools of rainwater settling between the ruts of mud. Most of the guards had since absconded, deserting their rapidly sinking ship. There was little noise apart from the occasional groan, and the stench of rotten flesh drifted across the camp in waves.

I thought a terrible thing there – that Lorenzo was lucky to have avoided this place. But every mutilated corpse I stepped over reinforced that feeling.

I became very ill at Bergen-Belsen, but was still able to get blankets to keep warm and find a cabin to shelter in. I also searched the abandoned stores for any morsels of food. I didn't find any. For days I did little more than rest, my stomach in knots, my head feverish.

That is about as much as I remember from the camp itself.

Reading over my words after all these years – words that have, incidentally, taken me almost two years to write between bouts of dark mental confusion – I feel that this last section of my war experiences deserves some sort of climax, perhaps one of those inspiring, rousing scenes you get at the end of old war movies.

But it wasn't a movie.

The truth is that it was a slow and laborious nothingness, a descent into death that I simply didn't care about at the time. I'm told that when the camp was liberated I weighed six and a half stone. That's a tall, broad-shouldered man tipping the scales at about ninety pounds. And I'm sure there were many worse than me.

The first I knew about liberation was when I noticed people who were well fed and properly clothed walking around the cabin. I sat on the edge of the bed and gazed across to them. They came closer but I couldn't focus. Neither could I talk, although I could hear every word they spoke. I remember two in particular talking about me as if I wasn't there. I even recognized one as having a Scottish accent. Although I was too weak to talk I felt elated inside, thanking God for this gift.

I was taken to a nearby temporary hospital for tests, and did nothing but sleep and eat a kind of bland baby food. I later learned it was a restricted diet as anything rich might have killed me. Week by week I improved, at first talking to the nurses, and then taking slow, gentle strolls, which made me feel like I was learning how to walk all over again.

Then I was transferred to a convalescent home in Berkshire. It was there that my mother and father saw me for the first time in years. Mother held me to her chest and sobbed, Father too, although he quickly wiped away any tears.

Then I became confused. Their joy gave way to expressions of thinly veiled disgust, and it took me a few moments to realize it was because I had lost so much weight and must have looked pale and gaunt in spite of the weeks I had spent recovering.

They weren't the only ones crying. I found the experience upsetting as well as exhilarating, and was glad my heart had had those weeks – I'm not sure it could have taken the strain otherwise.

Within weeks I was dispatched home. Fixed. Mended. A1.

So I was told.

It was only when I was back home, living with my parents and listening to the radio broadcasts, that I really accepted the end of the war, that I was free to walk wherever I wanted, to keep myself clean, to eat food fit for a human being. I came to relish a jacket potato with a chunk of cheddar cheese atop, or a slice of bread and jam, or simply the clean crunch of a freshly picked apple. Even looking outside and not being able to see sentry guards, barbed wire and lookout towers gave my stomach a butterfly or two of the pleasant variety, and brought a tear to my eye – a tear I was never quite sure was from joy or fear.

And then, as the weather turned autumnal, I spent many hours kneeling down in front of our coal fire, luxuriating in the warmth, doing nothing more than reading or listening to the radio. In time, I appreciated the fact that whenever I had the urge to walk along the Thames and see the swans, ducks and moorhens, and enviously watch the rowers slipping past me, I could do exactly that.

I got a job with the council – just to tide me over until I decided what I wanted to do with my life. By the summer of 1946, and with the help of my mother's home cooking, I had regained the weight the Third Reich had taken from me, and when finances allowed I joined the rowing club and spent many a pleasant evening gliding along the Thames with others or, preferably, by myself.

Life was good. Absolutely every day was a sunny day for me.

I put my energies into rowing, but never matched the performances I'd achieved before the war. I used to complain that my shoulder – the one I hurt when the truck crashed – was giving me pain. In hindsight that was an excuse. The urge to excel I'd had as a teenager was gone; there was no spirit left in me for pushing my body to its limits. I think quite a few per cent of my physical endurance – that crucial extra bit that makes winners – still lay in Auschwitz. No, I was just content to enjoy the ride. And the freedom. Over the next few years I started doing more coaching and general helping out at the club – organizing trips and regattas. I had to accept I'd lost my competitive edge for good. I gained no thrill from rowing faster than others, only from rowing itself.

I had my memories. My friendship with Lorenzo, meeting Rosa's mama and papa, the pretty village of Valleverde, and the one time I met Lorenzo Junior and Anna.

And Rosa? Over the years I convinced myself it had been merely a wartime romance – fleeting and precious but ultimately of its time and nothing more. At times I wondered what Rosa saw in me – thinking that sometimes in wartime you take passion where you can. One thing I never, ever did was forget her.

But I was still a young man, and it was a part of my life I didn't care to dwell on. I tried to look to the future rather than the past. I think everybody did in those days of unfettered optimism immediately after the war.

As well as not having the spirit to push myself physically, I soon realized I had also lost any career ambitions to the war. I simply had no hunger to start my own business and work hard. I stayed in my sedate, but secure, job for years, not really caring much beyond appreciating the basics in life. I started seeing women, and after a few liaisons came my marriages to Glenda and Patricia. And after those came living with my parents again. In time Mother was diagnosed with stomach cancer and didn't last long. Father was distraught and his heart couldn't take the loss.

So finally, sadly, I was on my own, and have been on my own ever since.

⁓

It's now 26 April 1992.

Alone in the cellar of 77 Victoria Road, Henley, where I've written all of this, I've been looking back on what the writing experience has brought to me. Has it calmed me, helped me sleep more soundly, undisturbed by nightmares, as Doctor Green suggested it might? Well, if nothing else it's occupied my mind during my first couple of years of retirement, and it's brought back one or two happy memories as well as many horrific ones.

But I've also started to recap my life and what might have been. As my mother and father shared such a happy and close marriage I now wonder why my two attempts have been abject and very painful disasters. Have I ever really come to terms with what happened to me during the war? Or is there still some sort of void in my life?

⁓

13 May 1992.

It's 6 a.m. as I start to write this, and I haven't slept properly for over a week.

I feel awful, dejected, fearful that writing about the war has been a complete waste of time – no, worse than that, that it has stirred up feelings of resentment I've managed to lock away until now.

Last week I took a walk over Henley Bridge, past the Leander Club, and headed north along the Thames footpath. I passed a couple, arm in arm, and for the first time in decades had a feeling I thought I had got rid of forever: burning jealousy in my heart. I had been in the man's situation – arm in arm with a woman – many times, so at first my feelings puzzled me. I turned and looked more closely. He was tall and broad-shouldered – a born rower. The woman was full-figured with slightly darker skin and solid, black hair. But it was the way she tossed her hair back that grabbed my attention and refused to let it go. This was Rosa, and the man was me. At least, in another, better world.

I turned and hurried away, then quickened my pace to get my lungs working. I thought that was the end of my aberration until I went to bed that night. I almost dropped off to sleep, but the image of that couple came to mind, jolting me awake. I settled down again, but the same thing happened. I was agitated, and went downstairs for a cup of warm milk. I told myself not to be stupid, not to obsess about events in another time, another place. I returned to bed and slept soundly for two hours, only to wake again and have the same restless feelings.

The next day I felt better – if a little groggy – but that obsession returned like all obsessions, good or bad. I went to the doctor and told him I couldn't sleep. He gave me some sleeping tablets, which helped. For a couple of days.

I increased my dosage of tablets, but they made me feel dizzy the next morning, like I'd been drinking the night before. And they only worked for another couple of days. I returned to the doctor. He asked if there was anything bothering me. I said there wasn't, as far as I was aware. He asked whether I had ever had therapy, that perhaps some memories were deeply buried and were affecting me without my knowing it. I told him I wasn't mad, just insomniac. He prescribed stronger tablets.

But his question struck a chord with me. As I was about to take the tablet that night, staring at my haggard old face in the mirror, I thought long and hard about what had kicked off this episode of insomnia: seeing the woman who looked like Rosa.

I considered the possibility that perhaps I haven't yet come to terms with what happened all those years ago after all. More importantly, there is still a part of me that muses on what became of Rosa. I always assumed she'd been killed in Auschwitz. I have no proof of this, I simply convinced myself for my own convenience that that was what had happened; I did this to enable me to get on with my life.

Nevertheless, I was physically drained and desperately in need of sleep, so I took one of those newer, stronger tablets.

I slept, but not as well as I'd hoped, and again, felt ill the next morning.

I saw friends, did some shopping, attended the rowing club that evening to help with coaching. Yes, that would help me sleep.

It didn't. I had to take another tablet.

The next day there was no rowing club meeting, so I went for a long walk to tire myself out. And last night I still couldn't sleep. Again I stared at myself in the mirror as I held a tablet in my hand. My face was pallid, my eyelids sagged. In one instant it hit me that I would die – cease to exist – without ever experiencing a happy marriage or children. I wondered whether I might have had that with Rosa, had things been different all those years ago. She would have survived, I would have married her and gone to live with her in Rome, we would have had three or four children and run the farm that rightfully belonged to her family.

And my daydreams of that other, perfect world brought with them a new and frightening memory – a flashback.

When I'd proposed to Patricia and Glenda many decades ago, I'd had an eerie feeling – similar to déjà vu but much stronger, and like I was somewhere else.

And that night – staring into the mirror at my ageing features – I knew why I'd had that feeling; my flashback told me why.

I'm back in Auschwitz-Birkenau concentration camp. I have just found my Rosa and we are talking. There is mud. There is rain. A dead body lies at my feet. We are both young but also very ill. We haven't seen each other for many months. We embrace and talk.

Now I remember what we talk about.

We talk of how much we've missed each other. I tell her I will come to Valleverde when the war is over, that we will be together.

'Marry me,' I say. 'Rosa Di Vito, please give me the pleasure of becoming my wife.'

She cries. In spite of the rain I know she cries.

'Yes,' she answers. 'Yes, a thousand times. I will marry you.'

That sounds like a dream, a wishful fantasy.

No.

It happened.

But my flashback ended there.

I know there was more. I know we talked more.

I tried to remember more, but all I could see was my own sad face staring back at me from the mirror.

In the end I took the tablet. The next day I vowed it would be the last time I ever took a sleeping tablet because I had such terrible nightmares. I dreamed of what happened to Rosa. No, not what happened, but all the terrible things that *could* have happened to her. The fact was I didn't really know the truth. I spent the next morning feeling quite ill, but knowing that these thoughts were eating me up inside, churning and festering and stopping me thinking of anything else, causing me much more agony than either of my broken marriages had ever done.

It came to a head last night, when I collected all my sleeping tablets together – the old and the newer, stronger ones. I emptied the bottles out into two small piles.

What if the memories, the nightmares and the considerations of a life lost to those memories – what if all of that got too much for me? Could this be a way to bring a curtain down on my suffering?

But no. I wasn't like that. I was for health and fitness, for using natural means to solve my problems where I could.

Then the 'other voice' came into my head. Good intentions are no more than that; perhaps the tablets could be my insurance policy – in case the memories got too much for me and I couldn't face years and years of this wretched existence.

It was then, with my mind in some sort of altered state, that I knew there was more. I had no idea what it was, but there was definitely some element of truth in the doctor's suggestion that this writing exercise might help my mind. Eventually.

When I was married to Glenda we went to the local theatre to see a hypnotist. He started off by saying there was more to the mind than the conscious. I laughed. I'd always been sceptical of their claims up until then, but that night I saw people – local people I knew not to be stooges – making fools of themselves. After the show I told Glenda it was all trickery, and she responded by saying I wouldn't accept the truth, that I had built a wall around what I thought to be true and was fiercely defending it. I dismissed her thoughts.

But last night, with my head full to bursting with thoughts of my proposal to Rosa, I was finally accepting the truth. And the truth was – the truth *is* – that I'm good at building walls. That's how I survived Auschwitz. But now I'm seeing more. Whether it's because of the frailty of my age or some desperate inner yearning, I'm now seeing the wall crumble, brick by brick.

There is more.

More to the mind than the conscious.

There *is* more – more to my memories than I know. My daydream was like viewing a scene through a frosted window, desperate to see but unable to focus properly. Something else happened at Auschwitz – something I've blotted out of my mind. But what can I do about it all these years later?

Yes. There is something I can do. Some hope.

Many years ago I heard the news stories about the museum they opened at the Auschwitz site, but, as usual, I immediately decided it was irrelevant to me, because in Mac's world old scars are weak and you leave them alone, all the better to heal. I was always a 'looking forward not backward' type of person.

But last night I wasn't looking forward or backward; I was looking at two piles of sleeping tablets.

I made my decision. I knew what I was going to do. I threw the sleeping tablets in the bin and went to bed. As soon as I turned the lights out my demons wheedled their way into my mind and stopped my mind from settling, but in time I found a little sleep. I slept because I knew what I was going to do the next day.

Today is that next day.

Those same thoughts, however, are the ones that interrupted my slumber and made me get up this morning well before the sun – but for the right reasons. I simply had to write all of this down, for now I'm surer than ever that I'm doing the right thing and the details need to go in my notebook.

It's now just after eight o'clock. By the time I've had some breakfast the shops will be open, so I'm going into town.

I'm going to book myself onto the next flight bound for Krakow.

CHAPTER TWENTY-NINE

I t was about twenty past seven in the evening.

Nicole came into the house and grabbed a cold can of cola from the fridge. She drank half straight away, sat down next to her mother at the kitchen table, then finished it, letting out a satisfied gasp at the end.

Her mother momentarily flicked her eyes up from the *Henley Evening Gazette* towards Nicole and said, 'How was rowing?'

How was rowing?

Rowing had been a little less than enjoyable. It had been her first row in a four with three other girls. She hadn't wanted that, but Austin and Shaun were rowing together – rowing seriously, training for some minor competition – and neither seemed to have time for Nicole. Well, Austin had time to say 'Hello again' before being dragged away by Shaun.

The three girls she rowed with weren't exactly rude, not unless you count spending ten minutes talking about which of their mates they'd seen at the nightclub at the weekend and how much they'd drunk and who had started dating who.

Nicole's mind being elsewhere didn't help. Even after they'd started rowing there was a fairly regular clash of oars, which prompted one of the girls to ask Nicole whether she'd 'actually rowed before'. Nicole said 'not really' and three pairs of eyes bounced skywards.

'It was cool,' Nicole told her mother. 'I rowed in a four for the first time.'

'Sounds like progress,' her mother said, nodding while reading newspaper. Then she said, 'So what did you get up to the rest of today?'

'What?'

Now she looked up. 'Well, you weren't here when I got home from work. Did you go to the college to sort a course out?'

'Oh, I . . . erm . . . I saw Dad again, at the café.'

'Oh.' Her mother gave her tea a considered stir. 'So how was he?'

How was he?

Well, she could say he smelled a little bit, which was probably because he'd been at work all day and then had to drive up here to have a burger and fries at Benton's greasy spoon café because it was the only realistic way he could meet his daughter.

Or perhaps she could say he asked yet again how 'your mum' was, whether she was bearing up under the strain, whether she was looking after herself, whether she was seeing anyone (not that it mattered to him or he had any right to know about her 'private affairs'), and whether she would object if he came round to the new house rather than always meeting his daughter at this 'rather insalubrious place'.

She could even say he told her that although he was pleased she was starting to make new friends courtesy of the rowing club, she should get herself on a course at the college.

Just as Nicole was about to tell her mother that he was fine, something else hit her.

She froze and looked straight at her mother. When her look

was returned she said, 'He's good. Well, not good, but okay.' She continued staring.

'What?' her mother said. 'What is it?'

'It's just . . . that's the first time you've asked how he is.'

'Only being polite,' her mother said with a shrug.

Nicole waited, preparing herself for a rebuttal, then said, 'Do you mind if I bring him back here next time he visits?'

Her mother's head tilted to one side, weighing up her answer.

'It's a horrible place, Mum. You wouldn't want me eating there.'

Her mother paused for breath before saying, 'I've told you before. It's your house, bring back who you want.'

'But it's awkward if it's Dad. You said I had to make sure you weren't in if he ever came here.'

Her mother waved her hand dismissively. 'Oh, don't worry about that.' She gazed through the window for a few seconds. 'I've got to meet him sometime. And I guess when that happens we've got to be adults about it.'

'It's just that . . . I know you hate him.'

'Oh, if I'm honest I don't really hate him. He's just a 24-carat idiot.'

'I think he knows that, Mum.'

She nodded firmly. 'Good.'

'Mum, could I ask you something?'

Her mother gave her a suspicious sideways look. 'Ye-*es*?'

'Do you . . . miss Dad? I mean, at all?'

She spluttered. '*Excuse me?* Do I miss the man who cheated on me?'

'But . . . do you know for certain he did that?'

There was no answer.

'Anyway,' Nicole said, 'I know you hate him, but . . . well . . . you must miss him a bit?'

'We were together for over twenty years, sweetheart.'

'But do you think about him?'

The flesh on her mother's face seemed to drop a fraction. She stammered for a few moments, then eventually said, 'Darling, please don't do this to me. Not now. Just . . . just invite him over if you want to, but don't involve me. All right?'

Nicole lowered her gaze and nodded.

Her mother stood up, poured the remaining half of her tea away, and stepped towards the door.

But she stopped.

She sat back down, edged the chair closer to her daughter, and put her arm around her.

'Nicole,' she said. 'Now listen to me.'

Nicole looked up.

'I know it can't be easy for you. But there's no point giving you any false hope. You know I couldn't consider staying with a man who did that to me.'

'He knows he was stupid, Mum. But he says he didn't—'

'Oh, I don't care what he says.' Her mother groaned, then tightened her arm around her daughter. 'Nicole. Just don't even go there, okay? I know it's hard for you to accept, but your dad and I are . . . well, we're pretty much certainly getting a divorce.'

Nicole nodded.

'And I know it doesn't sound like I'm helping, but we both love you, nothing's changed with that. And the only thing I can say is, well, it's not all bad. Worse things happen.'

Nicole didn't answer.

CHAPTER THIRTY

It's now 24 May 1992. Late last night I got home from my visit to the Auschwitz museum – in a roundabout way, at least. And I have so much to say that my mind is outpacing my ability to write down the details.

I had about a week to wait for my flight over there. On the days leading up to it I slept even less than I had been doing before, becoming agitated and frustrated that I had to wait. But during those dark night-hours my resolve to find what I was looking for hardened. I wanted to come away with some idea of what had happened to Rosa all those years ago. What had become of her? Had she perished in the gas chambers? Had I myself burned her body – bloody, dirty and unrecognizable – without realizing it? Or had she even been on the death march with me, perhaps a hundred or so bodies behind me?

I was also kept awake by my own stupidity. The questions I was now asking myself had always seemed half a world away, as if my time in Valleverde, Fossoli and Auschwitz had been lived by someone else. There were times when I didn't want to go, and, equally, there were times when I cursed myself for not going earlier.

*

On the day of the flight I left my house uncertain of what answers I would find, if any at all, but hopeful I would have clues as to how accurate my frosted memories had been.

On my trip I kept a diary of sorts – a reminder of the one my mother gave me when I stepped onto that ship bound for Tunisia all those years ago. And I used it. My records are all bits and pieces scribbled feverishly whenever a thought came to me. And many did. I wanted to start writing them up into something coherent as soon as I got in, but I was too exhausted. However, now I'm putting them in the correct order before I forget. It gives me a reason to live, although not the reason I had originally hoped for.

Although I had trouble sleeping on the nights leading up to my trip, on the night before the flight I slept relatively well, as if I could sense some sort of closure approaching.

But on the plane to Krakow I couldn't relax. I found myself checking the face of every elderly woman I saw, trying to imagine Rosa as she might have been now, almost fifty years later: probably fuller in the face and body but, I knew, still radiant and attractive. I tried to stop obsessing about her, but I was almost hallucinating – no, *fantasizing* – whenever my eyes locked onto likely suspects. The only way I could control myself was to keep my eyes shut. It was hard.

As they announced we were entering Polish airspace I had a panic attack. I hurried to the toilet, doused my face and my hair in cold water, and sat on the seat, gasping for breath, unable to move.

Eventually I regained some composure and returned to my seat. By the time the plane landed I thought I'd recovered, but still was asked by a couple of people whether I was all right. I nodded, tried to smile, and I'm sure they put it down to fear of flying.

I wasted no time. I could have rested or checked into my hotel, but I seemed to have regained that single-mindedness I'd had as a youth and had somehow lost during the war years. I took a train to the site of the concentration camp – now a museum – and within a couple of hours was once again approaching the sign that proudly proclaimed '*Arbeit Macht Frei*'.

Getting here had been no trouble. Taxi, plane, train, bus. But would actually entering the place be quite as easy?

And then, just when I thought that seeing what remained of the place might heighten my anxiety, might make me weak and faint, I somehow felt stronger.

I stopped and looked up to take a good look at those big, bold letters. A cloud drifted along behind them, almost mocking them, or ignoring them at the very least. A little fear trickled through my veins, and I can't pretend it didn't. But I also rejoiced that *I had survived this place*.

It had lost. I had won. That was something to rejoice over.

In fact, the whole site would have fallen to the attrition of nature and the industry of thieves long ago had it not been for the efforts of the authorities in preserving it as a museum.

Those authorities had done a fine job. Hair, spectacles, artificial limbs, shoes, toys – all were on display. Once upon a time people had relied on these articles to live their everyday lives. If they had continued to do so – if history had been telling us a different story – these articles would have been lost forever. Now they were on display, and a little of the real people behind them was still remembered.

As I strolled between the restored brick buildings, however, I started to feel less confident. I might well have survived this place when so many hadn't, but in a sense it had still taken my life from me. My drive, my energy for life – my very water of life – now revolved around this place and my memories of it. That shouldn't have been so; my energies should have been put into my career and my marriage and family. The very fact that I had returned forty-seven years after dragging my weary, broken body away from it was testament to the fact that it still had its claws in my back even now.

I saw a mock-up of one of the original gas chambers – dark and dank and sinister. I can't say it brought back any memories. Then I saw where the original chambers had been and where one of the crematoria had stood. The latter had long since been blown to kingdom come, and was now only a pathetic, defeated pile of rubble, left there as a symbol of an ethos in ruins. It was then that I retraced my steps between the chambers and the crematoria, which caused some glimmers of memories to return to me. I thought of how Lorenzo and I would have to part the bodies of those who clung to one another in death; how we would tie those leather belts around the corpses and drag them out of the chambers; how the odd stray limb would hook itself around the door frame; how, in our weakened state, we would help one another hoist the corpses up onto the waiting cart and drag it off to the storehouse or a crematorium.

Yes, this really was the place where I had taken part in one of civilization's most degrading episodes. It seemed trite to consider my own current situation in all of this, when, for so many, the sunny days had stopped in such a cruel and premature manner.

Then I searched for the spot where I'd last seen Rosa, but the fences that had been our boundaries – our markers – were no more, and it seemed a hopeless task. The memories didn't come flooding back as clear and vivid as I'd dared to believe they might, and now every building and path looked much the same.

And then, just when it looked like my trip had been a waste of time, that I'd come here looking for answers to important questions and found nothing except ruins, I had my moment.

There was a display of the various items taken by the Nazis from the Jews, including accounts of the gold teeth and dental caps the SS had plundered.

I don't know why it affected me so much, because nothing there was new to me. But perhaps it was the location – physically being here – combined with thoughts of teeth being taken from their still-warm owners. Suddenly a tide of memories flooded into my mind. It was as though a dam had broken and the surge was as relentless as it was exhilarating.

I stood stock-still at the display and gazed at a picture of the gold that had been plundered by the SS. There were not only teeth, but also bracelets, rings and brooches. And there I tried to make reason and structure out of those memories.

I went to get a cup of coffee and to rest. And to wish I had a companion to make sense of it all, to give words to my thoughts.

But I was alone.

Then I closed my eyes, and I was no longer in the museum coffee bar.

I am still at Auschwitz, but now it is 1944 and I am a Sonder-kommando, dirty and weak due to starvation, but still a king of the times. I have been called out to take some corpses away from one of the main prisoners' camps.

But there I have found my Rosa, body ravaged and skin diseased, but still beautiful to me.

We talk, and at the time I think more of how much I miss her than what she says. It's only now – now I'm reliving the experience – that I remember our words.

Through the rain we talk of marriage, but in truth neither of us really believes that will be possible.

I tell her I'll never forget our days together in that cosy cellar in Valleverde.

Now there is pain on her face. She struggles to speak and I hold her.

'Rosa?' I say. 'What is it?'

Her hand holds mine. It's cold and the fingers spindly.

'There is something I have to tell you,' she says. She looks left and right, then whispers, 'There is gold.'

'What?' I answer.

Is she delirious? Her frame is pathetic and wiry, her face gaunt and imploring. But now there is adamant passion in her voice too.

'There is gold at the farmhouse.'

I shake my head and tell her, 'I don't want gold.'

'Mac. Listen to me. You remember the wooden trunk in the cellar?'

'Yes,' I say, puzzled. And I think back to the layout of that room, with the intricately carved wooden trunk that was always padlocked, which she told me held personal family items.

'Mac, I didn't tell you. I didn't want to keep secrets from you but it was better you didn't know. There was a small metal travelling case at the bottom of the trunk. It contained all our family gold, going back generations. Rings, bracelets, necklaces, brooches and pendants.'

'I've told you, Rosa. I don't care about gold.'

Now she pulls my arm with the strength of a small child begging for sweets. 'Just listen,' she says. 'You have to get the gold.'

'But . . . didn't the guards ransack the house?'

She shakes her head. 'I knew they might come. I moved it.'

And then a faint recollection hit me. I remember a time when it was locked with a large shiny padlock, and then I remember finding it unlocked, but not giving it any thought.

'You remember the old olive tree?' Rosa says. 'The one next to the farmyard?'

'Yes, but—'

'I am the only person who knows where it is hidden. Now you too. If you escape from this hell you must get it. From the trunk of the tree measure two paces towards the ridge where I first saw you.

235

Dig down no more than two handspans. There you'll find the metal case.'

'But I told you,' I say. 'I don't care about that; all I want is for you to survive this place and go back to Rome. Then I can go there too.'

Now she smiles. It's a sickly, crooked smile, but I still feel it. 'We'll see,' she says with no emotion. 'But get the gold. If not for us, then for Lorenzo. Tell him where it is in case he survives.' Then she grips my hand more tightly. 'Mac, if you do anything for me, do this. Make sure Lorenzo gets it, and if not him, then make sure it gets to Anna and Lorenzo Junior. Anything, but make sure the Nazis don't get it.'

'But what about your mama and papa?' I say.

'Dead,' she says flatly.

'Are you sure?'

She nods, then says, 'Me next.'

I shake my head feebly. 'Rosa. Don't say that.'

Still she holds my hand. 'Please do this for me,' she says.

I am still confused. Even if I survive, what does she want me to do with the gold? But I tell her what she wants to hear – what gives her a little happiness in her wretched state.

'Of course I'll get it,' I say. 'But . . .'

'Think of it as my last wish. Please. I . . . I am near the end.'

'No!' I shout.

Now the guard reaches us and starts shouting and brandishing his rifle. Rosa turns her back and walks away.

I am never to see her again.

At the museum coffee bar I almost collapsed in fear.

Fear of what?

I don't know.

But I was stunned and confused. Why was I remembering all of this now? Why not years ago when perhaps I might have been able to do something about it?

And I also knew that wasn't the end. There was more about the gold, another conversation. But with whom? I never saw Rosa again. Or did I? I was so confused. Now the memories seemed clearer but the implications for me less so. What happened to the gold Rosa told me about?

I left the coffee bar and visited another display, which told the story of the pits that the Sonderkommandos dug out as funeral pyres. It should have disgusted me, but my mind was blank. Did something happen when Lorenzo and I were digging together? I stared and stared at the photos of the piles of corpses, desperately trying to claw back those memories.

I felt like I was peeking through a door – glimpsing something yet knowing there was so much more to see – but not having the strength to push it fully open.

I wandered through the remains of the camp, past the endless barbed-wire fences, along the paths which now fought against nature, and tried to cast my mind back to 1944.

Did Rosa really say those things to me all those years ago? Stories of hidden gold seemed very melodramatic. And so many years had passed by. Could any of my memories – especially ones that had been hidden away for so long – really be that reliable? It had also been a period of my life when I was almost delirious with weakness, malnutrition and sheer mental confusion.

But the more I considered it, the more I knew that Rosa really had said those things.

I also knew there was definitely more.

I wandered aimlessly through the memorial grounds until my feet ached, and eventually had to admit defeat.

CHAPTER THIRTY-ONE

Nicole jolted as she heard the front door slam. She hid the notebook under her bed and crept outside her bedroom to the top of the stairs.

'Mum?'

There was a firm but not discouraging 'yes' from the kitchen. Then the light went on.

Nicole went downstairs to find her mother sitting at the table, her chin securely lodged into the 'V' of her palms.

'You okay?' Nicole said quietly.

Her mother smiled glumly. 'Yes, *okay* sounds about right.'

'Didn't it go very well again?'

Her mother shook her head dolefully. 'I'm not sure I want to talk about it.'

Nicole drew a chair from under the table and sat down without speaking.

'Anyway,' her mother said. 'Never mind me and my disasters, what did you get up to today?'

'Went for a walk into town,' Nicole said. 'And went to the college again.'

'Did you apply for anything?'

Nicole spotted the admonishing stare and looked away. 'No. I came back and had a pizza, then read more of my book.' She paused before adding, 'Well, it's not so much a book, more a journal about—'

'I tell you, I'm done with dating and I've hardly started. Absolutely fed up with it, I am.'

What could Nicole say to that?

Apart from, *How about you give up dating?*

'I'm sorry, Mum. But . . . I guess you've only seen three so far.'

Mum had told her about the other two. There was 'too nice' Derek from work and then Zac last night, who made it patently clear after half an hour that he was only interested in a one-night stand.

Had Nicole hoped for better things with tonight's date?

No, of course she hadn't. But she couldn't say that.

'Was tonight just as bad?' she said.

'Oh, *worse*,' her mother said, sighing and rolling her eyes at the same time. 'I can take boring men, and I can take sex addicts if they keep to themselves, but if there's one thing I can't stand it's men who drive like lunatics.' Now she looked at Nicole and her head shook. 'You know, I seriously thought I was going to die, and all he could do was laugh at me.'

Nicole shrugged. 'I guess he wasn't to know about . . .'

'That's hardly the point.' She tutted and shook her head. 'Call themselves a dating agency? *Pah!*'

'*Dating agency?*' Nicole's eyes widened. 'You've joined a *dating agency?*'

'Oh, yes, didn't I say?'

'No. No, you didn't.'

'One of these online things. But I'm going to *un*-join in the morning.' She shook her head, and Nicole noticed a jaw that seemed just a little less firm than it had been.

'I know I said Derek was nice. And Zac was interesting but just plain creepy. So what do they do tonight? They only go and set me up with Mad Max.'

Nicole gave a less than confident nod and glanced at her mother. 'Who's Mad Max?'

A laugh.

Nicole felt her heart flutter. *A laugh from Mum.* Then she felt her mother's hand reaching across and tousling her hair, something else that hadn't happened for months. It would normally have been very irritating. But not today.

Her mother's laughing died down. 'It's an old movie. What I mean is, he was like an eighteen-year-old boy trying to impress his sixteen-year-old girlfriend. And trying so hard she realized he cared more about himself that he did about anything else. So, *no*, definitely not what you'd call *nice*.'

'I see.'

'I've just started with the dating thing and I've had enough already.' She covered her face with the palms of her hands.

Nicole hesitated. *Was Mum crying?* She waited for her to regain a little composure – or at least show that she wasn't crying – before speaking.

'I guess sometimes nice is good,' she said.

'Yes,' her mother replied. 'You're absolutely right. Well . . . Oh, I don't know. I'm confused.' She looked up, and Nicole saw there was a slight wetting of her eyes, but no more than that. 'I'm sorry, Nicole,' she said. 'You shouldn't see me like this.'

'No.'

'But you know whose fault it all is.'

'It's not all bad,' Nicole said. 'Worse things happen, you know.'

Her mother laughed again, and this time it was the full works: warm eyes, craggy crow's feet, a little red glow to the cheeks.

It was beautiful.

Nicole's mother held both hands up in surrender. 'All right, all right. You got me fair and square on that one.' She exhaled deeply before saying, 'And at least I've got you.'

While Nicole was still bathing in her mother's joy, her mother turned to glance at the clock, then planted her hands on the table as if to get up.

'I'm seeing Dad again on Saturday,' Nicole said.

Her mother settled back into the chair. 'Oh, Saturday? I erm . . .' She shrugged casually. '. . . I might well be in on Saturday. I mean . . . it's possible.'

'Oh, he won't be coming here. He's going to pick me up from town and take me to Windsor for the day.'

'Oh.' Nicole's mother's face dropped a fraction. 'Well, you did tell him he could come here, didn't you?'

'Erm . . . I wasn't sure you'd like that.'

Another shrug. 'Well, I . . . I'm not too worried. I mean, I'm not too fussed either way. After all, we can't go on avoiding each other forever.'

'Well, I could ring and ask him whether he wants to come here?'

'I don't see why not.' For a second a concerned frown played on her forehead, then just as quickly disappeared. She pointed at the window. 'You know it's going to be pouring down with rain all weekend, don't you?'

'Is it?'

Her mother nodded. 'You'll get soaked in Windsor.'

'Well . . .' Nicole paused, eyeing up her mother's face. 'I could invite him here to eat?'

Her mother gave a conservative nod. 'As long as he doesn't mind.'

'Cool. And d'you think you'll . . . ?'

'Oh, I can't promise I'll be here, of course. Stuff to do. Food shopping and all that. But we'll see.'

'Sure,' Nicole said. 'I'll let Dad know and leave it up to him.'

CHAPTER THIRTY-TWO

The museum was closing.

I thought I would never find out the full story of what happened in those dark days at the end of the war, and as I passed under those fabled wrought-iron words, I turned to take what was likely to be my last look.

And I didn't want to leave.

I was angry with myself for not remembering more.

Perhaps if I stood and stared the memories would come back to me.

I closed my eyes and churned the things I *could* remember over in my head, trying to concentrate on the sounds and smells, hoping they would evoke the memories I knew were there, hidden somewhere in the dusty corners of my mind.

I heard the coach driver telling me she was about to leave, then opened my eyes to see the place being locked up for the night.

Still I wanted to stay here. I had come all this way. I just *had* to remember.

But no.

My common sense got the better of me. I got on the coach, which set off for the railway station. I looked out of the window and thought perhaps I could come here again the next day – or even next year, because modern transport meant it wasn't that far away, and I was sixty-seven – not that old. By now there was a whip of rain in the air. Yes, I thought, perhaps I should come back when there was snow on the ground like there had been on the death march.

It was then that the bus passed a group of young men shuffling along the side of the road, turning their jacket collars up against the wet weather. I immediately imagined snow all around them, and my mind filled in the rest of the picture. These men were on the death march, walking for miles with nothing in their stomachs and little more than cotton bags on their feet. And in my mind I was among them.

It is January 1945 again. I am with Lorenzo on the death march. We are both cold, hungry and exhausted. He has fallen down onto the ground for the first time. I have tried to pull him up and he is struggling to even speak, let alone march. I am trying to keep him alive by talking to him – shouting his name. Anything will do; anything to give him a reason to live.

I put my head close to his. Now I whisper words to him.

'There is gold,' I say. 'I know where your family gold is hidden.'

He squeezes his bloodshot eyes almost shut in bewilderment.

'Rosa told me where it is,' I say. 'When this is all over you can have it and make a new life for yourself. I can look after Rosa and you can have the gold.'

There is a weak grunt from him. 'You think I care about gold?' he says.

He is right, of course. I don't care about it either, but the thought has made him talk; he is interested. I have no answer to his question, however. Out here, where we are cold and hungry and exhausted, gold – especially mere thoughts of it – has no value.

243

'Dying,' he says, hissing the words out. 'Feel it in my legs. Can't walk.'

'I'll help,' I say. I try to pull him up but he cannot even help by taking a little of his own weight.

'No,' he says. 'Can't . . . feel . . . legs.'

'But, Lorenzo . . .'

'It's the end,' he says. Then his hand falls on my sleeve. I think he is trying to grab it but hasn't the energy. He slumps, chin on chest, just as the guard arrives.

Now I plead with the soldier, but he doesn't understand and points his rifle at Lorenzo. I tell Lorenzo to think of his family. In desperation I pull him up and we continue walking, him leaning on me so much I struggle to stay upright.

In the stuffy atmosphere of the bus I felt my throat turning dry, and suddenly longed for some wetness on my tongue – snow, even – just to remind me I was alive, perverse as it sounds.

And then the thought hit me like a chilled breeze. Now I knew what I had been searching for all these years. I had to get off and walk in the rain – walk anywhere – because my mind was alive with the thought.

I grabbed my bag and hurried to the front of the coach. I told the driver I needed to get off straight away, repeating it when he made excuses.

Seconds later I was walking along the side of the road in the rain. I had no idea where I was heading; my mind was churning the thought over and over until I was certain there was no fault in my simple logic.

Back in the concentration camp, Rosa had told me she was the only one who knew where the gold was hidden. I know Lorenzo didn't tell anyone. I know Rosa wouldn't have lied to me, so if the gold wasn't there anymore – if it had been dug up since the war – Rosa was possibly still alive. On the other hand, if the gold was still in its hiding place I could be certain that my dear Rosa had perished in Auschwitz.

It wasn't a choice I wanted – Rosa being certainly dead or possibly alive – but at last I had *something* to hope for. It was quite possible that someone else had accidentally stumbled upon the gold or had chopped the tree down in those intervening years, but what if they hadn't?

For the next few hours I felt like I was committing some sort of illicit or dangerous act. In fact, all I did was walk to the railway station, call the hotel to cancel my reservation, and get on the overnight train to Rome. I ate on the train and slept well in spite of my apprehensions about what I might find in Valleverde.

The next morning I was woken by the jolt of the train coming to a halt at Rome. I hurriedly got dressed, put my suitcase in a locker and headed into the city. There I managed to buy a small shovel, then went to the taxi rank. I asked the driver to take me to Valleverde. That was the first time I'd heard the word in almost fifty years and the sound of it breathed life into me.

I had little meaningful memory of the village itself, only a dim mental picture of the cellar that had been my home in 1943, but as the taxi wound its way around the cobbled streets it all came back to me. I couldn't have described the street layout, but there was something about the place that seemed to heighten my powers of recollection. Perhaps the freshness of the air, perhaps the faint aroma of herbs, bread and cheese that hadn't changed in all those years.

The taxi dropped me off and I wandered those streets for ten or fifteen minutes, seeing more of it than I had when I'd been in hiding here. The winding, walled streets and cobbled paths made every house look the same.

But then I saw it in the distance. It was like a face you struggle to describe, but when you see it, you know. It was the terraced house the Di Vito family had been forced to live in after being removed from the farmhouse. This had been Rosa's home, and mine too in those precious times. The doors to the house and the basement were different, but the brickwork was unchanged except for a little more lichen and some water staining. Even the metal guttering and pipework was the same but for a few meetings with paintbrushes over the years. I could easily picture the door creaking open and Rosa stepping out into the clean Mediterranean sun with her bright red headscarf and grey flannel work suit.

Oh, if we could all choose one time in our lives to revisit.

I stood looking at the exterior for a few minutes. I felt my eyes moistening, and dabbed them with a handkerchief. I felt a hand on my shoulder, and turned to find a fresh-faced young man who said something in Italian. He spoke very quickly and there was no way I could have understood the words, but his expression asked me if I was all right. I nodded, thanked him, and we smiled goodbye.

I smiled goodbye to the house too; there was somewhere more important I needed to go.

I sauntered along the cobbles, surprised at how much I was enjoying the walk. It felt like I'd come home even though this was a mission more than a holiday. One or two road junctions stumped me, but not for long. Eventually I walked down the steep lane leading to the farm that Rosa's mama and papa had owned before Mussolini's laws had thrown them out.

At first I didn't recognize the layout of fields. There had clearly and understandably been many changes, more fields with horses and fewer with crops. Even the farmhouse had undergone changes. Half of it looked much the same as it had in 1943, albeit with different doors and windows. But it had been extended, the slightly lighter coloured mortar betraying the join. There was also a large, rambling wisteria vine threatening to envelop it.

Throughout all of this it was still recognizably the same farmhouse I'd stumbled upon in 1943.

Then I looked to the far left and felt my skin prickle. The old olive tree, its trunk like an extruded sugar sweet, just that little bit more twisted than it had been all those years ago, was still standing on the other side of the farmyard. I scanned the scene all around me for onlookers, then headed for the tree, almost having to stop myself breaking into a trot, which wouldn't have been wise at my age.

The fields beyond the tree – those I'd stumbled over after escaping from the overturned cattle truck – had now been turned into a housing estate, and a road ran along the ridge I remember having to lie down on to spy on the farmhouse.

I reached the olive tree and had the most curious feeling. In those fifty years the tree had hardly changed, whereas I had become old and decrepit – and perhaps insignificant. I was a mayfly in comparison to this beast.

I stopped daydreaming and looked at the weed-ridden earth around it. Yes, there were roots snaking from the trunk, but there were no tell-tale signs of excavations of any sort. It would have been hard to dig due to those roots. Perhaps Rosa had known that.

Clever Rosa.

I looked all around me for signs of human life and saw none. I pulled out my shovel, took two small paces towards the ridge, then knelt down. I used the shovel's sharp edge to make my mark. It was only one stroke on the ground, but one stroke that could provide so many answers.

Then I heard a door open and stood up as quickly as I was able, hiding the shovel in my shoulder bag. I turned to see a middle-aged man walking from the farmhouse towards one of the horses. He glanced in my direction, stopped for a few seconds, then started heading for me. Once he was within earshot he started speaking

Italian, but I interrupted him and said I was English. He stared at me, almost sneering, but started speaking English.

'So you are English,' he said looking me up and down. 'But why are you on my land?'

'I was here during the war,' I replied. 'I was a British soldier.'

'Oh,' he said, a heavy frown suddenly appearing on his forehead. 'I see.'

I was anxious to explain, to let him know I didn't mean any harm, so I continued. 'It was in 1943. I'd been captured. I was being transported near here when the truck overturned and I escaped. The family that owned this farm took me in and looked after me.'

'You live in house here?'

I shook my head. 'They owned the farm until the government took it away from them. Mussolini's laws. When I was here they lived in a house through there.' I pointed to the lane I had come down. 'But we met here, by this tree.'

He patted the tree with his dirty hands. 'We think about chopping down when we start on farm.'

'I'm glad you didn't.' We paused for a few seconds to admire the big beauty. I wanted to ask whether he had heard of Rosa Di Vito, whether he knew what had become of the family. But something was holding the words back. Only later did I realize what it was: fear of finding out.

'How did you come to own it?' I eventually said.

He eyed me suspiciously.

'Sorry,' I said, offering my hand out. 'My name's John.'

He shook my hand but didn't tell me his name. He did smile, though.

'So, did you buy this farm?' I asked.

He looked me up and down, paused for a moment, then shook his head. 'Not me. Papa. He buy from government. After war. He say . . .' Then he gritted his teeth and looked down to the mud. 'I don't know if is true but . . . Papa say other owners, they don't come back, they die in war.'

I think my face cracked, for I feared the worst – that they had all perished – although I couldn't be certain. He must have noticed my disappointment; he said he was sorry, which was kind of him.

'It's not your fault,' I said. 'You are the rightful owner.' I nodded to the farmhouse, complete with its new extension. 'And you've kept the house well. It looks beautiful.'

'*Grazie*,' he said. 'Er . . . thank you.'

He sighed and slapped his hands together. 'So. I have work. Sorry.'

'Do you mind if I stay here a while longer?' I said. 'I have . . . memories.'

He showed me a warm smile and a wink. 'Me too,' he said. Then he took a few steps back and said, 'I leave. I leave you to . . .' A twirl of his hand finished the sentence and he turned and started striding towards one of his horses.

He had taken no more than five paces before I reached for the shovel again. I knelt down and started striking the earth where I'd made the mark.

At first it felt like I was trying to dig through concrete, and I put so much effort into breaking through the surface I had to sit back and rest. But a few inches down the soil was sandy and moist. I dug like a madman, occasionally looking around to check nobody had spotted me.

Once or twice I almost gave up; two handspans is a long way to dig with a small shovel and I wondered whether Rosa really had done this, or whether I'd misheard her. Or even whether the whole thing was a fabrication of my imagination.

I took another rest, wiped my brow, then dug again.

There was nothing.

I wondered whether I had been wasting my time, sweat and hopes. But I dug to either side, then back and forth.

Seconds later the shovel hit something hard.

I plunged it down onto the same spot again. The same noise. I cracked the shovel onto a nearby stone and compared the sounds.

I leaned down and started digging frantically with my bare hands, burrowing sideways from the hole, shivering with fear at what I might find. I felt flat sides and my senses heightened. I cut myself but didn't care. This was definitely metal.

As I handled the top panel – rusted and brittle as biscuit – it gave way and my hand fell through.

It was only a small tin, and I now could feel its rusty panels from the inside. I could also feel a variety of shapes, all cold and hard. I grabbed what I could and pulled it out, laying it on the dry earth next to me. There were bracelets and necklaces, bright and pristine gold contrasting with the loose dirt they were mixed with. I searched more, ripping the box apart until it collapsed, empty.

But I had the gold.

Rosa's gold.

There were brooches, bracelets, pendants, rings and necklaces – all Di Vito gold, and still gleaming after all these years.

Then I realized what it all meant.

I fell back and started weeping at the thought.

Now I had my final proof of what had happened to Rosa. It hurt so much to accept the truth, but now I knew she had no years after the war. She didn't find a man who made her happy, she didn't get married to him and have lovely children. She didn't share seemingly endless holidays with them, she didn't blossom into a mature woman in her middle years, and there was no graceful decline into old age. She was, truly, forever young.

For all my adult life I'd been searching for something, although I didn't know quite what it was at the time. Now my search had come to an end, here under the canopy of the old olive tree where I first saw her.

I felt broken – just as much as I had done in 1945 – and sat under that old olive tree until my tears dried up.

By the time I was being driven away from Valleverde in a taxi, I had regained a little composure – at least enough to hide the gold in my pockets. But now I struggled to accept my old maxim that every day was a sunny day. In all those years since the war ended I'd experienced a few bad times, but there had been so many sights, sounds, experiences, good people, good food, laughter and more. So much that Rosa had missed out on. I looked through the taxi window and up to the skies. Perhaps, I thought, perhaps one day I would be able to share those good times with her.

As I looked at the roadside speeding past me I also thought of Lorenzo, and our trek together that was, for him, a trek too far. That was when I had my final visitation from the past.

He is on the ground by the roadside, fallen for the second time, with dark oblivion in his eyes.

I try to pull him up, but can't.

He croaks a few words out. I lean closer to him to hear.

'Promise . . . promise me something,' he says.

'Anything,' I answer.

'Anna and Lorenzo Junior,' he says, a single tear lending life to his face.

'What about them?'

'If you live, if it's true about the gold, make sure Anna and Lorenzo Junior get it. Tell them I'm sorry. I should have . . . I should have been a better father.'

I tug him by the coat, almost roughly. 'Lorenzo, listen to me,' I say. 'It won't come to that.' I try to lift him again. But I am too weak.

'Please, Mac. Please promise me.'

'Of course,' I say. 'I promise you.'

'*Grazie*,' he says. There is a smile on his face the like of which I haven't seen for months. But those are his final words before succumbing to the cold, the hunger and the exhaustion. I shake him a couple of times, but I know what I have in my hands isn't Lorenzo anymore. Then the guard appears. He doesn't shoot Lorenzo; we both know the bullet would be wasted. I am too exhausted to cry. I am beyond tears.

I walk on, alone.

It was then, thinking of his last words, groaned to me through the freezing air, that the balance of my mind changed. Of course, *there was more*. Lorenzo's last words to me were the same as Rosa's. They both said I was to make sure Anna and Lorenzo Junior received the gold. Yes, *they* were its rightful owners.

This was not the *end* of my search, but the *beginning*. After all, I was retired now and had the time. I would get home, search for Anna and Lorenzo Junior, and pass the Di Vito family gold on to them – for the memory of Rosa.

The taxi took me to the railway station to collect my suitcase, and from there to the airport. At the booking desk I asked about the next flight to Heathrow. I was told there were three places left, and almost fainted with joy. I tried to sleep but was too scared of missing my flight. A few hours later I passed through security with my heart thumping, then fidgeted all the way, unable to rest or eat for fear I would be searched.

Even when we touched down I couldn't settle, my thoughts a haze of trepidation as I drifted through customs. And in the taxi from Heathrow to Henley I gripped my pockets tightly as if some thief were sitting next to me waiting to pounce if I dropped my guard.

When I got back to 77 Victoria Road I locked the door behind me and let out the calmest breath to escape my lips for many hours. I was hungry but too tired to eat. I hid the gold in my old briefcase in the cellar, then staggered up to my bedroom. I took off my shoes, slipped into bed fully clothed, and was asleep within seconds.

CHAPTER THIRTY-THREE

Nicole slowly put the notebook down and listened. Her mind's ear heard the front door shut, then a few gasps, followed by the slow thump of elderly feet on the stairs.

A shiver spread up her back to her neck, and she tried to shake the thought from her mind.

Was it the ghost of Mac wandering through the house?

No. She didn't believe in ghosts.

She steadied herself and listened again.

Nothing. It was just her imagination.

She flicked through the notebook. There were only a few pages left. She steadied her nerves, ready to find out what Mac had done when he'd come home, exhausted, that night in 1992. She started reading where she'd left off a few minutes before.

Then she yelped and dropped the notebook as she heard the front door slam shut.

This time it was for real, just as real as the hurried footsteps on the stairs.

The bedroom door opened and Nicole held her breath tightly.

'Evening, love,' her mother said.

Nicole's body sank down as she sighed in relief. 'Mum. God. You frightened me.'

'Why? Who did you think it was?'

'Oh . . .' She sighed again. 'Oh, nobody. It doesn't matter.'

'Right. Good.' Her mother let out a long groan. 'Boy, am I glad to get that week out of the way. I think I need a drink. Have you been okay today?'

I was until a minute ago, Nicole wanted to say. Instead she just nodded.

'So what have you been doing all day?'

'Not much. Bit of ironing, watching TV, reading and stuff.'

Her mother's eyes darted to the notebook. 'Is that what you've been reading?'

Nicole gave a guarded nod.

'I thought you were reading a book. What's that? What is it?'

Nicole grabbed it. 'It's nothing.'

'Let me see.'

'It's nothing, Mum. Just what I'm reading. No big deal.'

'Strange-looking thing. Looks ancient. Where did you get it from?'

Nicole clasped it to her chest. 'Let me finish it first. I'm nearly at the end.'

Her mother still stared at the notebook, and looked like she was fighting a puzzled expression. 'Oh, all right,' she said eventually. 'Anyway, time to get the working week out of my system.' She stepped back towards the bedroom door, but lingered there and looked across at Nicole's face as though examining it. 'Nicole, you are all right, aren't you?'

'Yes.'

'I mean, you would tell me if anything was troubling you – I mean, anything I don't already know about?'

Nicole nodded. 'I would, Mum. But I just need to finish this.' She tapped the notebook.

'Okay, love. Are you going to rowing practice later on?'

'I don't know.' She raised her eyebrows at her mother and nodded to the door.

Her mother tutted, then left.

Nicole picked up the notebook and started to read again.

CHAPTER THIRTY-FOUR

Today is 8 September 2006.

I suppose you might call this an author's epilogue.

It still seems strange to think of myself as an author, and even stranger that this is the last part of this piece of work I'll ever write.

And for what?

Will anyone ever read it?

Who knows?

Way back in 1992, when I left Valleverde for the second time, I found I had a new purpose in life. And I acted on that purpose, writing innumerable letters to various American agencies, Jewish refugee associations and Holocaust survivor groups trying to trace Rosa's niece and nephew. Of course, the replies were polite, stressing the scale of the diaspora of Jewish refugees across the globe, of the problems recording their whereabouts and keeping track of them as they moved from country to country. They said Anna and Lorenzo Junior might even have been adopted and given different names. All of this was well meaning, but it didn't help me.

After about five years I gave up – called off the search. That was hard, but I came to accept it. After all, I had no idea where they'd gone apart from a vague notion it had been America.

In 2000, as we all celebrated the new millennium and hoped for better futures, the positive, joyous atmosphere convinced me I should mark my seventy-fifth birthday by trying to find Anna and Lorenzo again. Now I realized they could have gone to any of a dozen or more countries, so I tried writing to the same types of organizations in Canada, Australia and New Zealand. All I got was more of those polite letters. I'd previously assumed they would want to stay as far from Europe as possible, but eventually reconsidered – out of desperation, I suppose – and tried here in the UK too and even Italy. The latter was in spite of my feeling that they would almost certainly have returned to Valleverde if so, and hence I would have known about them from my visit.

Again, I drew a blank.

In 2005 I tried a third time. I took my book to many literary agents with a view to getting it published, the theory being that if it got published it would get a little publicity, which might have reached Anna and Lorenzo, wherever they were in the world.

None of them were interested.

So now, in 2006, I finally have to admit defeat. I've put so much work into this project – it's sixteen years since I started my memoir – that I feel it's part of me. But I've given up all realistic hope of anyone being interested in reading it – or of me ever finding the people I seek. It hurts, but only in my mind, and then only if I let it. So now I'll bow to the wisdom of Dylan Thomas; I've done my work, and now I'll take that rest I've found, thank you very much, Mr Thomas.

Also I'm now in my eighty-second year. My heart feels heavier with each passing year, my willpower weaker. Not to mention my eyesight. So I'm finding it increasingly difficult to summon up the enthusiasm to go down to the cellar – my writing room. Of course, that could be fear that my knees, more arthritic with each passing year, won't be able to bring my sag-bag of a body back up.

To be accurate, my head has admitted defeat; in my heart there remains a whisper of optimism. I've written to a huge number of people over the years, both in formal approaches to find the children, and in trying to get the book published. There's always a chance that someone will write back to me with details. I took my Rosa's gold out of the briefcase long ago; now it's safe and appropriately hidden, should that 'someone' ever contact me.

Whether I get such a letter or, more likely now, die with the story, I know I've led something of a charmed life. Many would disagree, but it's the way I feel. And it's the way I *want* to feel.

Sometimes you just have to put your losses to one side, see that the sun still shines, and force yourself to smile up to it.

Because to me – even now, with my failing health – every day is still a sunny day.

CHAPTER THIRTY-FIVE

Nicole sat up on her bed. She flicked back through the handwritten pages of the notebook, and forward through the blank ones.

That was it. That really was the last part of Mac's memoir.

Before she knew it she was struggling to hold back the tears. *Why did the story have to end like that?* It took a few confused minutes to work it out, but it made sense. Mac's story *did* end there. The stroke must have come soon after that, followed at some stage by whatever illness had killed him.

The gold hardly seemed to matter; Mac's last wish mattered.

She read the last line of the 'epilogue' again, and slowly closed the notebook.

A few minutes later she heard Mum's footsteps on the stairs, followed by a knock at the door, and it seemed pointless trying to hide the thing now. She blew her nose and said it was okay to come in.

'When are you going to your—?'

Her mother stopped there. Nicole could feel her glare.

Red eyes and nose; was it that obvious?

'Oh, *Nicole*.' The last word was drawn out, so yes, her mother had definitely noticed.

Complete giveaway.

She sat down next to Nicole and put out a hand, hesitating at first, then gently stroking her hair. She had that pained expression reserved for the sympathy speech.

'Oh, love,' she said. 'I'm sorry. I know it's hard for you – new town, not seeing your dad and all that.'

'What?'

'Look, Nicole. I've said you can bring your dad back here any time you want; it doesn't matter if I'm in or—'

'It's not always about *you*, Mum.'

The hair stroking stopped abruptly, and she looked at her daughter's frown. 'I beg your pardon?'

'I said, *It's not about you*. Or Dad. Or living in Henley.'

'Oh. I see.' Her mother frowned. 'So . . . why have you been crying?'

Nicole slapped a hand on the notebook beside her. 'This.'

'What do you mean? What are you talking about?'

'It's Mac's book.'

'Mac who?' Her mother's face froze for a second, then lit up slightly. 'You don't mean the old man who used to live here?'

Nicole nodded. 'The book's about the war. He was in the war.'

'So?'

Nicole handed her the notebook. 'Read it. Go on, just read it.'

'But I . . . I can't.'

'Why not?'

Nicole's mother took the book from her hands, then flicked through the first few pages. 'I just can't, love. I don't have time for reading books. And if I did have time it's . . . it's not my sort of thing.'

'But it's *important*, Mum.'

Her mother flicked through the whole book this time, with a sluggishness that said 'uninterested'. Then she screwed up her face slightly and said, 'Oh, come on, love. Is it *really* that important?'

'It's important *to me*,' Nicole replied, her teeth gritted.

Her mother looked at her face for a few seconds. 'I've never seen you like this before, Nicole. Are you sure you're okay?'

Nicole thought about it for a few moments.

Well, she wasn't okay; she felt sad. But maybe reading the story hadn't been the wisest thing to do. Maybe Mum was right and she was getting things out of proportion.

She shook her head and said, 'Oh, I don't know. I'm just feeling a bit sad because of Dad and trying to sort out college and . . .'

'I can understand that, love. It's been a difficult time for us all. Me included. And whatever's wrong, you'll get over it. I know you will.'

Nicole paused, then drew a sharp breath. 'Actually, d'you know what, Mum? I'll take that back.'

'What? What do you mean?'

'It's nothing to do with Dad or the new town or college. It's about a man's life.'

'Don't be silly, darling. What do you mean, "*a man's life*"?'

Nicole reached over and tapped her finger on the notebook a few times. 'You need to read this, Mum, you really do. Then you'll understand.'

Her mother placed the notebook down on the bed and stood up. 'I can't, love. I know it might mean a lot to you. I get that. But . . . well, let's see.'

'But, Mum, there's gold. I think there's gold somewhere in this house.'

Her mother gave a wide smile, then said, 'Darling, it's only a book. And by all accounts the poor man wasn't all there in his later years.' She tapped her index finger on her temple.

'But—'

'Remember what next door said. The old man even got upset when they wanted to chop a few trees down or dig up the garden.'

Nicole wanted to speak but couldn't get the words out.

Her mother continued. 'Anyway, I think I'll stay in tonight.' She checked her watch. 'And you're going to rowing practice, aren't you?'

'Well, I was, but . . .'

'And I think you still should.'

Nicole grimaced and placed her hand on her forehead. 'You know, I'm not sure I feel up to it.'

'No. It'll do you good. Definitely. You go, and I'll have a meal ready for when you get back. Okay?'

'Well . . . okay.'

'Good girl.' Her mother kissed her on the top of the head and left the room.

Half an hour later Nicole still hadn't decided whether or not to go along with her mother's idea. Her mind kept flitting back to the gold, hidden somewhere in the house.

Could there be a secret compartment in one of the rooms? The place was small enough for that. But no, it was unlikely; old Mac wouldn't have bothered with plasterboard and paint, and definitely wouldn't have involved anyone else.

Under the floorboards was more likely, but where? And if he had problems getting up those steep steps from the cellar he surely would have had problems kneeling down and reaching under the floor.

One thing was certain: when he'd taken the jewellery out of his briefcase – to put it wherever he'd put it – he'd forgotten one ring.

Yes. One ring.

Yes. That was it. If she showed the ring to Mum it might persuade her there was something in this story, something that wasn't just the fantasy of a bumbling old fool.

She jumped off the bed and trotted downstairs.

'Mum?'

Silence.

She tried again, but heard only the faint zoom of a car passing outside.

But Mum would have told her if she was going out.

Then she went into the kitchen and spotted her mother at the bottom of the garden, on the phone. Nicole laid a hand on the door handle, then looked across at her mother again. Something was wrong.

Mum was gesticulating, shaking her head, occasionally shouting, as far as Nicole could see.

Who the hell was she on the phone to?

Whatever. Perhaps this wasn't the right moment.

Actually, perhaps it *was* the right moment – the right moment to get out of the house.

Yes, perhaps Mum had a point. A couple of hours away from this house and exercising on the river might make her think more clearly.

She ran back upstairs, gathered her sports kit, more or less threw it on, then ran downstairs.

Grab a cold drink from the fridge to take to rowing.

When she closed the fridge door the back door opened.

'You're going then?' her mother – her *very red-faced* mother – said. 'Good.'

'I . . . I thought you were right, I should go. I mean, if that's cool with you.'

Her mother stepped towards her. 'Come here,' she said quietly. She curled an arm up and around Nicole's shoulder. They hugged briefly.

'You go, love. It'll do you good.' She reached up and kissed Nicole on the forehead.

Nicole nodded. They parted and she headed for the front door.

'About two hours, isn't it?'

'Usually about that, yeah.'

Nicole left.

A few minutes later, at the end of Victoria Road, Nicole took a few deep breaths and shook the cobwebs from her head.

Round past the corner shop.

Yes, she felt a bit better already. There was time to sort Mac out later, whatever she decided to do, whatever Mum thought about the whole thing.

Straight on to the river.

But she would do something. She would.

At the river she halted. She looked towards town, to where the pawnbroker shop was, where she'd almost sold the ring.

Well, she hadn't. That was a *good* thing.

She started walking again.

Oh, God, she thought. *Yes, I want to get rowing. I need to get my mind off Mac for just an hour or so. He would understand; he knew the escape rowing brought with it, pulling your body down a river under your own steam.*

Over the bridge, turn right, and the usual suspects were waiting at Danver's Shed: a few girls, a few boys, a few boats.

'Bit late,' Shaun said.

Nicole froze for a second. 'Sorry, I was . . . I was . . .'

'He's kidding,' Austin said.

Shaun produced a winning smile, winked at Nicole, then said, 'Just ignore me.'

'Everyone else does,' Austin added.

They started off with some stretching exercises, then Nicole went rowing with the same three women again. She steeled herself to do better than the last time, to hold her own, but very soon oar struck oar, the occasional groan was heard. Nicole tried again to zone in on the rhythm, to concentrate.

But something stopped her. She just couldn't keep her mind focused. Something was getting in the way.

She apologized. Then there was a barely disguised huff. One of the girls said, 'Give her a break,' and turned around to give her a twisted smile. 'We've all got to start somewhere.'

Another glanced at her and said, 'Guess so. Sorry.'

Austin and Shaun passed them in a double scull, crimson-faced and puffing away but also all sinewy strength and synchronized grace.

The women reached the turning point just in time to see Shaun and Austin set off again back to Danver's Shed. Austin gave her a brief smile, then his face returned to that distinct relaxed concentration and they were gone. Likewise, the women rested for a few minutes, took a drink, then rowed back towards Danver's Shed.

When they got there the other three girls hopped out, leaving Nicole struggling to balance.

'How'd it go?' Austin said, holding the boat steady for her.

She made a face like she'd just smelled something gone off. He laughed. She laughed.

'I'm beginning to think . . . perhaps rowing isn't for me.'

'Rubbish,' he said. 'You've got the body for it. After that it's usually just practice.'

'Thanks. But really, I'm thinking perhaps I should go home.'

'Oh, don't go.'

'But my mind's not really on it.'

'No, no.' Austin wagged his head from side to side. 'You're missing the point. Just relax your mind, take yourself away.'

Nicole took a drink, and glanced across the river. Towards home.

'Don't go now,' Austin said. 'You're not even halfway through the session yet. Look, I'll take you out. In the double.'

Nicole looked at his face, a puffy red, and his body, glistening with sweat. 'But you must be exhausted. You two were really going for it back there.'

He shrugged, stood tall, and squirted a few slugs of fluid into his mouth. He swallowed and said, 'Come on. I could do with a warm down.'

'Cool,' she said. 'You're on.'

'Great.' He pointed his bottle towards Shaun, who was wiping himself down with a towel and also talking to a middle-aged man. 'Anyway, Captain Bullshit's busy talking to his old man. I'd be on my own otherwise.'

'Oh, thanks. That makes me feel special.'

'Perhaps you are, perhaps you're not.' A lop-sided smile appeared on his face. 'But . . . I think you might be.'

Nicole blushed and told him to shut up.

They got in and soon were rowing along in slow but strong strokes.

That was better. More relaxing.

After a strenuous ten minutes they steered the boat towards the bank, let it drift slightly, and stopped for a rest.

'See?' Austin said.

Nicole turned to the side so she could see him. 'See what?'

'That was good. You're better than you think.'

'Yeah, right.'

Austin laughed. 'No, really. You're doing the right thing. Don't let anyone tell you otherwise.'

Nicole thought for a moment.

Mmm . . . Don't let anyone tell you otherwise.

Her mind ran with the words.

You're doing the right thing.

She drew breath, then said as casually as she could, 'You know Mac?'

Austin let out a gentle chuckle. 'Are you still on about him?'

'I'm serious. It's *important*.'

'I know but . . .' His mouth straightened when he noticed her expression. 'Oh. Sorry. I didn't realize.' He pointed back in the vague direction of Danver's Shed. 'Listen, when we get back why don't I introduce you to Shaun's dad. He knows everything about him.'

'Would you?'

'No problem. If you really want you can arrange to meet him.'

Nicole frowned. 'Meet Shaun's dad, you mean?'

'Well, yeah. Meet Shaun's dad.'

'Yes.' Nicole sighed.

'And then meet Mac too if you like.'

For a second Nicole struggled to find words – any words at all; the only things she was conscious of were the lapping of the water and the slightly boggy smell of the mud a few feet away.

She turned around in the boat a little more, almost tipping it over. 'Erm . . . What do you mean?'

'Watch it,' Austin said, grabbing the hull, trying to steady the boat. 'What I mean is what I say, you can meet up with Mac if you really want to.'

'But . . . he's dead . . . isn't he?'

Austin spurted out a laugh. 'Dead? Old Mac? Who told you that?'

'But I thought . . . The house . . .' She glared at him. 'I thought the house was sold by the council or something. He died and the council . . .'

'Look. I'm sorry. Didn't mean to laugh. It's just . . . I thought you knew. He went into an old folks' home on the outskirts of town. I'm guessing the council must have sold his house to pay for his care. He's not too well these days, but he's alive and kicking.'

'Are you sure?'

'Yeah. Shaun's dad goes and visits him every week.'

Nicole froze for a few seconds, then she said, 'I need to get out,' and stood up.

'Woah!' Austin grabbed the hull again.

'I need to get home.'

'Okay, okay. Just give me a second.' Austin settled back into his seat and rowed slowly towards the riverbank. 'If I can get an oar close to—'

Before he could finish the sentence Nicole had taken a leap into the shallow water.

She heard a splash from behind but carried on paddling, then clambered up onto the grassy edges of the riverbank. She turned around to see Austin knee-deep in water, lifting the boat sideways, tipping water out of it.

'Sorry!' she shouted.

He shrugged and shouted back, 'What did I say?'

'Tell you some other time!'

She started running.

Nicole felt the need to stop at some point for fear of bringing on one of those headaches, but was still out of breath by the time she reached the corner shop, and broke into a jog again as she turned into Victoria Road.

She fumbled, fingers trembling, and cursed as she dropped the key on the path outside the front door. A quick swipe grabbed it, and she was in.

'Mum?' she shouted out as she slammed the door.

She ran into the living room and halted, panting but standing stock-still. Staring.

'*Dad?*'

She looked at him, then across to her mother, sitting on another chair. Her eyes darted between them.

'Hello, poppet,' her father said, as casually as if . . . *as if they were all still living together.*

'Been for a jog?' he added, then noticed her feet, wet and muddy, and pointed at them, speechless.

'Wh . . . what's happening?' Nicole said.

'You're home early,' her mother said. 'Didn't expect you back yet.'

'How long's Dad been here?'

Her father motioned to a full cup of tea in his hand. 'About two minutes.' His head hopped between Nicole and her mother. 'Look, will one of you tell me what's going on?'

'Why's Dad here?'

'Your mum asked me over, she said—'

'I don't think I did,' Nicole's mother said. 'I called you up and told you about Nicole, and you insisted on coming over.'

Her father fiddled with his hands for a few seconds and said, 'Well . . . I mean . . . What does it matter? You said you thought Nicole was acting a bit strange and—'

'Oh, well,' her mother said. 'No, it doesn't really matter. I was just saying I didn't actually ask you over, you—'

'Mum! Dad! Will you both please *shut up*!'

Her father's face was like ice, her mother's like thunder.

'I haven't been acting strange.' Nicole dropped herself onto an armchair. 'But never mind that now. Mum. Listen.' She took a breath. 'Mac's *alive*!'

'Alive?' her mother said. 'But—'

'Mac's alive and well. Austin just told me. He's in a care home somewhere in Henley. The council sold his house to pay for it. He's alive, Mum. *He's still alive!*'

'Who's Mac?' her father said.

'I told you on the phone,' her mother replied. 'You should try listening. Nicole's been reading this notebook. The man who lived here before us wrote it. It's his war memoirs. I just thought she was taking it a bit too seriously.'

Nicole's father snorted a laugh. '*War memoirs?* Not your usual read, Nicole.' His face straightened. 'And who's Austin?'

'Oh, it doesn't matter,' Nicole said, shaking her head. 'There's lots of gold too. And Anna and Lorenzo. Somewhere. He was looking for them. But he just wrote letters and stuff because it was before the internet, but I *know* we can find them for him, I'm *sure* we can.'

'Who are Anna and Lorenzo?' her mother said.

'Just a minute.' Her father drew a shallow breath. 'Did you say "*gold*"?'

Nicole looked at each of her parents in turn. 'And the thing about the gold,' she said. 'I can show you. There's one gold ring in the cellar, and I'm sure there's a lot more somewhere in this house.' She went to speak further, then checked herself as she saw the expressions of suspicion on their faces. She sighed before continuing, 'I know you think I'm mad, I know you think I'm only seventeen and don't know anything. But . . . Look. Long story short. You both really, really need to read this notebook.'

Her father stared at her for another few seconds, his mouth open. 'Erm . . .' he said, and looked to her mother, who just shrugged.

'Yes,' he eventually said. 'Okay. We can read the notebook, but . . .'

'But what?' Nicole said. 'What's the problem?'

He squirmed in his seat. 'All this talk of gold – gold that doesn't belong to us. If it's true perhaps we need to get the police involved.'

Nicole gave her head a firm shake. 'We don't need them. We can find out what happened ourselves. And . . . I want to do something for Mac myself. We can use genealogy sites and all sorts of online user groups.'

'But this sounds like pretty serious stuff here, Nicole. Don't you think . . . ?' He turned to her mother. 'Karen?'

They both looked to Nicole's mother.

She went to speak, checked herself, then tried again. 'I think . . . Nicole's seventeen. I think perhaps we should go along with what she wants, and help her as long as we're not doing anything illegal.'

Her father pursed his lips in thought for a moment, then gave a cautious nod. 'Okay,' he said. 'So you want us to read this notebook? I'll go with that. It's just . . .'

'Just what?' Nicole said.

He glanced at his watch. 'That's going to take time. I mean . . . I could come over tomorrow instead? Or I could . . .'

Nicole looked at her mother. 'Mum?'

'Mmm . . .' Her mother looked down again. 'Well . . . I guess . . . under the circumstances you could stop the night.' She looked up and gave him a stern stare. '*On the couch.*'

Nicole's father frowned. 'Oh, of course, of course.' He turned to Nicole. 'So we need to read this book thing, and then what? What's this gold you're talking about?'

'It's somewhere in the house,' Nicole answered.

'So . . . we look for it?'

'Well, yes. But there's something else we need to do, something much more important.'

'What's that?' Nicole's mother said.

'I'd have thought it was obvious,' Nicole said. 'We need to find out where Mac lives and pay him a visit.'

Her mother and father looked across at each other and nodded.

CHAPTER THIRTY-SIX

Nicole and her parents spent the rest of Friday evening poring over Mac's notebook. It was a skim read, with Nicole filling in the gaps and her mother jotting down the important details.

They took a break to eat a delivered Chinese meal, then continued to study the book until Nicole started to get a headache and her father insisted they all stop and get some sleep.

As Nicole settled into bed the headache subsided, quelled by the warm feeling that the man she'd been reading about was still alive. Being able to get a goodnight kiss from both Mum and Dad probably helped too.

The next morning it didn't take long to find out where Mac was living; there weren't too many care homes in Henley and Nicole's mother and father took turns to ring them, each time saying they were old family friends and confidently giving 'Uncle John's' full name and date of birth.

Finding the gold took longer.

Nicole's father insisted they look for it. 'Just to see where we stand,' he said. 'Just so we know what we're dealing with.'

'What do you mean by that?' Nicole asked.

'Well,' he said, 'if we find Mac it wouldn't be a good idea to give him false hopes if, for instance, we find out the gold's gone missing.'

Then he and Nicole's mother exchanged one of those knowing glances Nicole hadn't seen for some time.

'What?' she said. 'What is it?'

Her father frowned. 'The other possibility, of course . . .'

'Yes?'

'Well, it's only a story as far as we know.'

Nicole looked at him, slightly aghast, then looked to her mother.

'Your dad's right,' she said. 'We don't really know anything for sure. Mac might have made it all up.'

There was a grim silence before Nicole's father jumped up from his seat and said, 'We're just trying to be realistic, love. But come on, let's look.'

Nicole searched upstairs, her father downstairs, and her mother the cellar. Each was looking for signs of false walls or ruffled carpet or loose floorboards or some sort of partition.

None was successful.

In the middle of the morning, over a cup of tea, they came to the conclusion that the gold – if it existed – must have been in the cellar somewhere, because the rest of the house had been cleared out. So they all went down there and took a more purposeful look around.

There were small containers everywhere that they hadn't searched – old margarine tubs, old glass jars, tin jars, small wooden boxes.

'Come on,' said Nicole's mother. 'It won't take too long to check all of these.'

'Could be a waste of time,' her father said with a sigh. 'I mean, if it exists it could be buried in the garden or anywhere.'

'Mmm,' her mother said. 'I'm trying to remember. Did he say

it's hidden in the house, or hidden at home, or hidden at 77 Victoria Road?' She turned to Nicole. 'Can you remember?'

Nicole shook her head. 'He just said . . .' – she thought for a couple of seconds – '. . . *appropriately hidden*, I think.'

'What does that mean?'

'Search me,' Nicole answered. Then she looked around the cellar, her eyes running along the two rows of tins and jars on the shelf above the makeshift table. Her gaze rested on one in particular.

'What about that one?' She pointed to it.

'The wooden cylinder thing?' her father asked.

'No. The tin one, top shelf in the corner.'

'You mean the one with the . . . what *is* that on it?'

Nicole's mother completed the sentence: 'The one with the rose on it.'

'Definitely sounds appropriate,' her father said. He looked to Nicole, she nodded, and he started clambering onto the wooden door that formed the makeshift desk.

'*Careful!*' her mother said.

He turned around, and gave her a lingering look.

'Sorry,' she said. 'It was just . . . you know, force of habit.'

'Thanks anyway,' he said, then edged to the far side, where he carefully got to his feet and reached up and across. It was an old biscuit tin, and it had something the texture of gravel inside by the sound of it. He lifted the lid and stared into it. His jaw fell and his face paled a shade.

'Well?' Nicole snapped.

He tilted the tin towards them. Even in the dim light there was no mistaking that yellowy lustre, almost as if it was giving out its own light.

'Oh, God,' Nicole's mother said. 'Oh . . . God. You were right.' She stood still, staring at the pile of gold brooches, bracelets, rings, necklaces and pendants. 'Nicole, you were right.'

Nicole's father gave a swallow and puffed a breath out. 'I . . . I have to admit half of me was just going along with it.' He turned to the other two. 'We have to take this to the police,' he said. 'We really do.'

'No, Dad,' Nicole groaned. 'I trusted you. Please don't mess it all up.'

'But, love, this must be worth thousands,' he said. '*Tens* of thousands.'

'It's not ours,' Nicole said. 'Wait and see what happens – what happens with Mac.'

'What if it gets stolen?' he replied. 'I'd never forgive myself. We *could* take it to the bank.'

'Put it back,' Nicole said.

'But—'

'You know the story, Dad. It's been in that tin for years.' She turned to her mother. 'Tell him, Mum.'

'Well?' her father said.

Her mother drew a breath before answering. 'Let's do this Nicole's way,' she answered. 'Put it back.'

Her father nodded, put the lid back on, and carefully placed it back where it came from, the furthest point of the highest shelf. 'God knows how an old guy put it up there,' he said as he clambered down.

'I guess it shows how determined he was,' Nicole's mother said. 'How much it meant to him.'

He nodded. 'Yes. Of course. Sorry.'

A few hours later their car pulled up on the driveway of the Shiplake Care Home with a rough scrunch of gravel.

'You sure you want to see him alone?' Nicole's father said.

'I'm sure.'

While he rang the doorbell, her mother gave her a hug and wished her good luck.

'We'll be waiting in reception,' she said. 'If you need us, if any-thing . . . happens.'

'I'll be fine,' Nicole said, with hint of flutter in her voice. 'It'll freak the poor guy out if all three of us pile in.'

But the flutter grew as she asked the receptionist what room John MacDonald was in.

'You mean Mac?' the woman said cheerfully. 'He'll be pleased; he doesn't get many visitors.'

She gave directions – down the corridor, room sixteen – and Nicole followed them, mouth getting dryer the closer she got. She took two deep breaths and looked round the open door of room sixteen.

The décor was dated, although it was a functional room, with little more than an armchair, a single bed, a small TV and a sink. But it was a little impersonal, with no photos to be seen. An old man was sitting in the armchair with his back to the window. It could have been any old man – grey trousers, blue patterned zip-up cardigan, thinning backcombed hair – sitting upright, hardback book in hand, thick glasses perched on red-marbled nose.

Nicole gave the door a few gentle taps with her knuckle.

He looked up, peered over his glasses, and appeared to be squeezing his eyeballs towards her, one side of his face reluctant to follow the lead of the other.

'Are you Mac?'

'That's what everybody calls me.' His voice was low and hoarse, the odd syllable hanging onto his larynx, refusing to come out, and one side of his mouth moved more than the other.

'Can I come in?'

He straightened his back slightly. 'Of course, but are you sure it's me you're after?'

Nicole nodded. 'Didn't they tell you to expect a visitor?'

'I'm sorry. Yes, of course. But . . . I must have forgotten who you are.'

'You haven't.' She walked over and sat down next to him, holding out her hand. 'I'm Nicole. We've never met before.'

He put down his book and glasses, and shook her hand. His hold was firm, his skin thin and smooth.

'How are you?' she said.

He gave a curious smile as his gaze ran over her face. 'Bit puzzled,' he said. 'Not complaining seeing as how I don't get many visitors, but a bit puzzled.'

'You see, I need to talk to you.'

A chuckle escaped from his mouth, like one from a naughty schoolboy, and there was a sparkle in his eyes that was at odds with the overhang of saggy skin around them. 'Say what you want, love. My usual visitors are middle-aged men.'

Nicole couldn't help but smile.

'And you don't need to speak,' he continued. 'Just sit there and I can look at you.'

'Mac,' she said with a calm firmness. 'I'm trying to be serious here.'

'Don't want to be serious. Never serious. Life's too short for that. Well, mine is anyway. You'll be different, of course. What are you, seventeen?'

'How did you know that?'

'Just practice.' He laughed again, his bony shoulders bouncing up and down almost imperceptibly. Thin, cracked lips spread even wider. 'So aren't you going to tell me who you are?'

'I'm trying.' Nicole drew breath and tried to straighten her face. 'We've just moved into your old house – me and my mum.'

'Oh.' His smile faltered slightly but hung on. 'Oh.'

'Mac, I found the briefcase in the cellar. I've been reading your notebook – with all your wartime stuff in it. Yeah?'

His face took on the air of a balloon slowly deflating. Smile turned to fearful frown. He gulped and said, 'Did you read all of it?'

'Every word, Mac, every last word.'

The old man's hands rose to his face and covered his eyes for a few seconds.

'It's all right, Mac,' she said. 'All I want—'

'No, no, no,' he muttered. 'You don't understand.'

'What? What is it?' Nicole held the old man's hands, gently easing them down from his face.

'Been trying to forget it. I don't . . . I don't think I can talk about it.'

'But I want to help you, Mac. I know what you've been trying to do – to find Lorenzo and Anna. And I think I can help.'

Mac said nothing, just looked at Nicole, then turned his face away.

'What is it, Mac?'

The old man swallowed a few times, preparing himself before speaking.

'You say you've read the book, the notebook I wrote?'

Nicole nodded.

'I spent so long looking for those two kids. I wanted to tell them about their father, about their Aunt Rosa, about what happened.'

Two shiny tracks appeared below his eyes. Nicole tugged a handkerchief from her pocket and offered it up to his face.

'It's embarrassing, crying like this.'

'Nah. Everybody cries.'

He smiled and said, 'You know I tried to find them?'

'I know, Mac.'

'Anna and Lorenzo.' His jaw dropped and took three troublesome breaths. 'I tried for years, must have written hundreds of letters.'

'You didn't use the internet, though, did you?' she said. 'There's loads of stuff on the internet to help find people.' She watched a teardrop linger on the red rim of his eye, then breach its dam. She pressed the handkerchief up to his cheek.

'I know this must be a bit of a shock to you.'

'Damn right it is,' he said breathlessly.

She spent a few seconds listening to him wheeze himself back to recovery, then said, 'Look, I don't want to pressure you. Perhaps I should just leave it.'

He said nothing, but turned his face away from her and appeared to be examining the wallpaper.

'If it's too upsetting for you I'll just leave the whole thing. I'll bring the gold to you and I won't do anything else.'

He gasped and shot her a glance. 'You found it?'

She nodded.

He wiped his face again, looked down to his lap, and thought for a moment. 'No,' he said, shaking his head, jowls wagging. 'I'm just an old fool. Just ignore me.' Then he turned to her and grabbed her hand, squeezing it tightly. 'No. They need to know these things. They need to have what's theirs, what their father and aunt wanted them to have. If you've read my notebook you'll understand.'

'Oh, I do, Mac. I do.' Nicole looked at his furrowed brow and said, 'You sure you're okay?'

He looked directly at her. She saw the corners of his mouth twitching; she felt a lifetime of courage hit her from the glint in the old man's eyes.

'You do it if you can, love,' he said. 'Please.'

'I will.'

'Then it's a deal,' he said.

They smiled.

Then Nicole said, 'I need to talk to you, though, about Anna and Lorenzo. You need to tell me anything else you can remember – anything not in the notebook that might help me trace them.'

He pushed his strands of hair back across the top of his head. 'Oh, yes, well . . . I'm not sure I can think straight just now. My mind's a tizz.'

'Maybe you need a rest.'

He nodded. 'Think so.'

'Do you want me to come back this afternoon?'

Mac thought for a moment, then nodded. 'I . . . I really need a rest.'

'Of course.'

He reached out for her again and grabbed her hand. 'You will come back, won't you?'

'Try and stop me.'

He smiled. 'You know, sweetheart, if you do this for me you'll make an old man die happy.'

'Nah, tough as old boots you. You've got a few more years yet.'

Still Mac's bony hand held onto hers. He shook it slightly. 'I hope so. A few more sunny days.'

'Yeah.' Nicole started to beam a smile. 'Yeah. That's you, that is, sunny days.'

He lowered his voice. 'You know, sweetheart, if you can do this thing for me, I don't know how I can repay you. I'll just have to owe you.'

Nicole gave his hand one last squeeze as she got up to leave. 'I don't think so, Mac. You'll never owe me anything.'

The mood was sombre on the drive back to 77 Victoria Road.

'So, did he tell you anything?' Nicole's mother said after half a mile.

'I'd leave her for a bit,' her father replied quietly.

'I was only asking, that's all.'

'Yes, but she—'

'Stop trying to tell me what to do, Barry.'

'But she as good as burst into tears the second we got in the car. Give her a break.'

'Stop arguing,' Nicole said quietly, sniffing tears away. '*Please.*'

After a long pause her father said, 'Sorry.'

Her mother said the same, then added, 'Sorry to you too, Barry. I'm just a bit . . .'

'I know,' he said. 'No need to apologize, not to me.'

Nicole waited for them to carry on, but there was silence. 'We've got to go back this afternoon,' she eventually said.

'Oh?'

'He was too upset to talk just now, poor guy.'

'That's fine,' her father said. 'Whatever you want.'

'What I want is for you two to stop arguing.'

'Yes,' her mother said. 'I think we should.'

Her father nodded agreement.

'You've been getting on well so far,' Nicole said. 'That's the first time you've had a go at each other.' Neither of her parents spoke. She leaned over from the back seat, close to her mother. 'Mum, could Dad sleep over again tonight?'

'Oh, I don't know about that,' her father said.

'It would help me,' Nicole said. 'I mean, it would help me find Anna and Lorenzo.'

Her father glanced to the side. 'I've really enjoyed it,' he said, 'but I don't want to outstay my welcome. I'll drop you off and then get going.'

After thirty seconds of silence Nicole's mother said, 'You may as well stop over again. I mean, if you want, if you haven't got any other plans.'

He nodded. 'I'd like that. Thanks.'

'It'll help Nicole.'

'Yes,' he said. 'Of course.'

Later that day they all returned to the Shiplake Care Home, and Nicole found herself alone with Mac again. They talked for over an hour, after which he was elated but tired, and had told Nicole everything he remembered that wasn't in the notebook, which wasn't a lot.

That afternoon and the next day Nicole and her parents scoured just about every website in any way related to Holocaust survivors, posted messages on sites here and there, emailed the relevant organizations and researched the fate of the Jews who had fled Europe during the war until their heads were throbbing with stories of families split up and adoptions across continents.

And there were no arguments.

But there were also no replies.

At one point Nicole suggested mentioning the gold, and both her parents insisted that was definitely not a good idea. No, Dad had said, all it would take was time. Post the basic information wherever possible – that they were looking for Lorenzo and Anna Di Vito, that they had some information about their father, Lorenzo Senior, their mother, Donna, and their Aunt Rosa. Then they had to sit back and wait patiently. Mentioning gold would be sure to get quick replies, but not the sort they wanted.

Nicole quickly realized they were right, but by Sunday night, when her father returned to London, there were still no replies.

On Monday her mother returned to work, and Nicole was alone in the house. She spent most of the morning checking her email account every ten minutes, and by late afternoon this had become every hour.

She gave rowing a miss that evening, and instead had a meal with her mother, eaten in a subdued silence, and went to bed with her initial enthusiasm still alight but flickering bravely.

On Tuesday morning she checked her email. There were no replies.

She spent the morning doing a little cleaning and ironing like Mum had asked her to do, and checked her email again at lunchtime, which was as fruitless as before. Then she went for a walk – a stroll along the river, a half-hearted look in lots of shop windows, and a visit to the college.

She decided it was probably best to get home before Mum finished work, to be standing to attention at the ironing board when she walked through the door.

CHAPTER THIRTY-SEVEN

I n the city of Beacon, New York State, Mrs Belotti had spent Tuesday morning like every other Tuesday morning: twenty lengths of her local swimming pool followed by a few hours helping out at the care home that had looked after her husband so well in the months leading up to his death two years before.

After that, she returned home for an early lunch, which was fried pancakes with blueberry jam, eaten on the back veranda of her house overlooking the Hudson River. And then she did what she did most lunchtimes: switch on her trusty old laptop. Sometimes the creak of the keyboard made the contraption feel as old as her own bones – and reminded her how fragile she now was. If only she could get herself upgraded to a newer model. *Ha!*

She had now been retired seventeen years, and the novelty was most definitely starting to wane. Also, coincidentally, she had been trying to get to grips with what they called 'new technology' for seventeen years, which was a contradiction in terms if ever there was one, only now they called a 'contradiction in terms' an 'oxymoron' instead. Either way, the problem was that every time she took the trouble to try to understand something, her grandchildren almost immediately told her, 'Oh, it doesn't work like that anymore,' or occasionally, 'The industry is moving to a newer system,' or more often than not, 'You're not still using that old thing.' But she always laughed off the remarks as the impetuosity of the generation rather than rudeness. What did they know about real life? And anyway, at least their impetuosity helped her keep in touch with old friends.

While her laptop booted up, she gazed out and took in the view of Newburgh. This side of Beacon afforded a damn fine view of it, which she took advantage of most days and was seldom disappointed. The clear midday sun streaked across the drifting water, occasionally glinting in the windows of the cityscape on the other side. It wasn't all natural beauty, but even buildings had a beauty of sorts. At this time in the morning everything seemed at peace. That was something to be grateful for.

She logged into her email account, expecting some schmucks to be trying to sell her slimming pills or degree diplomas or even, *ha*, Viagra.

But there was only one email so far today, and she knew it wasn't junk email, or *spam*, as her grandchildren called it for some inexplicable reason. She clicked on it to open it, and pulled the laptop closer. It was from her old friend, Freida, who she'd met soon after arriving in America as a young child, and who had been as good as a sister ever since.

But something was wrong. Freida's emails were usually long sprawling epics; this one said, '*You'd better see this*,' with a link underneath it.

She clicked on the link and the screen blinked onto a new website.

She read the words on the screen again and again, all thoughts of pleasant veranda views and computer technology now an age away. She felt herself floating on air, her heart fluttering up and away from her. A sip of orange juice and a difficult gulp drove away the dryness from her mouth. She exhaled a few times through flaccid lips, then picked up the phone. It was hard to control the shaking that appeared to have taken her over, but she dialled.

'Come on, come on,' she muttered. 'What are you doing? Answer. Pick up the phone.'

But what if he was out? She had to talk to someone – no, she had to talk to *him*, nobody else would do. And he *had* to be in. And where else would he be at this time in the—

There was a click. She coughed more dryness from her throat.

'Hello?' she said.

'Anna?'

'Lorenzo, is that you?'

'Who else would it be?' Then a thoughtful pause. 'You sound upset. Is something wrong?'

'Yes. No. I mean . . . listen to me. I've received this email.'

'From who?'

'Freida.'

'So what's new?'

'No. This is important. There's a link to someone asking for help.'

Then he launched his warning-flare voice. 'Ah, now, Anna. You know what your daughter says. You have to be careful on the internet. All sorts of people trying to—'

'Oh, stop it, Lorenzo.'

'I'm sorry, I was just . . .' Now his tone was softer, more serious, inquisitive even. 'Please. Carry on.'

'It's about Papa.'

'Papa? What about him?'

'No, Lorenzo. *Papa Di Vito.*'

Anna heard nothing for a few seconds, then, 'Oh. *That* Papa.' And then she heard him swear under his breath.

'They know my name,' she said, 'and your name, our parents' names, and they mention Aunt Rosa and Valleverde.'

'Well . . . what do they want? Who is it?'

'They just say they're trying to trace us. There's an email address.'

'It could be a trick.'

'Oh, Lorenzo. What kind of trick? And who would know about us?'

'Well, Freida knows.'

'Freida's the only other person alive who knows anything about what happened in Valleverde, and I'd trust her with my life.'

'No. No. You're right. How about you send them an email, say we fit their description and tell them where we live – I mean, just what state we live in – and ask them what they want?'

'Sounds good. But I'll have to ring you back; I can't work the phone and the computer at the same time.'

Fifteen minutes later Anna rang Lorenzo again.

'Lorenzo?'

'Well? Did you get a reply?'

'I did. It's . . .'

'Well what? It's what? What did they say?'

'It's a woman called Nicole Sutton, in Britain. She says she knows someone who knew us at Valleverde, and who also met our father and Aunt Rosa at Auschwitz.' Anna waited for a reaction. There was none. She continued. 'They say this person can tell us what happened at Auschwitz.'

'Oh. My.' His deep breath crackled the line. 'My oh my. I wouldn't have thought it possible after all this time.'

'Well, that's what the email says. Doesn't mean it's true.'

'What does she want?'

'She wants us to meet him – this man who knows us. She says he's looking for Lorenzo and Anna, son and daughter of Lorenzo Senior and Donna, niece and nephew of Rosa. Apparently he's been looking for us for twenty years.'

The line went heavy with silence.

'Lorenzo?'

'Yes. I'm sorry. I'm just . . . I don't know what to say. I feel sick. Sick and happy and frightened and confused.'

'Me too. She says she has a story to tell us – the story of what happened in Italy and Auschwitz, and what Papa was like.' She paused, then listened for a moment. 'Lorenzo? Are you crying?'

There were some sniffs and sighs. 'I need to come over. I need to tell you something. Don't reply to the email until I'm there, okay?'

'Whatever you say, Lorenzo.'

∽

It was almost a quarter past five in the evening when Nicole heard the key in the lock. She jumped up from her chair, and was at the door before her mother had set foot inside.

'Mum, I got a reply,' she said, babbling the words out. 'I got a reply. *I got a reply!*'

'Hello, darling. Let me get in the door first.'

'But I got a reply. To my posting. From America. First there was nothing there – like there hasn't been for days. Then I went to make a cup of tea, then I had another look and it just . . . appeared.'

'Isn't that usually the way emails work?'

'Yes, but . . .'

'I'm sorry, love. That's fantastic. Great news, it really is. But did you reply?'

'Yeah. I told them a bit more – not about the gold – but I said there's someone here who wants to meet them, someone who can tell them what happened in Italy and in the concentration camp, someone who knew their dad. I only sent it off a few minutes ago. Come and look.'

Her mother slung her coat on the hook, then looked Nicole up and down. 'You know, I haven't seen this much life in you for months. I think it's brilliant news. Come on, show me, then we could ring your dad and let him know.'

❧

Anna Belotti let her brother in, and he had taken off his coat, been handed a cup of steaming coffee and sat down with her on the back veranda before either of them uttered a word.

'Anna. Before you go any further with this, I have something to tell you.'

'Okay.'

'It's . . . it's a confession.'

'I don't understand.'

'Just listen a while. It's something I've never told a living soul.'

Anna frowned. 'Tell me, Lorenzo. Whatever it is I'll be with you, you know that.'

He nodded. 'Thank you.' Then he groaned and swiped his fingers across his forehead. 'Do you remember when we went back to Valleverde in our twenties?'

'Of course.'

'And we asked around, looked up the records, tried to find out what happened to our family after we were evacuated. And they said the Nazis raided the house and took everyone away in November 1943.'

'How can I forget?'

'And you remember how upset I was?'

'But . . .' Anna thought for a couple of seconds, then said, 'You had a right to be, Lorenzo. Everything we had got left behind there – everything except each other.'

Lorenzo shook his head. 'It wasn't just that. There was something else.' He looked down into his coffee and paused to steady himself. 'You remember the British soldier?'

'Well, vaguely, I guess. Now, what did we call him?'

'We called him "Mac".'

Anna smiled. 'Of course. Now I remember. A nice man. Can't remember much more, though.'

'Well, I can,' Lorenzo said. 'Probably too much for my own good.' He lifted the cup of coffee towards his lips, but stopped, placed it back down, and stared into it with wild eyes for a few seconds. 'There's no easy way to tell you this, Anna, and I feel ashamed I haven't told you before.'

'What? Told me *what*?'

'When we went back there I asked some more. I found out that . . . well . . . when they raided the place and took our family away, they took the British soldier too.'

Anna thought for a moment, her jaw slightly open. 'And so?'

Lorenzo's face creased up, his voice became weak and whiny. 'It was *me*, Anna. It was *me*.'

She leaned over and held his hand. 'What was you, Lorenzo? Please, *tell me*.'

'I told the woman living next door. You remember? The one who kept calling us names?'

Anna stared into space, frowning, then nodded. 'Actually, you know what? I think I do.'

'Well, I got angry at her and . . . I don't know why, I've felt so wretched about it ever since. I told her we had our own British soldier who would keep us safe from people like her.'

Anna let out a gasp and shot the palm of her hand over her open mouth. She was motionless for a moment, then put an arm around him and rested her head on his shoulder. 'Oh, Lorenzo,' she said. 'You poor thing.'

'It was *me*, Anna. If I'd kept my mouth shut he wouldn't have been found. And who knows, if I hadn't told that woman they might not have even raided the place at all. Rosa and our grandparents might have lived.'

'But . . . you were only a boy, Lorenzo, you couldn't have . . .'

Her words trailed off and once again she slapped her hand over her mouth. She drew back and stared at her brother.

'What is it?' he said.

'The British soldier . . . Mac.'

'What about him?'

'I wonder if . . . if that's who it is. That's the man who knows, who wants to meet us.'

Lorenzo stood up and walked back into the kitchen. By the time Anna caught up with him he was rinsing his face in cold water.

'What do you think?' she asked him.

He gulped a few times, then said, 'Well . . . who else could it be?' He gave his head a shake. 'This changes things, Anna. I'm not sure if I can . . .'

'Hey.' She turned him around to face her, then reached up and held his head in her hands, pushing his solid shock of hair back into place. 'Now listen to me, Lorenzo. If this thing has been troubling you as much as I think it has, you can't afford *not* to go. We're not doing anything else that can't wait. I'm sure we can scrape the money together for the flight and a cheap hotel, but if you can't, then I'll pay for you too.'

Lorenzo's reply was no more than a sigh.

Anna gave his loose jaw a little shake. 'Look at me, my big beautiful brother, and listen carefully.' Lorenzo did as requested. 'I can still remember when I first came over here as a little girl without Mama or Papa. I was absolutely petrified, and I spent my first ten years hiding behind you, leaving you to take the lead and ask all the questions. You carried me, Lorenzo, *you carried me.* Well, think of this as payback time. A little late, I know, but . . .'

He tried to look away but she jerked his face back towards hers. Her voice reduced to a whisper. 'Now listen to me, Lorenzo. I don't care what you did there all those years ago, and if Mac's any sort of a human being he won't either. The point here is that you have nothing to lose, and everything to gain. So you're coming with me, do you understand?'

Lorenzo opened his mouth, but said nothing.

'You're coming with me. That's an order. *Do you understand?*'

He nodded, slowly at first, then more confidently.

'Anyway,' Anna added, 'I'm definitely going, and I need the company.'

CHAPTER THIRTY-EIGHT

A few more emails were exchanged, followed by one or two phone calls, after which it only took a matter of hours for Anna to book the flights and hotel rooms.

Three days later she and Lorenzo touched down at Heathrow.

At 77 Victoria Road an impatient Sutton family waited for them. Nicole's parents had both taken the day off work, and Nicole was pacing the living room, occasionally glancing left and right out of the bay window.

'Did you check the flight?' she said to her mother.

'Twice,' she replied. 'Twelve minutes late. They should be on their way here now.'

'Do you think they'll want to go straight there?'

'How would I know?'

'Or to their hotel if they're jet-lagged?'

'All right, let's all stay calm,' Nicole's father said. 'I'm sure they'll be tired so let's not bombard them with questions the second they get in the door.' He reached for the TV remote control. 'Let's just relax and wait.'

Nicole's mother stood up. 'I'd better get changed just in case they *do* want to go straight there.' She left the room.

Nicole and her father listened to the thump of feet on stairs, then spent two minutes watching the TV, he flicking between auctions, house renovations and game shows.

'Oh, I can't watch any of this,' he said, switching it off. He folded his arms tightly and spurted out a laugh. 'Look at me telling you to calm down, and I'm more nervous than you are.'

Nicole grinned briefly. Her father smiled back and checked his watch.

She watched him walk over to the window, look up and down the road, then sit down again.

'Dad?'

'Mmm?'

'Do you think Mum would ever want to move back to London?'

He smiled a painful smile and his head shimmied quickly from side to side. 'Sorry, poppet. Pretty sure that'll never happen.'

'Oh.' Nicole's head dropped.

'I mean . . . well . . .'

She looked up. 'Well what?'

'I guess I could move here. I mean, *at some stage* I could move here.'

'You mean, in with us?'

'Oh, I didn't mean that.'

'Oh.'

'I mean . . .' He glanced to the door and lowered his voice. 'That's not impossible. Of course, nothing would make me happier, but . . .'

'Mum?'

He nodded. 'I'm still not sure exactly how she feels.' He leaned forward and whispered. 'She won't talk to me about it. I mean, at least she *is* talking to me, but I daren't ask how she'd feel about . . . you know . . . eventually . . .' He drew breath and said, 'What do you think?'

Nicole ummed and aahed for a few seconds. 'Well, I know she's . . . No, I just don't know. Possibly. Eventually.'

'But she needs more time.'

'To forgive you?'

He sighed. 'Or accept she never will.'

Nicole nodded thoughtfully.

'You do believe what I told you, don't you? It's all about the accident, not . . . the other.'

'I know, Dad.'

The doorbell went.

Nicole bounced up and peered through the front window. 'It's a taxi,' she said, her eyes excited. 'It's a taxi. It's them.'

Before she could leave the living room her father stepped in front of her and put his arms around her. 'You know I'm proud of you,' he said. 'And so is your mum. Just let them relax. Let them breathe a bit.'

They heard footsteps come down the stairs and approach the front door, then went out into the hallway. There, Barry and Karen introduced themselves to Anna and Lorenzo, and there were broad smiles, handshakes and polite kisses on cheeks.

'And you must be Nicole,' Anna said.

The woman was almost a foot shorter than Nicole, and she needed to bend down to give her a gentle hug.

Her brother wasn't much taller, but had a stout body and a firm handshake. Nicole couldn't help but notice his small, straight nose, his full head of hair, and his solid chin.

'And you must be tired,' Nicole's mother said.

'Exhausted,' Anna replied.

'Can I get you a coffee and something to eat?'

Half an hour later Anna and Lorenzo – but mostly Anna – had recounted their life stories.

They talked of how their idyllic first few years had been thrown into turmoil by the political situation in Italy. They hadn't understood at the time why their aunt and grandparents had been so tearful when they were left in the care of their great-aunt. They spoke about how they'd settled in New York State and worked hard to get on. They also said that throughout those years their memories of what had happened to them and their family during the war had never stopped raising questions, but that they'd given up all hope of finding answers.

The others all listened attentively to the potted biographies, Nicole too engrossed to say or do anything, her father clearly the same, and her mother frowning in sympathy and at one point holding Anna's hand and squeezing it tightly.

At the end of her story, Anna thanked them for their concern and appeared to survey every wall of the room.

'So this is where it all happened, is it?' she said. 'Where Mac wrote his book.'

'Not exactly,' Nicole said.

'Did he have a writing studio?' Lorenzo asked.

'He wrote it in the cellar.'

'A cellar?' Anna chuckled. 'How appropriate.'

'Do you think we might see this cellar?' Lorenzo said.

'I'm not sure,' Nicole's mother said. 'The stairs are very steep.'

'Oh, we're both pretty good for our age on that score,' Lorenzo replied.

Anna placed a hand on Nicole's. 'And it would be nice to see.'

A few minutes later Nicole, Anna and Lorenzo were standing in front of the dusty old door that had been nailed onto its makeshift legs of wooden blocks.

'It's . . . not quite what I expected,' Anna said.

Nicole nodded. 'Hardly a writing studio, is it?'

Lorenzo scanned the rows of tins and jars of screws. 'Nice bunch o' hardware though.'

Nicole opened the old briefcase and lifted out the handfuls of letters Mac had written.

Anna stepped forward and read a few of them, her face grimacing as if in pain.

'There's more,' Nicole said.

'Oh yes,' Anna said. 'You mentioned a notebook?'

'That's with Mac. And there's something else he has – something that belonged to your family in Italy.'

'Oh, really?' said Lorenzo. 'What's that?'

'Probably best if you meet Mac and have a read of the notebook first. He's got a lot of important things to tell you.'

'How intriguing,' Anna said. 'But hey, whatever you say.'

Lorenzo looked all around them at the grimy brick walls and reached out for the briefcase, caressing its cracked leather. 'Yes, I'm pretty keen to see him.' He looked over to Nicole. 'I have something important to tell him too.'

Later that day they all drew up at the Shiplake Care Home.

Nicole's father parked the car and glanced behind him. 'Okay?' he said.

But something obviously wasn't. Nicole, her mother and Anna were all looking at Lorenzo, whose face was trembling, and whose breathing appeared positively asthmatic.

'What's wrong?' Nicole's father said.

Anna put an arm around her brother. 'Lorenzo isn't feeling too well,' she said.

'Do you need an ambulance?'

Anna shook her head. 'That's very kind of you but it's not a medical problem.' She gave her brother a gentle squeeze. 'You see, when we were children he did something stupid and he worries how Mac will react to it when he tells him.'

'Oh,' Nicole's father said. Nobody spoke for a few seconds, so he continued, 'We could go back to our place—' He clenched his teeth for a second. 'Sorry, back to *Karen and Nicole's place* – to talk about it and come back later.'

Nicole's mother nodded agreement. 'We can come back here any time—'

'Please, no,' Lorenzo said. 'You've been very kind, very hospitable. But I'd just be delaying the inevitable. I want to see Mac. And I have to tell him.' He took a few gasps of air and reached for the door handle.

They all went in and Nicole's parents stayed in reception, leaving Nicole to take Anna and Lorenzo to Mac's room.

She looked across to him and tapped his open door. Today he was dressed more smartly, in a suit and tie. He looked up and took a few troublesome moments to stand.

Anna was first to react, taking slow steps towards him. 'Oh. My. Word,' she said, holding him at arm's length and looking him up and down. 'It is you. It truly is.'

There were few more words. Anna and Lorenzo both studied every inch of Mac's face, and Mac looked at them just as lovingly. There was a warm embrace between Mac and Anna, then the men exchanged a handshake that neither, it seemed, was prepared to break off.

When it came to talking, Lorenzo showed less confidence. He smiled at Mac, then opened his mouth, but merely gulped in air before smiling again. 'Mac,' he eventually said, 'before we go any further, before you share your memories with us, I have a confession to make.'

Mac frowned at him. 'What? Now? You're joking, aren't you?'

'I'm afraid not. I have to tell you something. It's been eating away at me all my life – haunting me.'

Mac told them to sit down first, and they did, Anna and

Lorenzo on the bed right next to him, Nicole a little distance away. Everyone looked at Lorenzo, who took a deep breath.

'The house in Valleverde, it got raided soon after Anna and I left for America, didn't it?'

'It did that,' Mac said. 'It was horrible, but it's all in the notebook; you'll have to read it.'

'We were told that.' Lorenzo nodded dolefully. 'The thing is . . . well . . . before Anna and I left Valleverde I did something very stupid.'

Mac tutted. 'Stupid?' he said. Then he laughed. 'It was a war. What *wasn't* stupid?'

'No. Listen. Please. You probably didn't know, but there was an old woman living next door who didn't care for us much.'

'Oh, I know the woman you mean, and you're being very polite about her. She knew about me hiding in the cellar, you know.'

'Yes, that was her.' Lorenzo started breathing heavily.

'Wicked old thing,' Mac said with a shake of his head.

'It . . . it was me, Mac.' Now Lorenzo's voice crackled, hoarse and throaty. 'It was me.'

'What was you?'

Lorenzo gasped for air, his eyes large and fixed on Mac. 'I told her. I was so angry about her calling us names all the time. I wanted to get back at her, and in the end I . . . I told her we had a British soldier living in our cellar who would protect us from people like her.'

Mac slowly looked away from him, his gaze fixed in the distance.

Nicole just looked down at her feet.

Then Mac drew breath. He showed Lorenzo a painful smile, then looked away again. 'It was you?' he said. He gave a thoughtful nod in the heavy silence. 'You know, I was angry about that for some time,' he said. 'Many years, in fact. But after a while I came to accept that I'd have been found out soon anyway.' He laid a hand on

Lorenzo's arm. 'They were rounding up all Jews, and the authorities knew it was a house of Jews.'

Lorenzo wiped the wetness from his eyes and looked at Mac, but said nothing.

'And with Rosa and her mama and papa gone, I was on my own. Someone else would have taken the house and found me – perhaps shot me, who knows?'

Lorenzo gulped and said, 'So you're not angry with me?'

'Lorenzo Di Vito, if it's my forgiveness you want, you have it.'

'Oh thank you, Mac,' Anna said. 'That means a lot. To both of us.'

Lorenzo's tears flowed freely. All he could do was nod in agreement.

'For one thing,' Mac continued, 'you were a child. And for another, what sort of world do we live in if we can't forgive a moment's wrongdoing regretted?'

Lorenzo sniffed, wiped his face, and leaned over to pat Mac on the back. 'Thank you,' he said. 'Thank you so much.'

Lorenzo glanced at Anna. She raised her eyebrows at him. While he sat there, his mouth silently opening and closing like a goldfish, Mac spoke again.

'We've got much more important things to talk about, don't you think?'

'Oh, yes,' Anna said. 'Do you remember much of Papa and Aunt Rosa?'

Mac's face almost dissolved at the last word.

'Ah, your Aunt Rosa,' he said, 'I'm biased, of course. I was in love with her. And I still am.' He laughed and gave his head a languid shake. 'She was a beautiful woman – and all woman too, strong when she needed to be. She spoke very good English and always wanted to be an English teacher.' A frown appeared on his forehead for a second. 'What am I saying? That's not right. She *was* an English teacher. She was a very intelligent woman too, and courageous and kind.'

Mac paused, dropped a long sigh and smiled to himself. 'Look, I could talk about Rosa all day, but I can do that another time. I need to tell you about your father.'

'Oh, yes,' Anna said.

'Well,' Mac nodded to Lorenzo, 'I can see the family resemblance. Your father was a strong man in mind and body, one of the bravest people I've ever met. He campaigned against the Fascist government, and when your mother was killed during one of those demonstrations . . . well, he felt he had to leave you two and fight.'

'We were told by our great-aunt that he left us to join the underground movement,' Lorenzo said.

Mac looked him in the eye and said, 'That must have been hard for you to understand as children.'

Lorenzo struggled to get any words out, just nodding slowly.

'But you should know two things. For one, he left you somewhere he was sure you'd be safe – with your aunt. For another, he left you for all the right reasons – to create a better country for you to grow up in.'

'I can understand that,' Anna said. 'We've done our history.'

'But there's something else,' Mac said.

Anna and Lorenzo both leaned forward a little and looked to him, expectantly.

'What?' Lorenzo said.

'I was with him when he died.'

Anna gasped, her grip on Lorenzo's hand tightening. Then she froze, her eyes fixed on Mac.

'It's how I know him so well,' Mac said. 'I worked and lived alongside him in Auschwitz. We left there together, were side by side on the death march, and I was holding him when he couldn't carry on, when he died.'

'Oh, my,' Anna said. 'So, he wasn't shot?'

'Just exhaustion,' Mac said. 'Like so many others.' Then he took a few seconds to compose himself. 'And that brings me to something else.' He smiled at Nicole before continuing. 'You need to know that you were both in his thoughts when he died.'

At that point Anna put her hand over her face and started shaking. Lorenzo pulled a handkerchief from his pocket and handed it to her. She wiped her face, and Lorenzo put an arm around her shoulder as she wept a little more.

'I'm sorry,' Mac said. 'I don't mean to upset you.'

Lorenzo shook his head firmly.

'It must be hard after all these years, but you should know what sort of a man your papa was.'

'That's . . . warming to know,' Lorenzo said. 'Thank you.'

Mac smiled at him, and waited a few minutes for Anna to recover.

Nicole took the opportunity to fetch a glass of water for Anna, who took a couple of mouthfuls, then apologized to Mac for crying.

'No need,' Mac said. Then he looked across to Nicole and said, 'While you're up, sweetheart, would you mind shutting the door?'

She did, and then he said to her, 'Now could you look under my pillow, please?'

Nicole walked over to his bed, lifted the pillow, and let a proud smile appear on her face. It was the old tin with a scratched picture of a rose on it. She offered it to Mac, but he shook his head and nodded in Lorenzo's direction.

'This is for you,' he said. 'For you and Anna.'

'What is it?' Lorenzo said, puzzled and still comforting Anna.

'It's a present from your papa.'

Now Anna looked up, her face still red, but also with the air of a child on Christmas morning. 'But . . .' Her jaw fell open but no more words came out. She looked to her brother, but he was staring at Mac and frowning.

'I don't understand,' Lorenzo said as he took the tin in his hand. 'A present from Papa? How is that possible?' He examined it for a few seconds, and Anna leaned across to look too.

'Open it,' Mac said.

Lorenzo's knobbly fingers struggled at first, but then the lid popped off and he poured the contents into Anna's open hands.

Lorenzo and Anna did nothing for a few seconds but stare at the brooches, rings, bracelets, pendants and necklaces. All bright and pristine. All gold.

'I don't understand,' Anna eventually said.

'This is the Di Vito family gold,' Mac replied. 'Your Aunt Rosa kept it safe for you. And now it's yours, for both of you.'

'You brought this back in the war?' Lorenzo asked.

'It was your papa's dying wish that you should have it. And I know because I heard him say the words.'

'But how . . . ? Did . . . ?'

Mac gestured to his desk in the corner of the room. 'Over there you'll find my notebook. It's all in there, what happened in Valleverde, what happened to me and your family in Auschwitz, what happened to the Di Vito gold. All I need to do is add a chapter – a postscript, I suppose it would be – on how the gold got to its rightful owners. You could even do that yourselves if you want; it would be a nice touch.'

'We can't take this,' Lorenzo said, still touching the jewellery as if it were made of snowflakes.

'It's all in the notebook,' Nicole said. 'Just like Mac says. It's your family gold. It belonged to Rosa. She wanted your papa to have it, and he wanted it passed on to you.'

'It belongs to you,' Mac added. 'What you do with it, well, that's up to you.'

As Anna held a few items up to the light, Nicole said, 'We've thought about how you can get it back to America. You can wear it all between the two of you. You can just, like, walk through security wearing it and take it home.'

'And remember,' Mac said, 'it's a family heirloom. Whatever you do, take care of it. What you have in your hands holds history.'

Nicole stood up and edged towards the door. 'But having said all that, it's probably best if you put it away just for now.'

'Where are you going?' Mac asked her.

'I'm going to leave you to it. You've got so much to talk about, I don't want to be in the way.' Then she addressed Anna and Lorenzo: 'When you're ready you can ring us. We'll come and collect you, and take you to your hotel. Or you can pop back to our place first if you want.'

'Oh, my,' Anna said. 'That's so kind of you.'

Then Nicole spoke to Mac again. 'I'll see you again, Mac. We'll have to arrange for you to come over to our place, back to Victoria Road.'

'Be nice to visit my old place,' he said with a crooked grin. Then, as Nicole opened the door and turned to leave, he said, 'Thank you.'

'No worries,' she replied.

'That,' he said, 'will be my dying wish to you. But really, thank you.'

CHAPTER THIRTY-NINE

About three hours later a taxi pulled up outside 77 Victoria Road. It was a surprise for Nicole and her parents, but Anna and Lorenzo told them they didn't want to impose any further by getting Mr or Mrs Sutton to ferry them about. They'd called a taxi instead, but thought it polite to call in again – just for ten minutes as the taxi had been told to wait outside.

After accepting the offer of coffee they spoke of how they were both walking on air, and how they couldn't wait to tell the folks back home about Mac, and what they'd learned about their family history.

They also said they couldn't thank Nicole and her parents enough for posting the information on the web, for caring enough to try to trace them.

'Oh, Barry and I didn't do much,' Nicole's mother said. 'It's all down to Nicole really.'

Nicole blushed.

'We were all a bit apprehensive,' Nicole's father said. 'It's a relief to know it's all worked out so well.' Then he turned to Lorenzo. 'So, what happened about the erm . . . problem?'

At first Lorenzo frowned.

Anna noticed the frown. 'He means your confession,' she said.

'Oh, that.' His puzzled expression dissolved. 'I can tell you I feel one hell of a lot better about that.'

'What did Mac say?' Nicole's mother asked.

Anna piped up, 'You know, he said something really quite poetic. He said what sort of a world would it be if we didn't forgive a moment's wrongdoing regretted.'

They all considered that for a while. Nicole's mother nodded to herself, then glanced at her husband, who glanced at Nicole.

Anna took advantage of the pause to say she was tired and needed a lie down. She finished her coffee and stood up. She raised her eyebrows to Lorenzo, who immediately finished his coffee and stood up too.

'But I can't thank you enough,' Anna said. She grabbed Lorenzo's arm and pulled him close. 'I mean, *we* can't thank you enough.'

Lorenzo nodded.

'And you all must have taken the day off work for this,' Anna added. 'Don't think we don't appreciate it.' Then she stopped as if a thought had hit her. 'I hope you didn't think we were being rude,' she said, 'but I forgot to ask what you all do for a living.'

Lorenzo piped up, smirking: 'What she means is she forgot to be so nosey because she got distracted by everything else going on.'

'*Lorenzo!*' she said, firing him an admonishing stare.

'That's all right,' Nicole's father said, laughing. 'But it's very boring compared to some lives, I can promise you. My . . . erm . . .' He gestured to Nicole's mother, who continued.

'My husband and I both work in banking. Like he said, it's very boring.'

'And Nicole?' Anna said.

'Yes,' Nicole's father said. 'Nicole, she . . . erm . . .'

'I'm studying at the local college.'

Her mother and father exchanged puzzled looks.

'Well, soon,' Nicole continued, 'I haven't signed up for it yet, but I'm going to.'

'Oh, good,' Anna said.

'What are you studying?' Lorenzo asked.

'History?' Anna suggested.

'Sports Science,' Nicole replied. 'I row on the river too.'

'That sounds excellent,' Anna said. 'I always said to my children you should do something with your life. Do anything that takes your fancy, but do *something*, work hard at it, and don't waste your life.'

'You forgot one,' Lorenzo muttered from the side of his mouth.

'Because life's a gift,' Anna added.

'That's the one,' Lorenzo said, sending Nicole a wink.

Anna elbowed her brother, Nicole laughed, and her father said, 'I like that, I really do.'

They all made their way to the hallway, where more kisses and hugs were exchanged, and Anna and Lorenzo said they'd call by tomorrow.

'Actually, I should say goodbye,' Nicole's father said. 'I'll wish you a safe journey back to America because I won't be here tomorrow.'

Nicole's mother turned to him and said, 'Well, you could be. We'll see.'

He looked confused for a moment, then corrected himself. 'We'll see.'

'Either way,' Anna said, 'we need to keep in touch.'

A minute later the visitors were gone.

'What was all that about?' Nicole's father said. 'The "*We'll see*"?'

Her mother shrugged. 'Just thought you might want to stop the night again.'

'Oh. All right. If you don't mind.'

'No. I don't mind.'

He nodded. 'Okay.'

'Okay,' she said.

∽

At ten to five that same day, Nicole put on her training gear and headed out.

She walked along Victoria Road, around the corner shop, and soon was walking alongside the river. *Over the bridge and turn right.* She was almost doing the journey on autopilot now.

As she approached Danver's Shed there was a little bounce in her step that had been missing lately. Perhaps this place was starting to feel like home.

Shaun and Austin were in lively conversation with two other guys, and four girls were steadying themselves to get into a quad scull. Austin glimpsed Nicole, turned, and hollered, 'Be with you in a minute!' Then he turned back and continued talking.

Nicole gazed upstream and downstream, then up at the sky, which couldn't decide what to do either.

She looked down at the double scull rocking gently at the water's edge. She glanced back to the rowing guys, then along the river again. She stepped into the double scull, removed the back pair of oars, and carefully eased herself onto the front seat.

She'd grabbed the oars and rowed a few feet away from the bank by the time anyone noticed.

Austin was the first to react.

'Hey!' He ran towards her. 'What are you doing?'

She ignored him, but noticed him burst into exasperated laughter. Then he cupped his hands around his mouth and shouted out, 'You're mad, you are!'

But she rowed on, and soon was out of earshot, in a world of her own. It felt a little eerie, but now the speed seemed to come easily, as if there were someone in the seat behind her, helping her pull the boat along, strengthening every stroke of hers.

And she looked up to the skies. It still wasn't bright, but somehow, today more than any other before, it felt like a sunny day.

ACKNOWLEDGEMENTS

I would like to take the opportunity to thank Delphine Cull for her content editing and unstinting encouragement throughout the development of this piece of work, and also Jill Worth for her copy-editing advice and occasional storyline suggestions.